SMOKE AND FIRE

Acclaim for Julie Cannon's Fiction

Breaker's Passion is…"an exceptionally hot romance in an exceptionally romantic setting…. Cannon has become known for her well-drawn characters and well-written love scenes."—*Just About Write*

In *Power Play*…"Cannon gives her readers a high stakes game full of passion, humor, and incredible sex."—*Just About Write*

About *Heartland*…"There's nothing coy about the passion of these unalike dykes—it ignites at first encounter and never abates. …Cannon's well-constructed novel conveys more complexity of character and less overwrought melodrama than most stories in the crowded genre of lesbian-love-against-all-odds—a definite plus." —Richard Labonte, *Book Marks*

"Cannon has given her readers a novel rich in plot and rich in character development. Her vivid scenes touch our imaginations as her hot sex scenes touch us in many other areas. *Uncharted Passage* is a great read."—*Just About Write*

About *Just Business*…"Julie Cannon's novels just keep getting better and better! This is a delightful tale that completely engages the reader. It's a must read romance!"—*Just About Write*

Visit us at www.boldstrokesbooks.com

By the Author

Come and Get Me

Heart 2 Heart

Heartland

Uncharted Passage

Just Business

Power Play

Descent

Breakers Passion

Rescue Me

I Remember

Smoke and Fire

SMOKE AND FIRE

by

Julie Cannon

2014

SMOKE AND FIRE

ISBN 13: 978-1-60282-977-0

This Trade Paperback Original Is Published By
Bold Strokes Books, Inc.
P.O. Box 249
Valley Falls, NY 12185

First Edition: January 2014

CREDITS
Editor: Shelley Thrasher
Production Design: Susan Ramundo
Cover Design By Sheri (graphicartist2020@hotmail.com)

Dedication

To all the men and women who put their lives
on the line every day for someone else.

PROLOGUE

The fire. It was always the fire. The smoke. The heat. The taste. The smell of burning flesh. She was afraid she would die and she prayed to God to stay alive. Then she felt nothing. Nerve endings seared, unable to send pain signals.

Then, weeks later, as nerve endings healed, contaminated dead skin was removed, the pain was excruciating. Day after agonizing day she prayed to a different God to take her.

Chapter One

I don't want to go."

"It doesn't matter what you want. You're expected to be there."

"Do I look like the type that enjoys that dog-and-pony kind of shit? Because you know that's exactly what it's going to be. Come on Flick, give me a break."

Brady watched her crew chief's eyes travel from the top of her oil-stained hardhat, slowly across her face, to the top of her steel-toed flame-resistant boots before returning to look directly in her eyes. Before she entered the somewhat clean crew office, she'd unzipped and shrugged out of the top half of her filthy coveralls, tying the arms of the dark-blue protective suit around her waist. She knew he saw exactly what she wanted him to see—a mirror image of himself.

"No, none of us would, but damn it, Stewart, you're the one who pulled Steckman out of that fire and the brass is proud of you. Hell, we're all proud of you, and you should be too. HQ just wants to recognize that."

Brady tipped her head back, stretching her tired neck muscles. She was ten hours into her eighth twelve-hour shift, and she was bone tired. Not that she would let anyone see just how dead on her feet she was. She knew her limits and was still on the right side of them. When you push too hard for too long that's when mistakes happened, and she'd seen the results.

"I didn't do anything anyone else wouldn't have done, and you know it, Flick. For crying out loud, he wasn't even on this crew."

Brady had volunteered to fill in for a few days on a different crew for one of the guys who had hurt his back.

"That may be, but *you* were the one that did." Flick Jordon, Brady's immediate supervisor, pointed his pudgy finger at her, then glanced at his watch. "You've got one hour to clean yourself up, dig out something decent to wear, and have your ass on that chopper."

Brady pivoted and, as much as she wanted to slam the door in frustration, she closed it gently behind her instead. "Fuck, just what I need, to pose for pictures with the queen almighty."

Brady stepped off the bottom step, her thick safety boot landing in the middle of a puddle of mud. It didn't faze her in the slightest. If she cussed every time she stepped into something wet, gooey, greasy, or slimy she'd be swearing nonstop. After twelve years of fighting oil-well fires on every continent of the world, Brady had gotten into the habit of mimicking the language of her peers.

"What a fucking waste of time," she mumbled as she walked to the crew quarters.

CHAPTER TWO

Y ou ready, Nicole?"
"Yes, I'm ready," Nicole replied calmly, biting back her irritation at Buck Hightower's unnecessary question. She was never late for anything. Except that one time. And look where that got her. Sitting behind a desk, covered in a shroud she would never let anyone see beneath. Practically speaking, her scarred body was draped in a suit, blouse, and shoes that cost well into four figures, her shoulder-length blond hair and nails professionally attended to. The only jewelry visible was the oversized titanium Eco-Drive watch on her left hand, a wide band of intricately carved butterflies on the ring finger of her right hand, and a sturdy platinum chain around her neck that disappeared beneath the collar of her royal-blue blouse.

Nicole closed the report she'd been reading, took off her reading glasses, and stood. At five feet ten she was taller than almost all the women she knew and shorter than most of the men that worked for her. She used her height to her advantage when necessary, but more often than not people were intimidated by the image she projected. She was always in complete control and could recite facts and figures off the top of her head that amazed even her most vocal critics. She rarely raised her voice and was the most powerful woman in the male-dominated industry of oil-well blowout suppression. She would never relinquish control of her emotions, her surroundings, or her company. And being late to a meeting with employees was no exception. As the president of McMillan Suppression she set the example of what the company stood for: reliability, respect, and dependability.

Four years ago when she stepped into her father's shoes, Nicole knew the business inside and out. From the age of ten she was at her father's side learning everything she could about the company he'd built from scratch thirty years ago. At eighteen she was on the front line fighting fires. Six years ago at twenty-nine her life changed forever. Today, Nicole was far too busy to look in the rearview mirror and avoided any mirror, for that matter, as much as possible.

Buck's dull voice continued, oblivious to her underlying mood. "We have a last-minute addition to the meeting, Brady Stewart. Stewart pulled John Steckman from the flames at the Zulo wellhead in Brazil last week." Since stepping in when her father fell ill, Buck had become her right- and left-hand man, taking care of everything from offering advice to executing her decisions. He was well respected in the oil-field community, having grown up as a wildcatter in western Oklahoma. Buck looked exactly like an older Rock Hudson, with dark hair graying around the temples and a thick salt-and-pepper mustache.

"Buck." Nicole interrupted him, her patience evaporating. "I know it's your job to get your message across at every opportunity, and as a PR guy you do a great job, but sometimes you repeat yourself too often. I know this. I read the report last night, the press release and the files of everyone coming today, and," Nicole said, taking her jacket from the back of her desk chair and slipping it on, "you've told me, several times as a matter of fact." Nicole eyed her favorite staff member with exasperation. "Six employees are being recognized for their contribution to safety, including Brady Stewart. One of the guys on the crew got tangled in the line and went down when the head reignited. Stewart dropped the line, ran into the fire, and dragged him out. They both suffered minor burns, and if it hadn't been for Stewart, the guy would probably be dead, his wife a widow and his five kids fatherless. Stewart has an exemplary safety record and high praises from everyone on the crew."

Nicole reached for the purple folder on her desk, careful not to lean too much of her weight on her right leg. It ached all the time but recently much more than usual. Over the last few weeks, she'd been skimping on her physical therapy and was starting to pay the price. Gritting her teeth against the pain and refusing to let herself limp, Nicole walked out her office door and down the hall.

❖

Brady spit out the toothpaste, rinsed her mouth, and looked at herself in the hotel bathroom mirror. She needed a haircut, her short brown hair sticking out at odd angles. To anyone else it looked stylish, but to her it was shaggy and in desperate need of a major overhaul. Reflected in the mirror over her left shoulder, the naked woman lying on the king-sized bed stirred. *Rachel? Roberta? No, Robin. Thank God.*

An offhand glance across the lobby bar last night had resulted in a much-needed reaffirmation of her sexuality. She'd been celibate far too long this time and planned to rectify that situation as much as possible the three days she was in Morgan City. Sex was a release for pent-up stress, a welcome distraction, a reward for still being alive.

Walking toward the bed she saw that Robin was awake and watching her. "Where are you going, stud?"

Brady cringed at the incorrect characterization of who she was. Sure, her hair, clothes, and overall carriage would lead any lesbian to believe she was much more butch than she actually was. Brady had little time or interest, for that matter, for courting, dating, making small talk, or any of the other get-to-know-you rituals that were a prelude to sex. She worked hard and had little time off, and when she did she made the most of it.

"I've gotta go and so do you," Brady said, dropping Robin's clothes on the bed between them. She hated morning-afters and did whatever she could to make sure she didn't find herself in this exact awkward position. She must have been pretty tired last night.

"Why don't you come back to bed and I'll make it worthwhile. You know I can," Robin crooned, and stretched in what she obviously thought was a provocative pose. Brady just found it annoying.

"As much as I'd like that I have to go, and you can't stay here," Brady said more forcefully. She handed Robin's clothes to her and didn't let go until the woman sat up.

Ten minutes later, her "date" in a cab, Brady was sitting in the backseat of the Town Car McMillan Suppression had provided for her short ride across town.

CHAPTER THREE

The office hadn't been at all what Brady had expected. Twelve years ago, when she'd applied for her first job, it had been at the local field office in Cameron, Louisiana. Little more than a refurbished single-wide mobile home, it smelled like stale cigar smoke, banana peels, and dirty socks. The woman behind the counter could only be described as a broad. With her big hair, long pointy fingernails, and the requisite blue eye shadow she could have very easily starred in any number of B-grade movies made in the early eighties. The nameplate on the scarred desk read Sylvia, and the pitch of her fake Southern drawl had hurt Brady's ears.

"Can I help ya?" Sylvia asked, snapping her gum.

"I'd like to fill out an application to be a firefighter."

Sylvia wasn't shy in the way she'd looked her up and down, as if her personal attire, demeanor, or height was the first prerequisite for the job. When she'd smirked and handed Brady the application it was obvious she considered Brady one step above trash—maybe.

Brady had long since stopped caring about what people thought of her. She'd grown up in a trailer park and was considered by many as nothing but poor white trash. Her parents' priorities were drinking, fighting, and fucking, more often than not in that specific order. Their line of sight didn't often include their only child, and after one too many smacks to the back of the head Brady learned how to stay out of that line quite effectively.

She was teased in school for being too skinny, on welfare, and wearing clothes from the local church donation box. When her parents did muster up enough interest or obligation to make a showing they were brash, outspoken, and every teenage girl's worst nightmare. It had been her eighteenth birthday when she stood in front of Sylvia's desk vowing to have more money than God and never look back.

Since then she'd traveled tens of thousands of miles, was on her third passport, and was a seasoned oil-field fire veteran. She'd done a lot of stupid things, crazy things, and brave things, the least of which was saving a coworker's life. She didn't think it was a big deal, but the boss obviously thought otherwise.

Stepping through the revolving door, Brady thought about the woman everyone called the boss. The pictures of Nicole McMillan in the company's annual report and trade magazines seemed to reinforce her reputation of being cold, hard, and all business. Her eyes were dark, her expression serious, and she had a take-no-shit look that Brady secretly admired. Brady couldn't remember ever seeing a picture of the boss smiling, and if she believed half of the crew gossip she was a real ball-buster. Her boss epitomized the saying about a woman in a man's world. Oil was a man's world. It didn't matter if you were drilling for it, pumping it out of the ground, or putting out its fire, there were at least a thousand men to every woman. And a woman at the top, well, suffice it to say Nicole McMillan was in a league all her own.

Alone in the elevator, Brady plucked the crease of her khakis, centered the buckle of her belt, and buttoned her navy-blue jacket. She turned her head left then right, looking at her neck, and breathed a sigh of relief that the she didn't see any signs of last night's entertainment. The elevator was quick, and the soft melodic voice announcing the eighth floor was soft and sexy. Stepping out, Brady wondered what the boss thought of *that* every time she heard it.

The offices of McMillan Suppression lay directly in front of her. The floor-to-ceiling glass doors were intricately carved with a scene of an oil rig on the left and an oil-rig blowout on the right. Evenly spaced across the top was the name of the company in four-inch-high brass letters.

Very impressive, Brady thought as the thick jade-green carpet muffled her footsteps. She pulled on the door handle and the heavy door opened with a slight *whoosh*. Sitting behind a large, U-shaped desk was a woman with dark-brown hair talking to absolutely no one. Before Brady had a chance to say anything the woman looked at her, held up one finger as if to say one moment, and signaled to her left ear with the other.

Brady realized she must have a headset or Bluetooth receiver in her ear covered by her long curly locks and casually glanced around the ornate lobby. The deep-red walls were offset by oversize tan leather chairs. The coffee table held several issues of *Oil Field Technology* and today's *Wall Street Journal*. A photo of a wellhead on fire filled the cover of a *National Geographic* and Brady picked it up, recognizing the name of the well as one of the fires she'd fought six or seven months ago.

"May I help you?"

Brady replaced the magazine on the table and faced the pretty receptionist. "I'm Brady Stewart. I'm here for…" Brady didn't get a chance to finish.

The woman's professionalism couldn't hide her momentary look of surprise before she said, "Yes, Ms. Stewart, we're expecting you. If you'll have a seat, Ms. McMillan's assistant will be out shortly."

Brady was ten minutes early, and, expecting she'd have to wait, she did as she was instructed, flipping open the *National Geographic* to the cover story. Scanning the article Brady was pleased to see that the general theme of the story concerned the ecological damage caused by oil rigs that gushed oil unabated or, in the case of the rig in the photo, burning oil as it shot out the top of the rig.

Brady could verify the author's description of the thick, black smoke billowing into the sky and practically obliterating the sunshine. The air around an oil-well fire was thick and caustic, forcing everyone within several miles to stay indoors or risk severe respiratory distress. As a member of the hotshot crew whose job it was to extinguish the blaze, she breathed through a specifically formulated mask, similar to a gas mask. It was claustrophobic to wear the mask ten or twelve hours a day, but the alternative wasn't an option. Even with the protection, her lungs rattled and her eyes burned. It took three crews eighteen days to extinguish the fire and another seven months for the air to clear.

"Mr. Stewart?"

Brady looked up and into the questioning eyes of a complete stranger. This must be the assistant, she thought to herself. Judging by the woman's expression, Brady wasn't at all what she expected.

"I'm Brady Stewart," she replied, not particularly upset to be mistaken for a man. Her name and profession drew everybody to the same conclusion. Of course her short hair, flat chest, and nonexistent ass didn't help either.

"Excuse me, Ms. Stewart," the woman said, obviously flustered. "I apologize, I…"

Brady waved her off. "Don't worry about it," she said, dropping the magazine back on the table.

"I'm Ann Franklin, Ms. McMillan's assistant. Would you please follow me?"

Brady nodded to the receptionist, knowing she'd be the talk of the office pool for the rest of the day. She was so glad she didn't have to listen to office gossip.

"May I get you something to drink? Coffee, orange juice, water?" Ann asked as Brady followed her down the hall.

Brady wanted a second cup of coffee but was afraid it would prolong the meeting she didn't want to be in in the first place. "No, nothing, thanks."

Ann knocked twice on the door before opening it and stepped inside. She indicated Brady should follow.

"Gentlemen, this is Brady Stewart," Ann said, looking from Brady to the men standing around the coffee carafe at the end of the table. "Ms. McMillan will be in shortly. Please everyone make yourself at home."

A big beefy man with balding black hair, a large mustache, and an ill-fitting suit spoke first. "What role do you play in this show?" the man boomed. The coffee cup in his large hand looked like it came from a child's tea set.

Brady changed her mind about the coffee. She didn't know she'd be meeting with anyone other than the boss, and after counting all the men in the room, she figured this would take much longer than she thought. She needed that coffee now more than ever.

"Excuse me?" Brady asked, pouring the steaming liquid into the delicate cup.

"What do you do? You're not the photographer, cuz you don't have a camera. Are you the reporter from the *Morgan City News*?"

"Who are you?" Brady asked, baffled why she was in this room with these men.

"Jack Bingham. I have twenty-five years of a perfect safety record. More than I can say about any of the others on my crew. I'm with the Oxbow crew under Gill Heard." He pointed to the other men before he continued. "Hammerstone invented some new piece of equipment, Baxter and Cormier recommended a new process for storing the C4, and Marcus and Showalter are the heroes of the Hunts Crossing blowout. Each man nodded when Bingham said his name.

Brady recognized the name of the man's crew and the other accomplishments he listed. She was beginning to realize this was more than a one-on-one meet and greet with the boss. It must be some kind of award or recognition event.

"Brady Stewart. I pulled some dumb ass out of harm's way," Brady said.

"No shit?"

"No shit."

"Well, I'll be damned," he said, shaking his head as if he couldn't figure out which was more surprising, saving a man's life or a woman on a crew who saved a man's life. He finally added, "Plenty of them to go around, that's for sure. What crew you on?"

"Nineteen. Flick Jordan's the chief. But I was a fill-in on another crew when that happened."

"Flick." The man paused and nodded. "I worked for him a few years back. Never had a woman on a crew I worked before."

"That makes two of us," Brady said as the door to the conference room opened.

CHAPTER FOUR

G entlemen, sorry for keeping you waiting," a man with dark-red hair said, entering the room. He stopped looking back and forth between the men and Brady, puzzlement clearly written all over his face. Brady knew the instant he realized who she was.

"My apologies," he said, looking directly at her. "I'm Buck Hightower. Ms. McMillan is a few minutes behind me. You must be Jack," he said, shaking the man's hand vigorously. "Congratulations on your safety award. We need more men like you at McMillan."

He turned to each man and acknowledged him in a similar manner. Then it was Brady's turn. "Brady Stewart," she said, extending her hand. She preferred to take the lead in uncomfortable situations.

"Ms. Stewart, I'm honored to meet you. Thank you so much for your heroic actions. I'm sure Steckman can't thank you enough either."

Brady didn't hear the rest of what Buck said, her attention drawn to the woman walking into the room.

The photographs of Nicole McMillan didn't do her justice. She was striking, elegant, and sophisticated, and she exuded power, confidence, and raw sexuality all in one nice, stunning package. She had what Brady had once read was described as presence. Impressive was the other word that came to mind. Other things came to mind as well, but Brady filed them away to think about later.

Nicole quickly glanced at the men in the room and hesitated when their eyes met. A slightly raised eyebrow was the only clue she gave upon realizing just who Brady Stewart was. *Jesus, does anyone in this company realize I'm a woman?*

Hightower introduced Nicole to each of the men, and she responded with a short comment about why each of them was here. Brady thought Nicole made small talk easily, a trait more aptly described as the gift of gab or the ability to bullshit with anyone at any time about anything. Brady didn't like to beat around the bush and said pretty much what was on her mind, if she had anything to say at all. Then it was her turn.

"Nicole, this is Brady Stewart," Hightower said.

"Ms. Stewart," Nicole said, extending her hand. "It's a pleasure to meet you. I've heard a lot about you and McMillan is proud of your work, especially the way you pulled Steckman out of the fire."

Brady was rarely at a loss for words, but the smooth, melodious way her name slid off Nicole's lips sounded like a soft rain on a warm summer night. It took several moments for Brady to remember her self-taught manners and shake the offered hand.

"Thank you, Ms. McMillan, but I was just doing my job. I told my crew boss that, but he seems to think it's a big deal," Brady replied, reluctantly releasing the strong, warm hand in hers.

"Well, it is a big deal, and I didn't want it to go unnoticed. Our lives depend on each other every day we're on the line, and without that we might not make it home in the same condition we left."

Brady detected a slight tremor in her last words but doubted if anyone else did. Her senses were on high alert with Nicole, from the subtle fragrance she wore to the perfect tailoring of her impeccable suit to the surprising flat dullness in her eyes.

Everyone at McMillan knew the story of Nicole. She was a firefighter herself and one day after over ten years on the line was badly burned in an explosion when the wellhead she was installing flared. She wasn't expected to live and, by what Brady had read and all appearances now, her recovery and months of recuperation were successful. Brady wanted to search for any signs of her legendary burns but forced herself to keep her eyes from straying.

Nicole was impressed by the woman standing in front of her. Brady Stewart wasn't at all what she expected. That was an understatement. Brady wasn't much more than an inch or two shorter than herself, her build stocky, and from experience Nicole knew she had to be strong and incredibly tough. Her handshake was firm but not overpowering, her eyes clear, and her interest obvious. The first was expected, the second mandatory, and if her racing pulse and pounding heart were any indication, the third a complete surprise.

"You've been with us for what...eight years?" Nicole made a mental note to have Buck research and report on how many other women were on the lines.

"Yes."

"You were on the A14 fire in Kuwait last year, right?"

"Yes, I was." Brady didn't appear to be the least bit surprised that she knew. Nicole had an almost photographic memory when it came to her company. She knew who had been on what fire, when, and how long it had taken to contain.

Nicole nodded, remembering the video of one of the largest fires McMillan had worked in the last year or two. It had taken five crews, dozens of pieces of equipment, and forty-eight days to extinguish.

"Well done."

Nicole had an overwhelming desire to sit down with Brady over a beer or two and talk with her. She wanted to know every little detail of the fire, wanted her to describe in minute detail everything that happened at the scene, wanted to experience it vicariously through Brady's words. Instead Buck took over the meeting and everyone sat around the large cherrywood conference table.

As Buck talked, Nicole mulled over her reaction to Brady. Since her accident, Nicole had not set foot on a site. The mere thought of a fire made her break out in a cold sweat and her stomach threaten to dump its contents on her shoes. After months of nightmares of being burned alive, her mother encouraged her to go to therapy. Instead, Nicole moved out of her parents' house, back into her own on the other side of town, and it was never mentioned again. She hadn't allowed herself to think about the details of a fire in years.

While Buck and the others talked she caught everyone except Brady staring at her at least once. She knew what they were looking for. Like everyone else who knew about the accident, everyone except the most polite people always were trying to catch a glimpse of the horrific burns that had scarred her body. Even though she understood their curiosity, it still hurt to have people envision her body as a canvas of scars. Through sheer luck or the grace of God, her hands, face and neck hadn't been exposed to the life-altering flames that had engulfed her years ago. The long sleeves and pants took care of the rest.

The meeting over, Nicole stood and shook hands again with the men who had made a significant contribution to the health and safety of her employees. She saved Brady for last and found herself asking Brady if she had time to come to her office after the tour. She knew Buck was watching her but she didn't make eye contact, focusing only on Brady when she agreed.

❖

Nicole paced back and forth in front of the three large windows in her office as she waited for Brady. After lunch Buck had taken the group on a tour of the McMillan company museum which, with the exception of the security desk and the bank of four elevators, filled the entire first floor. Her schedule was packed, which wasn't unusual, and Ann had frowned at her when she told her to clear her calendar for the rest of the afternoon. She had no idea what she was going to talk about with Brady. All she knew was that she wanted to spend more time with her.

Changing her pattern, Nicole wondered if it was because she knew Brady was attracted to her but just as quickly banished the thought. Other women had expressed interest in her, some subtly, a few with outright propositions, but Nicole had politely and firmly declined each one. Other than her physicians and a variety of other health-care providers, she hadn't let anyone see the extent of her injuries. High hedges around the pool in her backyard kept prying eyes from glimpsing her scarred and maimed body. When she needed pure sexual release she took matters into her own hands, and when that no longer sufficed, she called a discreet number her physical therapist had given her years ago. The lights were always off in an obscure hotel room, and no real names were ever exchanged.

How long had it been since she'd enjoyed the touch of another woman? The service, as she preferred to call it, was just that—a service. When she needed her hair cut she went to the hairdresser, when the sink was clogged she called the plumber, and when she was so tight with sexual need she called the number she had memorized.

If she wanted a job done right, she got a professional. Nicole turned from the window when Ann announced Brady had returned.

"Thanks, Ann, please have her come in." Nicole smoothed her already perfectly pressed blouse and took a deep breath. Her mind was a jumble, her stomach in a knot. She fought down panic as she looked from the chair opposite her desk to the more casual seating area in the other corner by the window. Should they sit with the desk between them, keeping it all business, or be less formal on the comfortable couch? Good God, Nicole thought. How difficult is it to just sit down and have a conversation? Brady stood in her doorway, a look of her own apprehension on her face.

"Ms. Stewart," Nicole said, somehow managing to sound calmer than she actually felt. "Thank you for coming."

"Thank you for inviting me," Brady said politely, but obviously uncomfortable.

"Please sit down." Nicole indicated the chairs closest to Brady. "Can I get you anything? Coffee, soda, beer?"

"Beer?" Brady asked, seeming genuinely surprised.

The smile on Brady's face made her knees weak, and Nicole glanced at her watch for something to get her mind back on track. "Okay, not beer. Even though it is after lunch, it's still a workday."

"No, I'm fine, really. Thanks. I've had enough coffee to drown a horse," Brady said, sitting down at the end of the small couch. She leaned back and studied the room.

Nicole followed Brady's eyes as they took in the magazines on the small table in front of her, the knickknacks she'd collected from various parts of the world on the bookshelf to her left, the photos of various fires that adorned the rich, tan walls, and finally settling on her.

"I didn't think crews could ever get enough coffee."

"Generally that's true. But when I'm not working, I try to be more civilized."

A flash of Brady uncivilized shot through Nicole's imagination, and she grabbed the back of the chair to keep from stumbling into it as she sat down.

"Are you all right?" Brady asked, concern in her dark eyes.

"Yes, just caught my shoe on the back of the chair." Nicole tried to find her composure that had so quickly deserted her when Brady walked in her office. "Do you get much downtime?"

Brady looked at her intently and answered evasively. "You know how it is. You grab any time you can anywhere you can."

"Yes, I do." For the first time in years someone was actually talking about her life before the fire. A mixture of nostalgia and familiar gut-wrenching fear settled in her chest. "Or at least I did."

"I'm sorry. I didn't mean to upset you. I should go." Brady started to get up but Nicole stopped her.

"No, please," she said, almost pleading. "I want you to stay. It's just that you're the first person in a long time who's mentioned anything about my time on a crew."

"Really? But I'd think that's such a big part of who you are, what you do today."

Nicole looked at Brady, and even under intense scrutiny Brady didn't look away. "You're very intuitive, Ms. Stewart." Brady laughed, and Nicole's grip on her stomach subsided a little.

"I've been called a lot of things, Ms. McMillan, but intuitive was certainly not one of them." This time Brady's eyes sparkled.

"Maybe you should expand the company you keep."

It was Brady's turn to study her. Nicole couldn't read anything on her face but could sense the wheels turning and a decision being made.

"Thank you, but I like the company I keep. Present company included." Brady let her comment sink in before adding, "And please don't call me Ms. Stewart. That was my mother and I'd rather not... well, anyway..."

"What's your crew name?" In addition to their given name it was tradition that every crewmember had a nickname, usually bestowed on them by their first crew chief.

Brady hesitated again before answering. "Bond."

"Bond?"

Brady nodded. "Yes, as in James Bond."

This time Nicole laughed. "Why? Are you a spy?" Brady laughed and Nicole's stomach flip-flopped.

"No, nothing that glamorous or sexy."

Nicole motioned for her to continue.

"As in doesn't say much about their life and," Brady looked directly at her, "gets all the girls."

The temperature in the room jumped ten degrees. Nicole's groin burned and her hands started to sweat.

"What was yours?" Brady asked back.

Nicole swallowed hard and tried not to lose whatever composure she'd recently found. She wet her lips and saw Brady watch her tongue and her eyes darken. *Holy crap, what is going on here?*

"Chipper. As in chip off the old block. My first crew chief said Chip was too butch for the boss's daughter."

Nicole could hear Heat Bickford's raspy voice as if he were standing behind her. She'd been assigned to Heat's crew the summer she turned eighteen. She had been begging her father for months to let her out on a crew and he'd finally relented, trusting his only daughter to the care of his best friend. Heat had never left Nicole's side the entire summer, calmly instructing, correcting, and praising her work. She'd returned to Heat's crew every school break thereafter until she graduated from college three years later.

Several seconds passed before either one of them spoke. Given the way Brady was looking at her Nicole began to wonder if she'd lost the ability to speak, let alone form a complete sentence. Not to mention a coherent one.

"I bet it was difficult being the boss's daughter."

Since it wasn't really a question Nicole knew she didn't need to answer, and she didn't really want to. It had been difficult, to say the least, but she did what she was told, when she was told, and watched and learned from the best firefighter in the world—her father. With perseverance and grit she'd proved she was just as capable as a man doing the same job. She wondered if Brady's experience was similar.

"And do you have any problems with the crews because of..." Nicole thought for a moment as to how to ask her question and settled on "the Bond element?"

Brady's laughter diffused the growing sexual tension in the air. "I can't say I've ever heard it referred to that way. I'll have to keep that in mind. Never know when you'll need a phrase like that."

It didn't escape Nicole's notice that Brady didn't answer the question. Instead, Brady asked, "Did you?" Brady paused a beat. "Have any troubles because of the Bond element?"

She dared a sip of her coffee, hoping her hands weren't shaking. It was pretty gutsy for Brady to ask. It could very well be a career-limiting move to imply the boss was queer. It very well could backfire in her face.

Nicole thought a minute, choosing whether to answer. If she did she outed herself, but if she didn't, Brady would know she was afraid. For some reason what Brady thought of her was important.

"No," she said simply.

"Was it because you were the boss's daughter?"

Nicole's respect for Brady went up another notch. She laid it all out on the table. "Probably. I never asked. I didn't talk about it, flaunt it, or hide it. If you make it a big deal it becomes a big deal. I consider it a nonevent."

"Again, tough being the boss's daughter."

"I hated it."

"I suppose you would." Brady's voice was soft and didn't hold a hint of "yeah, right," like she'd heard from so many others.

Feeling like her thoughts were being peeled away and she couldn't do anything about it, Nicole stood and walked to the window. As ridiculous as it was with her back to Brady she felt less vulnerable.

"I wanted to be treated just like everyone else."

"You didn't expect you would, did you?"

Brady's question surprised her. Not only was it blunt, but saying it to a superior could also be a career-limiting move. Brady's confidence impressed her. "I know. That doesn't mean I didn't want it. Don't you want things that sometimes you can't have?"

"I suppose."

"Yeah, well, you either pine over it, let it eat you up, or get over it."

"And you got over it?"

"Yes, I did. I couldn't change it. It was a fact of life. So I just got over it. It wasn't my problem. It was theirs. But if they couldn't deal with it and it became a problem, I dealt with it."

"I bet you did." Nicole detected a hint of admiration in Brady's voice.

Nicole had never talked this freely to anyone, let alone someone who worked for her. What surprised her the most was that she wanted to prolong the conversation. She had no agenda or anything specific to talk about, but in addition to simply wanting to, Nicole felt Brady would be very interesting. She had that no-nonsense, no-bullshit confidence guys on the crew had, and Nicole was in desperate need of regular conversation.

"How long are you here?" Nicole asked.

"The travel department booked my flight back to Moss Bluff tomorrow evening."

"Any plans while you're in town?"

"Nothing special. Sleep, maybe take advantage of the sights."

Something different in the tone of Brady's voice made Nicole wonder what sights she was referring to. She'd noticed the faint dark circles under Brady's eyes when they met earlier and had considered them a product of too much work and not enough sleep, a common occurrence on a site. Now she wasn't so sure it wasn't due to not-enough sleep *last* night. *Why in the hell am I connecting everything that had to do with this woman to sex?* The thought made her uncomfortable.

"Well, I won't keep you then," Nicole said, rising. "I'll walk you out."

"That's okay. I can find my way. You've got better things to do."

"That's where you're wrong." Nicole opened her door and followed Brady through her office reception area. "I've got things to do but not better things."

They walked to the elevator and Nicole said, "When you're in town again, give me a call. Maybe we can have lunch again."

"Sure."

Nicole pushed the down arrow and faced her. "If you ever need anything, please call," she said sincerely.

"I'll probably never be in a position to need to call someone like you." Brady didn't look at her but must have realized what her words sounded like because then she did look at her and quickly added, "I mean someone as important and powerful as you. You know, the boss."

A subtle *ding* indicated the elevator car had arrived on her floor. As the doors opened silently, Nicole extended her hand. Brady hesitated and finally grasped it. Her hands were rough and callused, and Nicole quickly wondered what they would feel like on her body. Flushed, she looked Brady directly in the eyes and said, "Never is a very long time."

Brady stepped inside and pushed the button to take her to the ground floor. Before the doors closed Nicole said, "Please be careful." The doors closed and Nicole was alone in the vestibule.

CHAPTER FIVE

The same driver was waiting for Brady when she exited the building. He straightened from his position of half-sitting on the trunk and hurried to the rear passenger door. After tipping his hat and opening the door, he said in a heavy Southern accent, "Where to, Miss Stewart?"

"Back to the hotel, I guess." Brady wasn't sure where else she could go. She lived about three hours away in a little-bit-of-nothing town called Moss Bluff and had gladly accepted the invitation to stay in town and enjoy a nice hotel.

"Miss McMillan called down and said I'm at your disposal all day."

Brady stopped before sliding into the luxurious backseat and looked at the driver, surprised.

"Yes, ma'am," he said. "Wherever you'd like to go. Doesn't matter where or for how long. I'm with you until I take you to the airport tomorrow evening."

"What's your name?" Brady asked.

"Milton, ma'am. Milton Farber." Milton stood a bit taller, as if pleased and proud someone had asked his name.

Brady didn't have much experience with hired drivers. Hell, she didn't have any experience at all and wasn't sure what the protocol was. She got the sense that Milton, a tall man with dark mocha skin, was a great guy. He called her and Nicole Miss instead of the safer Ms. "Well, Milton. May I call you Milton?" she asked before continuing. When he nodded she said, "I'm not used to this kind of thing. This being chauffeured around," she said, indicating the car. "What am I supposed to do?"

She was rewarded by a deep, baritone laugh and a smile that filled the old man's face. "Well, Miss Stewart, you simply tell me where you want to go, then sit back and enjoy the ride."

Brady thought for a minute. "All right, then, Milton, let's do it."

Brady had no specific destination in mind so she asked Milton to just drive around the city. Morgan City was more a large town than a city, and the countryside was beautiful, the houses alternately quaint small-town bungalows or large Southern estates.

As the miles passed Brady didn't pay much attention to the scenery around her, but was busy dissecting exactly what had happened this morning. The meeting with Nicole wasn't at all what she'd expected. She thought it would be dull, full of requisite platitudes from the bigwigs. They'd call them by their first name, stroke their egos, let them eat in the executive dining room with real cloth napkins and sparkling water, and dismiss them to go back into the field to tell stories that included a fancy hotel room and a chauffeur. For a little time and effort spent with a few workers, management would get untold free advertising and employee loyalty.

But that wasn't what had happened. Nicole had been warm and friendly and had quickly put everyone at ease. The men in the room weren't at all shy or tongue-tied around the boss and dominated most of the conversation. Brady was used to that and was quite content to sit back and observe.

After the shock of seeing how stunning Nicole was in person, Brady couldn't keep her eyes off her. It wasn't just because she was a beautiful woman; she'd seen and been with plenty of those. No, it was something else entirely.

Brady struggled to identify exactly what it was about Nicole that she found so intriguing. She said the right things, connected with everyone in the room, and had looked each of them in the eye. But Brady detected a haunted longing in her eyes that she masked whenever anyone was looking. She'd heard rumors that Nicole had lost all her hair in her accident and had looked at her hair, trying to detect if in fact it was a wig. If it was it was a very expensive one because Brady couldn't really tell. After a few minutes she thought what the hell difference did it make?

McMillan was the third company Brady had worked for, and she'd played every angle she knew to get hired. McMillan was known for its sophisticated hiring practices, at least more advanced than the other companies that mass-hired employees.

The job application was eight pages long, and in addition to the fill-in-the-blank sections, several essay questions were required. The interview process consisted of not less than three separate interviews with management and peers. The background check was extensive, and McMillan didn't accept anyone with a history of problems with drugs, alcohol, or crime. As a result McMillan employees were top notch, and the company was the most highly respected in the world.

How much of this was due to having Nicole at the helm? Brady had been hired prior to Nicole assuming command of the company, but her own interview process had been very similar to what it was today. She had read that when Nicole was younger she worked with her father in every aspect of the company and, with her degree in business, had taken McMillan to the next level.

Not that Brady had been around a lot of people in high positions, but somehow she knew Nicole was special. She used her hands as extensions of her expressions, her voice to modulate her question or comment on a story, and her smile as encouragement. She had every man in the room eating out of the palm of her hand but didn't seem to know it. But Brady was an expert at reading people, and she couldn't help but suspect something else behind Nicole's exterior. Not sinister or conniving, but her eyes were flat and her laugh a little forced. A haunted expression often passed through her eyes, and she seemed just a bit disconnected from those around her. Of course the men had no idea, and even if they did, Nicole seemed to be pretty damn good at concealing whatever was inside.

Brady hadn't said much during the meeting, learning long ago that, at times, it was better to not be seen or heard than it was to be seen and not heard. When she had been sitting in Nicole's office, Nicole had asked her about it.

"It's much more interesting and usually more entertaining to watch people. I'm not shy or intimidated, and when I have something to say I say it. Otherwise," she'd shrugged as if to say, "I keep my mouth shut."

"How 'bout we stop and stretch down by the civic center, Miss Stewart?" Milton asked, interrupting her thoughts. Brady looked around, the flat, expansive buildings to her left giving her a clue they were already there.

"You can grab a soda and take a walk on the seawall," Milton added. "It's not too hot and the bugs haven't showed up. Should be real nice." He extended the vowels of *real* to sound more like reeeel nice.

"Only if you join me," Brady replied. Whether it was her upbringing or simple politeness, she always treated those around her with respect, especially if their job was to wait on her. She'd seen too many service workers get no respect or get shit on by the customer who was "always right." She herself knew what it was like to be looked at from the wrong end of a snooty nose or a very large asshole.

"I couldn't do that, Miss Stewart," Milton said. "That just wouldn't be right."

"All right then, Milton." Brady decided on a different approach. "I'm afraid to walk along the seawall by myself. Will you walk with me?"

The old man didn't reply right away, the up-and-down movement of his broad shoulders in front of her giving away his laughter. "Yes, ma'am, I'd be happy to."

Milton held a Diet Coke and Brady carried a Dr Pepper as they strolled down the curved path. The seawall was a cement border keeping the Gulf of Mexico from spilling over into the park. From what Brady could see, the water was deep, and Milton explained that during certain celebrations, the boats would tie up at various points side by side along the entire wall. They were moored so close together the occupants would easily hop from one boat to another, usually carrying their alcoholic beverage of choice.

"Sounds like my kind of fun," Brady said.

"Yes, ma'am, it is."

"Do you have a boat?"

"Who, me?" Milton seemed surprised Brady would even think that.

"Why not you? You said you've lived here all your life."

"But that don't mean I have a boat, Miss Stewart. That's something I just can't afford, with my kids."

"How many do you have?"

"Nine," he said matter-of-factly.

Brady choked, her drink almost coming out her nose. "Nine? Nine kids? My God, Milton, what were you thinking?"

Milton joined in the laughter. "That I love my wife and wanted a house full of kids."

"That's not a houseful. That's practically a football team."

"Yes, ma'am. On Sunday when they all come over for dinner with their kids, it is."

Brady wondered what it would be like to be a part of a large family. More important, a family that loved each other like it appeared Milton's did. She'd never given any thought to having kids. They'd tie her down and get in the way of achieving her goals. Kids meant diapers, clothes, furniture, shoes, and toys. Kids had needs and wants, were constantly growing, and regarded parents as their personal ATM. And kids also meant commitment to one woman.

Brady had a goal and that was to have as much money as she needed to be able to do whatever she wanted, when she wanted to do it. She'd been poor and gone without all her life, and as soon as she'd realized it, she'd vowed never to be poor again. Never would money, or the lack of it, rule her life, and nothing or no one would get in her way of achieving that goal.

After another hour of driving around, Brady had Milton drop her off at her hotel. As she walked into the lobby she couldn't help but be amazed to be in such a fine hotel. Her typical lodging was the Motel 6 or Econo Lodge or any number of low-rate places she'd rather not remember. This place was upscale, even for Morgan City, and she took it all in as she walked across the lobby.

The front desk was to her left, with three clean-cut employees, each clad in dark-green matching blazers, white shirts, and ties. The only thing that separated them as individuals was the color of their hair and the shiny gold name badge. Brady recognized one of the men that had checked her in last night and gave a casual wave in his direction.

Across the tiled lobby and to the right was the restaurant, and the cocktail lounge was past that. Why was a bar called a cocktail lounge in a hotel but a bar anywhere else? They both served drinks and munchies and had the requisite three or four TVs mounted in the corners. It was in this bar last night where she'd met the woman she had to drag out of bed this morning. Brady risked a glance inside, hoping she didn't see her again. She couldn't remember her name and didn't do two nights in a row. That gave women the wrong impression.

Maybe Milton would know a discreet out of the way place that would suit her—what did Nicole call it—Bond element.

As she rode the large elevator to her room Brady was still trying to figure out why Nicole had asked her into her office. She had asked out of hearing from everyone and obviously after the meeting ended.

"Jesus, Stewart, what were you thinking hitting on your boss? And the big boss, for God's sake," Brady said to herself, looking around the hallway and relieved to see it empty. She slid her card key into the lock and turned the knob when the green light flickered.

It was late afternoon, and the maid had been in erasing any evidence of her nocturnal activities. The bed was perfectly made, the drapes open, the towels neatly folded and stacked on the large marble counter in the bathroom. The minibar hummed and Brady reached inside for a beer. Flick had told her that the company would pay for her hotel and meals, and Brady wondered if that included the $6.25 can of Michelob in her hand. Yikes, she thought as she read the prices on the menu inside the small door. She closed the door, popped the top, and sat in the chair next to the bed.

Why had Nicole wanted to talk with her? Judging by the questions she'd asked and what they'd talked about it wasn't anything special that she could put her finger on. She hadn't asked if she had the right equipment, good food, and a comfortable place to crash. She hadn't tried to get Brady to spill the beans or divulge any secrets about her team members, or anyone else for that matter. The other guys here today could have said all the same thing. Of course except for the part where Brady outed herself. She wasn't in the closet by any means, but she also didn't have to tell Nicole the full meaning behind her crew name. She could have just left it at Bond.

No way was Nicole interested in her. Sure, she smiled at her a little longer and held her hand a second longer than she had the men, but first, she was the boss, second she wasn't oil-field trash, and third, no way in hell was Brady even in the game, let alone in her league.

But that was okay. Brady had learned long ago not to nibble from the stove, and she certainly wasn't going to start with Nicole McMillan, even if she was interested in her. The interlude could be very interesting but it would be two big strikes against her game plan, and she didn't allow any changes in her plan, however attractive.

CHAPTER SIX

N icole, are you even listening?"

"Of course I am," she lied. She wasn't and hadn't been since Brady left her office earlier that afternoon. She had stood staring at the elevator doors for several moments after they closed behind Brady, trying to gather herself together enough to go back to work. But now, several hours later, she was still thinking about her.

Brady had completely surprised her. Other than the fact that she was a woman, and Nicole made a note to make sure she never made that mistake again, Brady wasn't like other women she'd known on the fire crews.

Nicole hated to stereotype, but those women were often crude, brassy, and generally big, beefy butches. And a bit scary as well. Most but not all were lesbians, but none were anything like Brady Stewart. Brady was tall and lean, showing a hint of the muscles that lay beneath the khaki trousers and her jacket. You needed both brute strength and raw finesse to fight oil-well fires, and from what Nicole saw, Brady had both.

She had read in the report that Brady had been burned on her right arm while rescuing that numskull Steckman from the fire. Nicole hadn't seen any indication of the injury, but then again the long sleeves of Brady's shirt and jacket didn't allow for much skin to be exposed. She knew too well how to hide scars behind layers of fabric.

"Then what did I say?"

"For God's sake, Buck, just say it again and spare me the humiliation of having to ask." Nicole's tone was uncharacteristically sharp and she apologized.

"I said Senator Mason wants you to meet with her committee the day after tomorrow. SB249 is due for a vote next month in her off-shore safety committee, and she wants to talk with you to make sure she fully understands all the ramifications of requiring companies to install redundant blowout preventers."

Since the Deep Water Horizon blowout in 2010, environmentalists and politicians greedy for re-election had been pushing to make it mandatory for every oil well to have no fewer than three very expensive pieces of equipment.

The cost aside, drillers were adamantly against the bill and had spent just about as much money on lobbyists to kill the bill as the Sierra Group had spent trying to get it passed. Personally Nicole was supportive of anything that would make drilling safer to humans and the environment, but Senate Bill 249 was, in her opinion, overkill. The cause of the blowout on the Horizon had been determined to be a variety of factors, with ignored or lax safety measures the primary one. The damage to the environment was heartbreaking, but another blowout preventer might or might not have prevented the disaster.

"Sure." Nicole responded halfheartedly. She was uncomfortable around Colleen Mason, the four-time senator from Colorado. Colleen was one of the few out lesbians in the U.S. Senate, and she'd made it clear, if very subtly, her interest in seeing Nicole on a personal level. Nicole had testified before the committee a few years ago, and Colleen had contacted her off and on since then for reasons both professional and personal. Lately she was getting a little more demanding and was not taking Nicole's "no" seriously.

"Something wrong, Nicole?"

"No, just letting my mind wander a little bit. Would you get me a Cliff-Notes version of the bill so I can brush up on it?"

After Buck left a few minutes later, Nicole sat back down at her desk and tried to concentrate on the pile of papers in front of her. She succeeded until the request for a new crane was next in the "approve" pile.

Brady was on the crew fighting the blowout in North Dakota. The owners of the rig had called after the pressure systems failed and all attempts to extinguish the blaze themselves were unsuccessful. The first blowout preventer was installed in the early 1920s, and with the advance of modern technology, well-control techniques, and personnel training, blowouts were infrequent. But when they occurred, the result was a monster.

Nicole remembered the endless discussions with her father about fires. When other little girls were listening to bedtime stories of princes and castles, Nicole was learning about blowout preventers, ignition sources, and fire-suppression techniques. She hung on every word and fell asleep dreaming about fighting fires with her dad.

Glancing at her watch, Nicole wondered what Brady was doing now. It was after six, and more than likely she was having dinner and getting ready to go out on the town. She said she was going to take in the sights, and Nicole knew exactly what sights she was referring to. Morgan City didn't have a robust lesbian community, but if you could read the signs and if you were as attractive as Brady was, you could find exactly what you were looking for.

Nicole noticed the paper in her hands was moving and realized her hands were trembling. How long had it been since she "saw the sights"? It had been several months since she last dialed the number, and she hesitated before reaching for the phone.

She'd met Katherine, or 17402, the employee number the agency had assigned her, the first time three years into her recovery. She was nervous and had chosen a hotel twenty miles outside the town limits. The last thing she wanted was for someone to see her going into a local hotel room. In Morgan City everyone knew everyone's business, and what they didn't know, they made up.

Nicole had waited for Katherine with the drapes drawn and only the light from the bathroom slicing through the darkened room. She paced back and forth across the small room, too nervous to sit still. She still wasn't sure she could go through with it, but she had to do something. She needed human contact, the touch of a woman, the release that cleared her head and made her feel alive.

Gina, her ex, had once said Nicole had an insatiable thirst for sex. Nicole, on the other hand, viewed it as her desire to make love to the woman she loved. In the beginning Gina didn't seem to mind, and many nights they only dozed before one or both of them would reach for the other. Whether it was just her nature or the fact that she'd seen several men die, Nicole lived life, knowing how quickly it could be extinguished. She and Gina had been together for eighteen months when Nicole told her she loved her and wanted to be only with her. It took Gina several weeks before she echoed Nicole's words, and they'd moved in together shortly thereafter.

Nicole was away from home for weeks and sometimes months at a time fighting fires around the world. Even though she'd many opportunities to cheat, and Gina would never find out, Nicole had always been faithful.

After Gina had walked out on her, Nicole had discovered Gina hadn't felt the same. Nicole believed that fidelity was the backbone of a relationship. It didn't matter if you were straight, gay, lesbian, or anything in between when you made a commitment to someone it didn't matter if it was for a month, weekend, night, or even an hour, you didn't cheat. What did the minister say at their commitment ceremony—thou shall forsake all others? Well, Gina must have mistakenly thought he said thou shall fuck all others.

Nicole didn't know who she hated more—Gina for walking out on her after the fire, Gina for cheating on her, or herself for being so naïve to believe Gina would honor their commitment vows. To Gina the "in sickness and health" part meant as long as you don't get sick, the "for richer or poorer" meant I get to spend all your money, and the "until death do us part" caveat meant that since Nicole's heart did stop several times in the first week after the fire, Gina fulfilled that criteria as well.

The breakup scene with Gina was loud and ugly. Nicole was home after several months in a rehab facility and was having what she called a good day. Her range of movement was improving, all but a few burn areas were completely healed, and she was tapering off the heavy pain meds that made her dopey but enabled her to get through the day.

The home-health aide had helped Nicole prepare Gina's favorite dinner of beef brisket with red potatoes and grilled corn on the cob. Gina, an architect who owned her own firm, had been coming home later than usual the last few weeks. Nicole had to guess when she'd be home as she prepared the simple but special meal. She put clean sheets on the bed, set the dining-room table with the good dishes and flatware, and lit the candles on either side of the small basket of get-well flowers that had arrived earlier that morning. The dimmer for the overhead lights in the dining room was low, creating a soft yet intimate setting. She had been planning this evening for days.

She missed Gina. Missed the connection they had, her touch, the way she made Nicole feel like she was the only woman in the world. Since the fire Gina had been there for her but yet not there. She was polite, helped when needed, but distant. Nicole's body would never be the same and she was still in the process of accepting that reality, but she was still the same woman she had been before her life changed. No, that wasn't true, she'd finally admitted to herself just that afternoon. No one could go through what she had and not change.

Maybe that was what was affecting her relationship with Gina. From the time she regained consciousness and could remember, Gina hadn't touched her. She didn't kiss her or hold her hand, one of the few places the fire hadn't affected. In the evenings they sat platonically on opposite sides of the couch and watched TV, or Gina disappeared into her office with the excuse of work, and tonight was no different.

They hadn't made love, and Nicole hadn't been comfortable exposing herself in front of Gina. Her therapist had explained this was common and that with time and Nicole's acceptance of her own body, she would know when she was ready. Nicole hadn't yet fully accepted her body but she needed to be with Gina, the woman she loved, to help her reaffirm that she was a desirable woman.

Gina was in bed, her back to her, lights off, the glow of the full moon sneaking through the shutters on the bedroom windows. Nicole hesitated before slipping her T-shirt over her head and sliding under the covers. The shirt did more than keep her warm. It was her shield, and discarding it left her completely exposed and totally vulnerable. Afraid she might lose her nerve, Nicole didn't hesitate to approach Gina. More than inches separated them in their bed, the place where love and laughter, tears and dreams had been shared.

Nicole moved close to Gina, lightly pressing against her back. Gina stiffened, and for an instant Nicole thought about backing away.

But she couldn't. She needed Gina, and they needed to reconnect as a couple, to start to rebuild their life together.

"I love you," Nicole said, slowly moving her unbandaged hand up and down Gina's side. Her skin was soft and warm, the familiar curves arousing.

"Nicole," Gina said, and Nicole knew that tone. It was the one that said, "You're kidding, right?"

"Gina, we need this. You've barely looked at me since the accident, and I can't remember the last time you touched me, even if it was just in passing." She no longer called her Nic either.

By unspoken agreement both she and Gina had made certain the other wasn't in the same room when they were anything other than fully dressed. Gina rose early and was off to work before Nicole was out of bed. The reverse was true in the evening.

"Nicole," Gina said, more forcefully this time, and moved away from her. She was already so far to her side of the bed Nicole was surprised she didn't fall out. She reached for her again.

"Gina…" Before Nicole had a chance to say more, Gina sprang out of bed.

"No," she said, her face clearly visible in the moonlight.

"Gina," Nicole said again, this time hearing the pleading in her voice. She hated it.

"No, Nicole. I can't do this." Gina waved her hands, indicating the bed.

Nicole started to sit up, the sheet falling down and exposing her scarred chest. Her breasts were the bright pink of new skin, though her nipples, thankfully, hadn't been damaged. She saw Gina look at her and just as quickly turn away. She pulled the sheet up to cover herself. "Gina sweetie, we don't have to make love. I just want to be close to you, feel you against me again. I've missed you."

"I can't do this," Gina repeated, and headed to the closet. Nicole heard her rummaging around and practically gasped when she emerged with a small suitcase and several business suits.

"What are you doing?" Nicole asked as Gina pulled open drawers and tossed underwear into the open case.

"I can't do this."

"For God's sake, Gina, stop saying that." Nicole was angry now. She grabbed her T-shirt from the floor and put it on before she turned on the light.

"Gina, honey, what's going on? You have to talk to me. We love each other. We can get through this. We just need a little more time," Nicole said, making up excuses.

"Nicole, don't start with this again." Gina gave a sigh of exasperation. Nicole had insisted they both attend therapy to deal with the accident. Gina had refused.

"We never finished it, Gina." They had had this discussion before, but Nicole was always too weak to complete it. Tonight she'd see it through to the end.

"Why are you here? Is it out of guilt? An obligation? A sense of duty?"

"Of course not. Don't be melodramatic."

"Melodramatic? I have burns over sixty percent of my body. I may never walk normally again, or ride a bike, or throw the ball for the dog. I certainly will never, ever wear a bikini. Hell, I won't even wear shorts again. I'm not melodramatic. I'm a realist." Nicole's voice carried across the room. Rosco, their springer spaniel, jumped up from his bed in the corner and quickly slinked out the bedroom door.

"For God's sake, Nicole, stop it." Gina looked around as if making sure she hadn't forgotten anything.

"No, I won't stop it. For weeks I peed out of a tube, shit in a pan, and ate through a hose that went up my nose and down my throat. I've been peeled naked by nurses, manhandled by therapists, and psychoanalyzed by shrinks. A little squabble's nothing to me."

"This is not a *little squabble*." Gina stopped as if deciding whether to continue. "I can't do this. I can barely look at you. My eyes stray to the bandages, the bloody bandages that make my stomach turn. In the morning I can hardly wait to leave, and I stay at the office until I can barely see I'm so tired because I can't do this. I don't want to do it." Gina stood still, as if her declaration took all the energy out of her. Then she continued.

"I know I didn't say what you wanted to hear, but it's the truth. I don't want to see your burns, change your bandages, and I certainly don't want to touch them. I can't do it and I don't want to." Gina repeated herself like Nicole was a small child and still not getting it. "You always said we have to tell each other the truth. Well, there you have it. Maybe I am a coward or a shit or whatever you want to call me, but at least I'm honest about it."

Nicole had been afraid this would happen. In the hours she was alone in her hospital bed or enduring the agony of the debridement of dead skin to avoid infection, her biggest fear was that Gina would find her scarred and bloody body repulsive.

Nicole shouldn't have been surprised, but it hurt nonetheless. She and Gina had been together for six years and were making a life together. They had shared broken bones, an appendectomy and tonsillectomy. Their love had endured long separations due to Nicole's job, yet they'd managed to carve out time to take vacations in places like Rome, Australia, and Fiji.

"Get out," Nicole shouted, lifting her bandaged arm and pointing to the door. "Get out of this room, my house, and my life." As if released from her shackles, Gina ran out of the room, sparing Nicole the agony of having to tell her again.

Now, leaning back in her desk chair, Nicole reached for the phone and dialed the number she knew by heart. Ninety minutes later she was in the same hotel, opening the door to the same woman who'd released her torment many times before.

Chapter Seven

*R*elax. Breathe. Don't think. Just feel. Nicole chanted inside
her head as Katherine slid her skillful fingers inside her. From
the minute Katherine entered the sterile room Nicole felt disjointed,
almost outside herself. The first time she and Katherine were together
was very different from this time.

It had been the same out-of-the-way hotel, and the clerk's smirk
had embarrassed Nicole when she said she'd pay cash. She'd signed
the register, took her key, and bolted from the plain but clean lobby.

Once in the room she was too nervous to sit. She had texted her
room number to the woman who was due to knock on the door any
second.

"What in the fuck am I doing? I'm about to have sex with a
complete stranger. I didn't even do that in college," Nicole said to the
empty room as she walked back and forth at the foot of the king-size
bed. "Shit, she might be a cop, and that'd just be perfect." Nicole
grabbed her keys and touched the doorknob just as the expected
knock came.

She didn't open the door. She didn't move and wasn't sure she
was even breathing. The woman knocked again. Nicole knew it was
a woman because when she'd called to make the appointment she
was asked her preferences, including male or female. Somehow she'd
stuttered out female and explained her physical situation before being
assigned a client number. The deal was cash paid up front.

"Ms. Haven," a muffled voice said from the other side of the metal door. Nicole didn't answer. Her hand was still on the knob, her knees weak.

Nicole hadn't given her real name when she made the appointment. When asked, she blurted out the first thing that came to mind. This woman would be her sanctuary, retreat, and refuge from the world she now faced. When Paul, her physical therapist, had referred her to the agency, he said that the employees were professionals, discreet and specialized in individuals with disabilities. She supposed that having scars over a majority of her body constituted a disability.

"Ms. Haven. My name is Katherine, 17402. I understand you're expecting me."

Her hand was shaking as she turned the knob and pulled open the door. Nicole hadn't known what to expect, but this woman was tall, well dressed in a familiar name-brand suit, and completely put together. The smile on her face was apparently meant to put Nicole at ease, but it only made her more nervous.

"I'm Katherine," she said, extending her hand in greeting.

Nicole responded more out of habit and was surprised to feel Katherine's hand was warm. She knew hers was damp and clammy.

"May I come in?"

"Yes, of course," Nicole stuttered, opening the door wider and stepping to the side. Katherine smelled like lilac and practically glided as she entered the room and turned around.

Nicole closed the door and had no idea what she was supposed to do or say. Did she hand her the money that was in a plain white envelope? Did she just get naked and lie down on the bed? Was any conversation allowed or encouraged? She'd paid for one hour, and at this moment that felt like forever. Katherine must have sensed her discomfort.

"Shall we sit down?"

"Yes, sure. Can I get you something to drink or something? There's soda, beer, and a few cocktail mixes." Nicole had looked in the minibar under the TV earlier.

Katherine's smile was warm and understanding. "No, thank you. I'm fine, but feel free to have something if you'd like."

Nicole couldn't help but smile. "I probably should, but I think I'll pass too."

Katherine crossed her legs and Nicole couldn't help but look. She glanced up and knew Katherine had caught her.

"I understand this is the first time you've called the agency."

Nicole nodded, trying not to look as frighteningly uncomfortable as she felt. "And I have no clue what to do or why I'm even doing this."

"I was told you'd been in an accident," Katherine said, her voice clear and deep.

"A fire," Nicole added, trying to ease some of the tension she felt. Katherine hadn't yet glanced over her body with curiosity, trying to detect any sign of her burns. She continued to look her straight in the eye. Nicole was impressed.

"I'm sorry that happened to you, and I'm glad you were referred to us and that you called. People with physical limitations or issues are no different in their need for human contact than anyone else. They find it difficult to…shall we say…connect with someone. Especially if they're single."

Nicole quirked her mouth. "I wasn't always single," Nicole blurted out without thinking. Good God. This woman wasn't her therapist—or then again maybe she was—her sex therapist. Katherine didn't say anything, and her expression said Nicole could continue or drop it. "She said she could barely look at me and certainly didn't want to touch me." Katherine still showed no reaction. "I told her to get out, and I haven't seen her since."

"Good for you. How long had you been together?"

"Six years," Nicole replied, still angry. Katherine didn't say anything else. "So, uh, how do we do this?" Nicole felt absolutely stupid. "I'm sorry. I didn't mean to sound so direct and crass. Its just that I've never done this before and have absolutely no idea what the protocol is."

"However you want to. We can talk, if that's what you want, or something more, or something in between. You don't have to do anything you don't want to or anything that makes you uncomfortable. I follow your lead. I know it's hard for you to believe what I say right now, Ms. Haven, but you can trust me. If you say no, I'll stop immediately. No questions, no explanations needed, and hopefully no embarrassment. This isn't about what I want or need. It's about you. You can participate any way you're comfortable with. I don't judge and I don't keep score. I'm here to help you in whatever you need, whether it's to help you regain sexual self-confidence or to get you off. I don't mean to be tactless, but at times that's all someone wants."

Nicole nodded, absorbing everything Katherine had just said.

"I've found that it's easier for people to say what they don't want rather than what they do. How about I ask and you can just give me a yes or no? Would that work for you?"

"Yes." Nicole was more comfortable now that she knew the ground rules.

"All right. Is there any place you don't want me to see?"

"I have scars," Nicole said, but couldn't finish. "I wear a wig. I lost most of my hair and it never really grew back."

"I understand," Katherine said quietly. "But is there any place you don't want me to see?" Katherine repeated her question because Nicole hadn't answered her.

"If I say yes?"

"Then I won't look," Katherine answered simply without hesitation.

Nicole felt comfortable with the clinical, straightforward questions.

"Is there any place you don't want me to touch?"

"I don't know."

Katherine's smile was filled with understanding. "Fair enough. We'll play it by ear on that one. Again, if anything makes you uncomfortable or you don't want me to do something, just say stop and I will. Immediately. No questions, no pressure."

She stood up. "How about if I step into the bathroom and freshen up a bit. You can do whatever you feel comfortable with. Is that okay?"

Nicole nodded again, understanding Katherine meant she could take her clothes off and get into bed or continue to sit there like a frightened virgin.

"Good. I'll be a few minutes, and I'll ask you if it's okay for me to come out."

"Yes, that'll be fine," Nicole replied, and Katherine silently left the room.

This was it. The moment Nicole had to make one of the biggest decisions of her life. She could leave right now, sit and chat with a beautiful woman for the next forty-five minutes, or retake control of her life. She stood on legs that felt shaky and started to undress.

As she carefully laid each piece of clothing on the chair, she felt increasingly vulnerable. Other than her doctors and physical therapists, no one had seen her naked. Not even Gina. Sadly, not Gina. And isn't that why she was here, in this out-of-the-way hotel with a woman she was going to pay to have sex with her? She needed to feel desired, like a woman, experience a woman's hands on her, and if she had to pay for it, so be it. Trying not to think, Nicole pulled the bedding down and slid onto the crisp sheets.

"Okay for me to come out?"

"Yes," Nicole lied. She held her breath, more nervous this time than her first time. She didn't have much experience with women. Before she met Gina she was constantly on the road on burning offshore oil rigs, in boondock-ville, or the middle of a country that stoned an unescorted female. Not much opportunity to meet women.

Katherine came into the room dressed exactly as she'd been when she left. If she was pleased or surprised to see Nicole in bed, her expression didn't give it away. She crossed the room and stood next to the bed.

"May I join you?"

"Yes."

"May I take my clothes off and get under the covers?"

Nicole found it interesting that Katherine was so specific in her questions. When Nicole said that Katherine could join her, she assumed she would be naked too. Katherine, however, made no assumptions.

"Yes."

Nicole watched nervously as Katherine removed her clothes. She was tanned, the muscles in her arms and legs clearly visible. Nicole flashed to a scene in the 1980s movie *American Gigolo*, in which the main character was working out to keep his body in top physical shape for his clients. Nicole wondered if Katherine did the same. Hers had looked like that once, though not from hours in the gym but hours fighting fires.

"Lights on or off?"

"Off," Nicole answered, and the room was immediately cloaked in darkness. She felt rather than saw Katherine slide into bed beside her. She couldn't see anything, at least not yet. It would take a few minutes for her eyes to adjust. When they did, Katherine turned to her.

"May I move closer?"

"Yes." Nicole turned on her side facing Katherine.

"May I touch your arm?"

"Yes."

Katherine's hand was warm and soft. Slowly she moved it up and down Nicole's arm several times, her eyes never leaving hers. Katherine took her hand and lifted it to her lips. She didn't say anything, but it was clear she was asking permission. Nicole barely nodded and Katherine's warm lips touched her palm.

Her lips were soft and warm, and what felt like a shot of warm liquid traveled up Nicole's arm, through her body, and settled low in her stomach.

"May I move closer?" Katherine asked between kisses.

Nicole nodded, and the bed shifted as Katherine closed the distance between them. As their breasts touched, a gasp of pleasure escaped before Nicole could stop it. It had been far too long since she'd felt the skin of another woman, and her body's reaction confirmed that it was indeed what she needed.

Katherine ran her hand over Nicole's shoulder and down her back. Nicole tensed when she touched the edge of the scar, and Katherine immediately stopped. Nicole smiled weakly and nodded for Katherine to continue. When she did she dropped her hand and cupped Nicole's butt. Nicole involuntarily arched against her, and Katherine pulled her closer.

God, that felt good. She'd missed this so much—the connection of two people who fit perfectly together, the feel of a woman in her arms, the building heat of desire. She moved against Katherine.

"May I kiss your breasts?"

Katherine's face was so close, Nicole felt her warm breath caress her cheek. "Yes," Nicole said in anticipation. She had a direct nerve from her nipples to her clit and would probably come the instant Katherine touched her there. She was wound so tight, and it had been so long.

Nicole rolled onto her back at the first touch of Katherine's mouth on her erect nipple, pulling Katherine with her. Katherine slid her muscled leg between hers, and Nicole moaned. The sensation was overwhelming. She wanted to come now, yet she wanted this to go on forever.

Katherine's mouth was magic on her breasts. Nicole came twice as Katherine teased one nipple then the other with her teeth and tongue. Nicole grabbed Katherine's long, dark hair and held her tight against her as her orgasms ripped through her body. Her heart was still pounding when Katherine lifted her head and shifted her attention to her chin, her neck, and back to her lips. Nicole was gasping for air when Katherine asked, "May I touch you?"

"God, yes, please." Nicole didn't care if she was paying for this; it felt wonderful. Katherine's fingers were as skilled as her mouth, and she came again as Katherine flicked her fingers over her hard clit.

"You okay?" Katherine asked, and Nicole blinked her eyes open. She was still breathing fast as Katherine continued to explore. Nicole didn't have the energy to do anything other than smile.

"I'll take that as a yes." Katherine leaned over, nibbled on her ear, and whispered, "May I go inside you?"

Nicole groaned, not sure if she could go again, but her body made the decision for her. "Only if you stop asking and just do it," Nicole growled in frustration. She was rewarded with another powerful orgasm when Katherine followed her instructions to the letter.

And here she was, three years later, paying the same clerk the same amount of cash for the slightly redecorated room where she waited for the same woman she called several times a month. They never kissed and didn't talk about personal things. The afterglow conversation was always light and easy. No promises were ever made, and neither referenced the white envelope on the dresser or when they might see each other again.

Relax. Breathe. Don't think. Just feel. Nicole chanted to herself, but it wasn't working. Maybe she was too tired. She'd been working too many hours for the past few weeks, and that was probably the reason. Usually when she worked too much she needed this release and usually came not long after Katherine entered the room.

"Haven? What is it?"

After three years Nicole hadn't told Katherine her real name, and she suspected it was the same for Katherine. "I'm sorry. I guess I'm a little distracted."

"No apologies, remember."

Nicole fidgeted on the bed, and the air-conditioning kicked on.

"Do you want me to leave?"

"Yes…no…I don't know." Nicole sighed. Her own hands and vibrator just weren't doing it anymore. She needed a release but was too keyed up for it to happen.

"Turn over," Katherine said, moving from between her legs. Katherine had seen her scarred back many times and Nicole was no longer self-conscious, but she'd never seen her with her wig off. That was personal. What she did with Katherine was professional.

"Just relax. Clear your mind. Feel my hands on you. Caressing you. Feel your muscles start to relax. That's right, deep breaths." Katherine continued stroking, moving lower, the same rhythmic caressing of her ass and legs. Nicole relaxed, but when each passing stroke came closer to her clit, she began to feel something else.

Thank God.

Katherine teased her with her hands moving up and down her inner thighs. Nicole opened her legs wider to give her better access to where she needed them. Katherine's fingers grazed Nicole's clit, and she moaned and lifted her ass to chance the contact. Katherine repeated the movement several more times, and each time Nicole whimpered when she pulled away.

Finally, Katherine entered her with agonizingly slowness. Nicole was bucking and Katherine finger-fucked her. Her thumb massaged the opening in her ass as if requesting entry. Nicole had discovered that this little treasure shot her right to the moon, and Katherine saved it for what she called special occasions.

"Yes." Nicole could barely breathe. Carefully Katherine entered her, and jolts of pleasure shot through her. Brady's face was suddenly in front of her—her smile, her expression when she was concentrating on something, the touch of her hand when they shook. Katherine's fingers were everywhere. On her clit, deep inside, and filling forbidden places. Katherine's fingers had made her come, but she came for Brady's face behind her closed eyelids.

❖

"No thanks, I'm just here for a beer," Brady said to the third woman who'd asked her to dance. She'd come to The Knock Out to—how had she phrased it for Nicole this afternoon?—experience the sights. She'd been here over an hour, and though the bar was packed she didn't see anyone who caught her eye. Damn. She'd been on site for weeks with nothing but her hand and imagination for company, and now here she was with a room to pick from and she felt nothing. The familiar zing of attraction, the unmistakable throb of arousal weren't in attendance tonight. The more she looked, the more she drank, the more confused she became.

She'd never experienced this. Every time she went out with sex on the menu, she always came back satisfied. She loved women. Their exterior features only provided a hint of what they were like in bed. Rarely did Brady find a woman unattractive. She could always find something desirable. She'd been with large women, petite women, tall and short. But they were all women, and she loved everything about a woman. They smelled wonderful, their skin soft and smooth, their voices husky in the dark. Some screamed her name, others came in the silence, but all gave her what she needed.

Yet tonight she just felt different. There was more than enough of a selection to choose from, but she simply wasn't interested. Sure, any of the women here could get her off, but she was looking for something else—something she couldn't quite put her finger on, something she'd seen in Nicole McMillan.

She signaled for another beer and pondered that thought. Nicole was sensuous in a sophisticated way. She was calm, confident, and serene. Brady didn't have much experience with that kind of woman. They certainly didn't live in her trailer park, and a woman like that didn't hang around the bars she frequented.

She was almost intimidating, but long ago Brady had refused to be intimidated by anyone ever again. She might not have more than a high-school education, but she was smart, honest, and rich.

When Brady had received her first paycheck she went to the local American Express Financial Advisor office and asked for an appointment with a woman to help her set up her retirement plan. Three hours later she had a money-market account and owned several blue-chip stocks and an IRA account. A year later she'd doubled those accounts and knew enough about diversifying her portfolio to start making her own investment choices. She saved every penny, and, since her meals and travel were paid for while she was on site, was able to put almost all her paychecks in her accounts. She was on track to retire at fifty-five and do whatever the hell she wanted whenever the hell she wanted.

"You've been sitting here by yourself a long time." The deep, seductive voice came from over her left shoulder, and a faint tingle tickled her stomach.

"And you would know that by…"

"Watching you."

"Have you now?" Brady took another swig of her beer.

"Yes, and I can honestly say I like what I see."

"Would you lie to me and say it?"

"No. Not enough liquor in this place for me to take home a woman I didn't want to see in the morning."

"That's good," Brady said, shifting a little to see the mystery woman's face. She liked what she saw and was tired of brooding. "Would you like to sit down?"

"Only if you don't have a woman back home. I do have my limits."

"How do you know I don't live here?"

"I've never seen you here. And this is the only place like this in town," the woman said, looking around the dark, noisy bar.

"Maybe I just moved here."

"My lucky night."

Brady thought about what was right here in front of her and what she faced once she returned to camp. "Nope, nobody at home." Brady moved the stool beside her and indicated for the woman to sit.

"Michelle," the woman said as she sat.

"Brady." She took the hand Michelle offered, and Michelle didn't immediately release it.

"So what is it? Local or transient?"

The tingle in Brady's gut had turned into a full-blown throb of desire. "Transient."

"How long are you here for?"

"Long enough."

"Do you want to sit here and make small talk?"

Brady shook her head.

"Neither do I."

Brady left a twenty on the bar, along with any thoughts of spending the night alone.

CHAPTER EIGHT

The heat washed over her first, sucking the breath out of her lungs. Then, the deafening roar, the blinding pain.

Nicole bolted out of bed and ran through the house, her heart racing, her breathing fast. Her hands were shaking, and if she stopped walking she might fall down. Her knees were that weak. Every light in the house was already on, but she still couldn't drive away the shadows.

"God damn it!" she shouted into the empty house. "God damn it to hell!" she said, changing directions. "One, two, three, four…" She counted until she got to twenty and then started again. The panic attacks rarely lasted more than a few minutes, but it felt like a lifetime.

The first time it happened she thought it was a heart attack. She was hot all over, her limbs shaking, her heart beating almost out of her chest. She was light-headed and had trouble breathing. Thankfully she was still in the hospital, and a battery of tests had confirmed nothing more severe than a panic attack.

Nothing more serious? What a fucking joke. Something that could paralyze her brain and terrorize her mind wasn't serious? Get real. She was prescribed anti-anxiety medication and talked about it with her shrink.

Nicole recited all the mind games her shrink had taught her, but it was several minutes before she started to calm down. She hadn't had an attack in months. Nighttime was the worst—the instant just before she fell asleep, when her mind started to drift. Even with medication, at times the attacks were so frequent she didn't sleep for days. She prayed they weren't starting again. The clock on the wall read two forty a.m.

Nicole walked around her house, concentrating on her breathing and her surroundings. The flashbacks always left her disoriented, and looking at familiar things helped ground her. Her house was new, designed by her and built only a year ago in an intimate enclave of seven homes on oversized home sites, each with a private boat dock. Turning off the alarm she walked through the main living area on the first floor, making a lap through the kitchen, around the large breakfast bar, and past her office. She continued through the great room with warm wood floors, surround sound, and numerous windows for natural light. She opened the French doors and stepped onto a large patio.

The stars were brilliant, and the constant breeze on the Gulf shore at this hour of the morning was quite cool. She drank slowly from the bottle of water she'd grabbed on one of her passes by the refrigerator. Inhaling the salty air several times and listening to the sound of the waves calmed her even more.

Sitting down on one of the Adirondack chairs, Nicole kept a close rein on her thoughts. If she let them wander she might find herself right back where she'd fought so hard to get out of—in that terrifying place between panic and sheer panic.

She thought about the recent financials Buck had shared with her last week. The company was profitable, had a large reserve of cash, and more fires were flaring in the world than McMillan could put out. Nicole didn't care if her company was the largest or extinguished the most fires. She cared that her father's legacy continued. McMillan was known in the industry to be fair, quick, and very, very safe.

Which made her think about the gathering yesterday morning. She wanted her legacy to be that McMillan recognized and rewarded safety at all costs. If a job took longer, so be it. If it cost more to extinguish a blowout due to safety procedures being followed, she paid it. If an employee ignored or intentionally bypassed a safety procedure, she fired him. She would never compromise on safety in the name of money.

Nicole reflected on the actions of the five employees who had gathered in the conference room down the hall from her office. The men were stereotypical oil-field workers—a bit rough around the edges, not highly educated, but very smart. Smart from experience and common sense, and innovative out of necessity. If the apocalypse ever came, she wanted to be next to these guys.

Brady, on the other hand, was different, even more so than the few other females in the industry. And even fewer put out fires. Nicole wondered how Brady got into this business. She made a mental note to look at Brady's personnel file in the morning. It was none of her business, but Brady was one of her employees so she did have the right.

Brady had been more an observer than an active participant today. Nicole watched her take in her surroundings in both the conference room and her office. She spoke when spoken to but rarely initiated a conversation or voiced her opinion. She listened and watched what was going on around her, which is what put her in the position of saving her co-worker's life. Was she the same way off the job? Was she the life of the party or did she hover just on the fringe?

What was Brady doing right now? What a stupid thought, she said into the dark. It's the middle of the night. She was probably sleeping, something Nicole needed to do. She had a long day tomorrow but would have difficulty falling back asleep, so she stayed where she was.

Was Brady sleeping alone? Was she from around here? During their conversation she didn't indicate that she knew anyone. But something like that wouldn't keep a woman like Brady from getting what she wanted. She was attractive and polite, and had all her teeth. Nicole couldn't help but smile at that last thought.

She rubbed her left arm above the elbow. The scar tissue had tightened over the past few weeks, and the ache that accompanied it constantly reminded her how her life had changed from being on the front line to being an observer.

The night chilled and her nipples stiffened. She didn't know how long she'd been outside, but now she was cold. Closing and locking the door behind her, she reset the alarm and went to her office.

Chapter Nine

Nicole sat in a straight-backed chair facing nine senators. They were seated on a raised dais, whereas her table and chair was on floor level. It was a power thing, and she thought it petty. She had been called to Washington to testify in front of the energy committee to give expert testimony on the technology and procedures around fighting oil-well fires. Since the blowout of the Deepwater Horizon well in the Gulf of Mexico several years ago, the committee was on a witch hunt for safety violations. To add to this zoo in front of her, every senator on this committee was up for reelection next year, including Colleen Mason, who just so happened to chair the committee and was sitting directly in front of her.

"Ms. McMillan, thank you for joining us today on such short notice to share your expert testimony with the committee."

"I wouldn't consider myself an expert, Madam Chairman. Just someone with a lot of experience. But thank you for inviting me." She hadn't gone back to sleep the night of her panic attack and hadn't slept much last night in the hotel either. She felt sluggish.

"Ms. McMillan, you underestimate yourself," Senator Mason said, and to Nicole her words sounded like a weak platitude. "Let's get started, shall we? Please walk us through the anatomy of an oil well and an oilfield fire, if you would."

Nicole glanced quickly at the other members of the committee. Several appeared to be interested, two looked completely bored, and Colleen Mason couldn't take her eyes off Nicole.

"Certainly." Nicole had prepared a few notes, but most of what she would more than likely be asked she would know without them.

"First, the hole is drilled above where they believe the oil is. The hole could be anywhere from a few hundred feet to several thousand deep and fifteen to over thirty inches in diameter. Once they reach the desired depth they place sections of pipe into the hole to prevent it from collapsing on itself. Then the crew lowers the drill string, or the drill pipe that is usually in thirty-foot sections, as a conduit for the oil to flow through up to the surface.

"Then the derrick is set up, which is probably the only part of the rig that most people can identify. It holds the drilling apparatus, including the drill bit, and is tall enough to allow new sections of pipe to be added as the drilling progresses. Once the reservoir is tapped the crew puts on the wellhead and the pumping can begin."

"Where does the blowout preventer come in?"

"The B-O-P, as it's known in the industry, was developed in the early 1920s to cope with extreme erratic pressures, also known as a 'kick,' and uncontrolled oil flow. When a kick occurs, rig operators monitoring the system or, in newer models, automatic systems close the valve, stopping the flow out of the pipe. Sand, mud, rocks, and other substances may be ejected from the hole in a blowout, in addition to the oil or gas."

"How does a blowout happen? Aren't they pretty rare?" the man to the right of Senator Mason asked.

"In comparison to fifty, twenty, even five years ago, yes, they are."

"If these B-O-Ps, as you call them, are designed to prevent blowouts, as the name aptly describes, how do they still happen?" One of the senators who looked old enough to be classified as a fossil asked the question.

"Blowouts are often ignited by sparks from rocks being ejected from the line or simply from heat generated by friction."

"Or by negligence," Senator Mason said quickly.

Again Nicole waited for a question. She didn't have to wait long.

"So, Ms. McMillan, what makes fighting this type of fire so challenging and so expensive?" a different senator asked.

"What makes it so challenging is the fuel that's feeding the fire. The oil flowing out of the ground is the fuel source and is coming out at a very high psi. Pounds per square inch," Nicole added for reference. "What makes it so expensive is that the conventional way to fight the fire doesn't work."

"How so?" Senator Mason asked.

"Oil rigs in general are located in remote areas. The availability and ease of getting to the site with water, and lots of it, is the first problem to solve. You need dozers, cranes, front-end loaders, power generation, pumps, and countless other things. The crew needs breathing equipment, water, portable generators, food, and quarters to rest in. All of that needs to be brought in from somewhere, and that somewhere is usually not local, and to add to the complexity, you need it right now."

"So how do you put it out?"

"Several ways, depending on the situation," Nicole answered, finally getting into the meat of what she knew. "In most cases the first thing we do is what's called 'raising the plume,' where a metal casing or pipe is put over the damaged wellhead, causing the fire to be above the ground." The confused look on the committee's faces told her she needed to be more specific. She reached for the laser pointer lying on the table beside her glass of water.

"I brought this diagram for reference," she said, pointing to the large poster board on a stand to her left and slightly behind her. Nicole proceeded to point to and call out the parts of the well she had mentioned earlier, using very simplistic, everyday terms. Every time she moved, she could hear the clicking of digital cameras freezing her for eternity on the evening news and the Internet. She was grateful that flash wasn't allowed in the committee room, or she probably wouldn't be able to see what she was pointing to.

"And this is the pipe that I referenced earlier when I talked about raising the plume," she said, pointing to the pipe that was sitting atop the wellhead. "Instead of the oil spewing out of the wellhead here," she used the red dot and made a circle around the part, "the pipe is brought in by a crane and positioned over the head, redirecting the oil and flame up and away from the head and ground so the work can be done." This time when she looked at the committee they appeared to understand.

"Liquid nitrogen or even water can be forced down the casing, suffocating the fire and leaving just the oil. On some sites we use dynamite. If you remember from grade-school science, fire needs fuel, heat, and oxygen." Nicole pointed to three of her fingers for emphasis. "If any one of the three is missing, you won't have fire. We pour hundreds of thousands of gallons of water on the fire to control the heat. We can't eliminate it altogether but we can reduce it. Because the wellhead is damaged we can't stop the fuel, so we cut off the oxygen supply. For just a split second when the fire is deprived of oxygen, the fire is killed and all that's left is the fuel or, in this case, the oil. Then we install the replacement wellhead and the fuel source is extinguished," Nicole said, making it sound far simpler than it was.

"Am I safe to assume that an oil-well fire is more dangerous than a regular structural fire?"

"Absolutely. Red Adair once said that extinguishing the fire isn't the most difficult part of well control. It's what you do after the fire is out that's dangerous. As long as the oil is still flowing, the well could flash or reignite, injuring or killing anyone near it." Which is exactly what had happened to her.

"Ms. McMillan, how many fires did McMillan Suppression extinguish last year?"

"Twelve," Nicole replied, after a second's hesitation due to the abrupt change of subject.

"And the year before?"

"Eleven."

"And the year before that?"

"Nine."

"So, Ms. McMillan, would you say that you're seeing a trend of increased oil-well fires?"

Colleen Mason was looking to make a bigger name for herself than she already had. She was going after big oil, and everyone knew it. Nicole would answer her questions honestly but carefully, but she would not feed her ambition.

"No, Madam Chairman, that's not what I said. You asked me how many fires my company extinguished. Many other companies around the world do what McMillan does, and I can't speak to their numbers." Nicole saw a slight narrowing of Mason's eyes and knew she didn't like her answer.

"Ms. McMillan, do you think the number of fires is increasing?"

"Again, Madam Chairman, the only facts that I have are those that pertain to my company."

"Come on, Ms. McMillan, you're an expert in this area. You would know these things."

Nicole detected a note of sarcasm in Mason's statement. "Madam Chairman, I'm an expert at extinguishing oil-well fires." Nicole felt her temper rise but refused to get pulled into the chairman's agenda.

"But surely, as a result, you're an expert in the industry. You know what's going on out there."

Nicole didn't answer. The McMillan attorneys had coached her carefully as to how to answer and to not get caught up in conversation innuendos or political grandstanding. If there wasn't a question on the table, say nothing. And if there was, only answer the question and nothing else. Don't answer with an opinion or color. So Nicole waited for a question.

"Ms. McMillan, what was your gross revenue last year?"

"Madam Chairman, McMillan is not a public company, and to disclose that information would put my competitors at an unfair advantage."

"Surely you made more money last year than you did the year before just by the sheer increase in number of fires you extinguished."

"The cost and therefore the profit of extinguishing each fire is dependent on many factors. Simply because we killed more fires than the year before does not correlate to increased revenue."

"All right," Senator Mason said, clearly not too happy.

The day tediously dragged on with each member of the panel asking the same questions but phrasing them somewhat differently. They were all posturing for their own sound bite to use in their reelection commercials. She answered each one and tried not to show her frustration with the entire proceedings. When Senator Mason banged the gavel signaling the end of her testimony, Nicole was parched and hungry, and had to pee.

She escaped into the ladies' room at the end of the corridor, and as she was washing her hands, Senator Mason walked in.

Fuck.

"Nicole, I want to thank you again for coming today." Senator Mason didn't step any farther into the room but propped herself back against the door like she was settling in for a long conversation and blocking anyone else from entering.

"Anything I can do to help the committee understand the complexities of the industry," Nicole answered, even though she knew the senator wasn't here to thank her. Was she going to make a move on her in the ladies' room of the senate building? That would be the tackiest thing she had ever experienced.

"Speaking of that, are you free for dinner tonight? I'm not sure I understand the kicking of the plume, or whatever you called it."

Nicole suppressed a shudder as the senator's eyes raked over her body. Dinner was the last thing on the senator's mind. After a day of answering the same question at least nine times, Nicole just wanted to order room service, curl up on the couch in her hotel room, and watch the ball game.

"I have a standing reservation at DeRitters." Senator Mason dropped the name of the finest steak-and-seafood restaurant in the city. "We can decompress over a glass of wine and sink our teeth into something hot and juicy when we're ready."

Nicole didn't have to see the leer on the senator's face; she heard in her voice that Nicole was on her menu tonight. "I'd love to, Senator, but—"

"Perfect. I'll meet you there at seven thirty," Senator Mason said just before she swung open the door to the hall. Nicole didn't even have a chance to utter her excuse. Instead she let more than a few expletives cross her lips before she followed the brash woman out the door.

Senator Mason was already seated when Nicole arrived. She had removed her suit jacket and scarf, and unpinned her hair. Her arms were bare, her neckline low, and her cocktail more than half gone. The waiter, or more likely the senator, had moved the second place setting from across the small table to the seat on her left. The seating arrangement implied intimacy. Nicole would have to be on full alert. She hid a frown. It was going to be a long evening.

"You look lovely, Nicole. May I call you Nicole?"

Nicole nodded.

"Please call me Colleen. We're off the clock. Would you like a drink?" She signaled the waiter as she finished her drink.

"No, water is fine." No way was she going to call her Colleen, and she absolutely wasn't going to drink.

"Nicole," Colleen laid her hand on top of hers. It was cold and clammy. "It's okay to have a cocktail."

Nicole casually reached for her napkin, effectively removing the intrusive hand without embarrassment. She didn't need to remind herself to keep her hands in her lap from now on. "I know. I just prefer water." Actually she wanted a stiff drink, and after the senator's come-on she wanted several—after a long, hot shower with a lot of strong soap.

"I'll have another," she said, not looking at the waiter but pointing to her now-empty glass instead. Nicole casually glanced around the small table, looking for the menu. The senator must have noticed because she said, "I thought we'd talk a bit before we order dinner."

Nicole had absolutely no appetite, but at least eating would give her something to do.

"It's good to see you again, Nicole. I enjoy the time we spend together."

"I'm glad the committee is interested enough to talk to those of us in the field." She had to keep this from becoming a personal conversation.

"How are you?"

Nicole was not going to acknowledge the personal aspect of why she was here. "Things are going well. McMillan's safety record continues to be the best in the industry. As a matter of fact, we had our quarterly safety-awards meeting this week."

"You're a very hands-on leader. Everything I hear about you shows how much you care."

"I do. I've been there. I know what it's like, what's important."

"Yes, I know what's important too," the senator said. She hesitated, and Nicole suspected she was expecting her to ask what that was. No way was she going there.

"I understand a bill for tax incentives for solar power sponsored by Senator Felix is working its way through committee." Nicole referenced the senator's peer from Colorado.

Senator Mason frowned at the shift of topic. "Yes, but I don't want to talk shop tonight. I do that all day. I want to relax, enjoy a drink and a good meal with a beautiful woman." She took another healthy swallow of her fresh drink.

"Senator, I'm not available."

"Available?" The senator shifted away, a false questioning look on her face.

"For anything other than a few minutes tonight. I have a call with one of my crew chiefs at eight." Nicole looked at her watch to make her excuse more plausible.

"Nicole," the senator said in a tone she probably thought was sexy. It wasn't. "I want to get to know you better. You're a beautiful woman. You can't blame me for that, can you?"

"Senator, I'm not available, and if I were I don't think it would be appropriate."

"Let me worry about that."

"I appreciate that, Senator, but *I* don't think it is. I'd be more than happy to talk with you and the other committee members in the committee room, not in a restaurant where the intent could easily be misconstrued." Nicole was as diplomatic as she could be, but if the senator didn't back off she could and would make her lack of interest perfectly clear.

"You're right, Nicole, the committee is completely focused on the safety of the public. We have to do what we think is in the best interest of the American public. Even if it makes your business much more difficult or expensive."

Nicole's back stiffened. "What are you implying, Senator?"

"I'm not implying anything," she countered, a smirk on her face this time. "I'm just clarifying the role of the committee."

"That you are the chair of."

"Yes, that I am the chair of."

"Well, Senator, you are highly respected and have an outstanding reputation for not letting your personal views affect what's right for the country," Nicole lied. "I'm sure you'll do the right thing. Now if you'll excuse me," Nicole said, standing. "I have to make my call. Good night."

Nicole turned and walked out of the restaurant feeling far more confident than when she'd walked in.

❖

Nicole fumed as she waited for the valet to call her a cab. Senator Mason was completely out of line, and when Nicole had rebuffed her advances the bitch had pulled the power card. Nicole had been through too much in her life to let someone like Colleen Mason bully her. Did she actually think she could blackmail Nicole into sleeping with her? How archaic and completely heterosexually male. The senator looked old, foolish, and desperate.

Still fuming, Nicole changed her reservation and caught an early flight out, and the next evening sweat dripped off the tip of her nose. She was breathing fast, the blinking red lights on the heart-rate monitor on the treadmill signaling that she was forty-seven minutes into the cardio zone. The TV in front of her was tuned to CNN, the volume high enough to be heard over the rhythmic pounding of her feet on the rubber track.

She used the large room on the far east side of the house as a workout room. Beside the treadmill to her left was a set of free weights and a stationary bicycle. Directly across was a seventy-pound heavy bag suspended three feet above the floor by a shiny chain secured to a rafter in the ceiling. Her training gloves lay where she'd left them on the floor underneath. In the corner a speed bag dangled from its mount, the letters of the brand worn off by her constant battering of the red leather.

Before the accident, her body had been toned from the hard physical work of extinguishing raging oil-well fires. She had run in the light of day, under the bright sunshine and fresh air, her hair pulled through the hole in the back of her favorite running cap. The music on her iPod was loud, her gait smooth as her long legs stretched across the asphalt, her clothing no more than a pair of shorts and a sports bra. The pictures of her smiling as she crossed the finish line of dozens of half marathons and a handful of full marathons, were in a box in the attic, a painful reminder of her previous life.

Tonight, like many nights, she ran mile after mile in the privacy of this fifteen- by twenty-three-foot room. She used to kickbox in a gym filled with other enthusiasts twice a week but now only sparred with the solitary heavy bag. She didn't swim anymore, and the only pedaling she did was reflected on a simulated mountain trail displayed on the video screen in front of her bike.

There were no mirrors in the room. She didn't need to ensure she had the right form, technique, or stance. No one would ever see her compete again or judge her on how well she controlled her body. She certainly didn't need to see what she looked like. She already knew.

Switching to the heavy bag, Nicole tightened the Velcro strips holding the gloves in place on her hands. She bounced on her toes and moved her head from side to side, stretching the muscles of her neck, shaking her arms as she moved. In her mind she saw herself as she used to look in the kickboxing ring—tan, with tight muscles under smooth skin preparing to do battle.

She hit the bag gently at first, then built up both her speed and power. The scar tissue on her leg was tight, limiting the range of motion and height of her kicks. Punching skillfully at the heavy bag, Nicole hit it harder than normal. Her hands would hurt in the morning, but she needed to release her anger and frustration, and the bag was always the safest outlet.

Nicole was in this room several nights a week. Normally a circuit around the room took the edge off her anger, frustration, and anxiety, but tonight it was taking longer than usual. A right jab for Colleen Mason's smirk during her testimony. A left for the way her eyes had traveled over Nicole's body in the ladies' room. A right, left combination to the midsection of the bag for the insinuations she'd made toward McMillan. Jab after jab, punch after punch, she let her thoughts of Colleen Mason drift away and replaced them with images of Brady Stewart.

It wasn't fair. But then again Nicole's father had always said, "Fair is a four-letter word and it starts with *F*." She was single, rich, in her thirties, and the head of a major company. She should have life at her fingertips, with her calling the shots and making the rules. She should be traveling around the world with her crews and building her future with that one special woman.

But she had narrowly escaped death, and because of that her life was anything but under her control. She hadn't been on a job site since the accident, hid her panic attacks, and could barely get out of bed some mornings. And there would never be that one special woman. Other than Katherine, there would never be any woman. No one to talk with over morning coffee, call in the middle of the day just to hear her voice, and reach for in the moonlight. She would live the rest of her life alone, wearing the tightly controlled mask she would never allow to crack.

She beat on the bag for what she used to have, what she had left, and what she'd never have. Her arms grew heavy and sluggish until she could barely lift them. Finally, after one last flurry of fists, and breathing hard, Nicole pulled off her gloves and let them drop to the floor, her tears mixing with the sweat dripping off her face.

CHAPTER TEN

B rady hated flying, which was a terrible position to be in with as much as she did. She could never understand how two hundred tons of steel got up in the air and stayed there for hours at a time. She had had several close calls, primarily in the small planes ferrying her to and from the well sites. But nobody knew. One of hundreds of things she kept to herself.

You didn't show any fear or weakness in this business, especially if you were a woman. When Brady had first started her career she was given every shit job and grunt assignment there was. As a woman she was an interloper. She didn't belong on the line, and the men on the crews she worked with made that very clear. Her locker had been stuffed with tampons, Kotex, and one particularly embarrassing time with several very realistic and very large dildos. She kept one.

The pranks weren't pranks. They were the men's attempts to get her to leave. She couldn't be fired; she was doing her job, but it was obvious she wasn't wanted. Even though the companies were American and were bound by equal-employment and sexual-harassment laws, those didn't apply out in the field. The field had its own rules. She could make them apply: file a complaint to her superiors who would probably turn a blind eye. She could go to their supervisors and continue to crawl up the food chain until she eventually got some resolution. But where would that put her? It would make her even more blackballed than she already was. She was teased, ridiculed, and several times actually put in harm's way. One specific incident had come too close to her actually getting hurt.

The man responsible had been in the crew quarters when Brady entered. She walked over to where he was sitting at a table with three other guys. The four were a pack, a nasty pack of wild dogs.

"Stand up, Wilson." The man in question ignored her as his buddies snickered. "I said stand up." Brady's body was coiled, ready to do battle. When he ignored her again Brady grabbed the back of his chair and pulled it out from under him. He hit the floor and his posse jumped up, ready to join the action. Brady glared at them. "Back off. This is between me and Wilson."

There was an unwritten code among crews that a man fights his own fight. Or in this case a woman. Not trusting the men, Brady watched them out of the corner of her eye as Wilson scampered up.

"You just made the biggest mistake of your life, bitch."

Brady was ready. She'd seen him fight before and knew his first punch was always a roundhouse with his right. She stepped away from the punch, and when his arm missed its target and breezed by her left cheek, she struck. She threw a solid left cross, followed by a right to his midsection that left him doubled over gasping for breath. Another left and he staggered backward, obviously dazed. Brady moved in.

Grabbing his crotch in one hand and the front of his shirt with the other she pushed him even farther back until he was flush against the wall. "If you ever come near me again I'll rip these peanuts." He screamed as Brady tightened her grip on the referenced body part. "And I'll shove them so far up your ass you'll choke on them. Don't think I can't or I won't do it." Brady looked up into his pain-filled eyes. "Do I make myself clear?" When he didn't answer she squeezed his nuts harder, and he screamed again with a combination of pain and acknowledgement. She let go and he slumped to his knees.

She loved her job. She enjoyed the physical work, the sense of independence, and the money. The money was what she'd started doing it for, but the love of the job was why she was doing it now. So she'd sucked it up, bit her lip, and endured. Eventually the men realized she wasn't going anywhere no matter what they did. But that nasty experience had been with another company.

When an opening came up at McMillan she jumped at it. The company had a reputation of fairness and respect on the job site, and, even though her job was very much a man's job, McMillan didn't tolerate any bullshit from their workers. The men there were a bit rough around the edges, but that suited Brady just fine. They were honest and didn't have hidden agendas, and what you saw was exactly what you got.

From the very first day she signed on with McMillan, she'd been treated with nothing but respect. Sure, she had to prove herself on the line, and she had the opportunity to do so without the previous bullshit that was intended to undermine her ability. She'd found a home here. The company didn't have a formal job-bidding system, but when there was an opening on Flick's crew, she sought him out and talked with him because she'd heard very good things about how he ran his crew.

When she met Flick she was surprised because he couldn't have been an inch over five feet five and probably weighed less than she did. He was missing his pinkie and ring finger on his right hand, but his handshake was firm and solid, and he looked her right in the eye. He asked questions that judged her firefighting ability and just as many about her personally. He stated that his crew was honest and fair and didn't do any of "that screwing and drinking shit" that was common in the industry. The locals might call them oil-field trash, but his crew would be anything but, he said proudly. All but two of the men were married with kids, and they didn't fuck around. They worked hard, played harder, but never crossed the line, or even came close to it, for that matter. He invited Brady to join his crew.

That was six years ago and too many fires to count. Brady respected Flick, his knowledge and his temperament, more every day. If she ever wanted to be a crew chief she had the perfect role model in him. He pushed his crew to their ability and just a little bit more, never sacrificing the safety of anyone on his watch. He had rules and expected people to adhere to them. If not, he banished them from ever setting foot near any fire his crew was fighting.

On more than one occasion Flick had bodily thrown a subcontractor or an employee of the well company off the site. More often than not it was due to a safety violation, for which he had zero tolerance.

Normally Brady couldn't wait to get back to the site, the job she loved, the life she knew. But this time something was different. Normally when she was off, all she could think about was getting laid, how she could get laid, and waiting anxiously to be called back out. This trip she accomplished the first, but for some reason it didn't have the same effect as all the other times. The second barely crossed her mind, and it wasn't that she didn't want to return to the site. She just wished she could have spent more time with Nicole McMillan.

An attractive flight attendant who made her interest clear served lunch. Any other time Brady would have taken her up on her offer, but today she ignored it. She picked at the meal, thinking about her boss. In the few hours she'd spent with Nicole she hadn't detected any sign of the hard-ass bitch she'd expected to see. Except for her crew, whenever anyone referred to Nicole in conversation they usually used words like *ball-buster*, *bitch*, and the ever-popular *dyke*. Flick would never permit such derogatory talk on his watch, and everyone knew it. Brady just thought that type of vocabulary showed the limited intellect of the speaker.

She, on the other hand, prided herself on not only her vocabulary, but her grammar and the fact that she was well read. After she'd been working for about a year, she hired a tutor. She'd never been really good in school. She was more focused on trying to keep her peers from noticing her and ignore the never-ending stab of hunger pains that greeted her every day.

Her tutor was a retired teacher, and though embarrassed at first, Brady quickly warmed up to him and thrived on his teaching style. He had her read the newspapers, as well as *Time*, *Newsweek*, and her favorite, *National Geographic*. He quizzed her on what she heard on the evening news, her financial portfolio, and the latest political events in Europe. Even though she had been almost twenty, she couldn't read at more than a seventh-grade level. He never made her feel stupid but challenged her with just the right amount of coaxing and praise. He didn't make a big deal when she accomplished something she didn't think she could but acted as though he'd expected it all along. Now she was a voracious reader, devouring everything she could get her hands on.

No one had any idea she was as diverse and educated as she was. Most, if not all of the men she came in contact with every day had little more than a high-school education. But they were good people, and she never once felt smarter or dumber than any of them. They were her crew, her buddies under fire, and she trusted them with her life.

She adjusted the headphones on her iPod and settled in to listen to the third lesson. She was learning to speak French from Rosetta Stone.

The flight back to North Dakota was short, and finally back on site, Brady endured the good-natured taunts and teasing from her crew. It was all in good taste and fun, and she gave back as much as they threw at her. They all looked out for one another and kept each other in line when temptation reared its beautiful head. She loved these guys. Flick was like the father she wished she'd had, Mast was a sailor in his free time, and Couch got his nickname from the furniture he sat on every moment he wasn't on duty. Rounding out the crew were Anchor, a tall, blond, extraordinarily handsome man who belonged in front of a camera, not behind the wheel of a bulldozer; Peanut, who never went anywhere without a bag in his pocket; and Crank, who refused to tell anyone where his nickname came from. Six other crewmembers were out on the line finishing their shift.

Dig, a tall, lanky twenty-year-old from Blue Springs, Alabama, handed her an ice-cold Diet Coke.

"How many?" Brady asked, taking the can and popping the top. Dig had recently asked her to stand beside him at his wedding, and he was counting the days until his "sweet little Sara" would be his wife.

"Seventeen," he said proudly, grinning from ear to ear.

"Did you miss me?" Brady asked, flopping onto the clean but stained couch in the crew quarters.

"Nope," Dig answered, opening his own can. The third finger on his right hand was missing from an accident early in his career. "Didn't even know you was gone."

"Bullshit," Brady replied. "You probably took my shift, ate my snacks, and used my toothpaste like you always do," she teased him. Of all the crewmembers Dig was her favorite. He had an air of innocent honesty about him that she found refreshing.

"Nope, but I did look at the pictures in your *National Geographic*."

"Heathen."

"Smarty-pants."

"Do you eat with that mouth too?"

"Every chance I get."

"All right, you two stop bickering like my kids." Flick interrupted them in a gruff voice but a smile on his face. "We've got work to do. This baby ain't gonna die without a little help. Anybody interested?"

❖

The fire was angry. The changing direction of the wind whipped the flames in every direction as it danced in the midday sky. Brady stood in the monitor shed surveying the scene in front of her. The shed, a three-sided box made of heat-resistant, flame-retardant material, shielded the firefighters from the two-thousand-degree heat. While she was at HQ the bulldozers had cleared away anything around the wellhead that could ignite and set up the first shed.

They had a twelve-person crew on this fire. Two were support staff while ten were certified firefighters. Five, including Brady, specialized in operating heavy equipment, and they worked twelve-hour shifts in whatever capacity was needed. For safety reasons they rotated positions every hour. Other crews took two- or three-hour shifts at their positions, but Flick insisted on only one. He believed that his crew was more alert when not exposed to the extreme heat and concentration each position required. That was a no-brainer in Brady's book and one of the reasons Flick's crew had the highest safety record in the company.

The direction of the wind was the key to the assault. Staying upwind of the heat and flames was a matter of life or death. The best approach was to fight the fire as the wind pushed away the heat. Retardant saturated the ground over oil that had spilled before the plume had ignited. Clouds of dense black smoke from thousands of barrels of burning oil spewed noxious gasses and poison into the air. The extraordinary heat melted anything that wasn't protected. The constant stream of water on the fire kept Brady and the other crewmembers from collapsing from the heat and the machines from melting.

Her safety gear depended on her job assignment and today consisted of flame-resistant long johns under her aluminized Kevlar Nomex assault coat. The corresponding pants, held up by the requisite red cotton web suspenders, had full-bellow cargo pockets, reinforced knees, and fabric take-up straps with a thermoplastic buckle. Steel-toed vulcanized rubber boots, also insulated to deflect heat and fire, were on her feet.

A Nomex hood like she'd seen professional race-car drivers wear shielded her head and neck from burns, while the bright-yellow full-brim hardhat protected her head from cracking. At least it used to be bright yellow. After only an hour on a site it quickly became smudged with caked-on oil, dirt, and smoke. Gloves and goggles dangling from an elastic band around her neck completed her turnout gear.

Pulling her goggles up to protect her eyes, Brady stepped away from the shed and immediately felt the intensity of the fire. She started to sweat and breathing became difficult. Even with hundreds of thousands of gallons of water pouring on the fire, she was constantly aware of her own personal hydration. In full gear she could sweat up to a quart an hour during a twelve-hour shift. She had to be careful that she didn't overheat or pass out without warning.

To her right a large excavator surrounded on three sides of the cab with its own protective heat shield slowly crept toward the fire, its 190,000 pounds leaving deep track impressions in the mud. The big rig was one of the most useful pieces of equipment on the site, consisting of a cab and bucket situated on a rotating pivot, as well as an articulated arm that did most of the work and carried another shed suspended from three large chains. Today Dig was driving the rig. His real name was Mark, but he was quickly given the nickname that was synonymous with the piece of equipment he had the ability to finesse like it was an extension of his own hand.

Two men followed him, using the big machine as their own heat suppressor. They carried a fire hose that, once the shed was on the ground, would hook up to their main water supply. Brady used hand signals to communicate to Dig where to place the next shed in the right place. Communication was difficult at best near a fire, and everyone on the crew knew the signals necessary to get the job done but, more importantly, could save their lives.

After Dig set the shed, the two men stepped out from behind the rig and quickly moved inside. Brady looked around to ensure nothing was in the way and signaled Dig he could leave. The hose was quickly hooked up and the water shot out of the cannon to cool the superheated flames. For the rest of the day and into the night, preparations were underway for the damaged well to be capped.

The new wellhead arrived the next day, and Flick, Brady, Mast, and Crank reviewed the plan to install the head. It was late afternoon, and between the setting sun and the black smoke filling the sky overhead they decided to wait until tomorrow to set the head. Flick sent them off with orders to eat and get some much-needed rest.

Exhausted from the physical work, Brady settled onto her cot. She didn't even try to sleep, knowing her mind wouldn't shut down but continue to review the critical steps necessary to complete this job.

Extinguishing the fire was only the start of the job, and installing the new head in place was when the most dangerous work began. Once the fire was out and the plume pipe removed, a steady stream of oil from the uncapped well was nothing but a huge ignition switch that could reignite. It wasn't too bad if it happened before anyone moved too close to begin the work but life threatening when they were. An explosion, the concussion effects, the flash fire, or both could kill crewmembers. That was what had happened to Nicole.

Brady involuntarily shuddered. She had seen several reignitions or flares, as some called them, and from what she'd read and heard about Nicole's accident she was very, very lucky to be alive. Brady rubbed the scar on her right forearm. The redness was fading, and ultimately it would be visible only to those who knew what to look for. Even though she didn't know the details she realized that Nicole wasn't as lucky with her burns.

Nicole had a beautiful face, and judging from what Brady had seen of third-degree burns, Nicole must thank God every day that her face hadn't been affected. In every picture Brady had seen of Nicole, every public appearance she was able to Google, Nicole was always covered from wrist to ankle. Her shirts were open at the collar but only the top button. Even at a charity black-tie event where Nicole had been photographed several times, she was wearing tailored tuxedo pants and a billowy long-sleeve top.

"Hey, Bond," Dig said from the cot next to hers. A sheet hanging from a white rope the length of her cot plus a few feet separated their sleeping area. It was her only form of privacy in the crew quarters, and Flick insisted on it. Even though it was only a thin piece of material she enjoyed having it.

"Yeah."

"Tell me about the boss. What was she like?"

"I don't know, like any boss, I guess. Strong handshake, big office, nice furniture, running water. You know, typical HQ stuff."

"That's not what I meant. Tell me about *her*." Dig emphasized exactly what he wanted to know.

"I told you. Like any other boss."

"Is she pretty?"

"Dig!" Brady exclaimed. "What in the hell are you asking for? You're marrying the prettiest girl in the state of Texas in two weeks, and you're asking if another woman is pretty. Are you sure you're ready to be married?"

"What?" Brady heard the confusion in his voice. "Oh, God, no, that's not what I meant. I love Sara," he said, as if that explained everything. "It's just that she was burned so bad. We take that risk every day. I guess I was just curious as to what she looked like."

"I didn't see any evidence she was burned. And yes, she's pretty, very pretty, as a matter of fact." Brady would have used more descriptive words like *beautiful, stunning,* or *striking.* What else could she say about Nicole? Her hand buzzed when she remembered what Nicole's hand felt like in hers. There had been some type of connection between them. Brady hesitated to call it chemistry, but maybe it was as simple as that.

Brady often acted on the attraction that sparked with another woman. And more often than not it led to a mutually enjoyable experience. But because of her work and the fact that it wasn't in her master plan to get tied down, she was where she was today—single, with no plans of being anything other than that. Yet she couldn't deny the attraction she'd felt toward Nicole.

Brady had to admit this was a first. The first time she was attracted to a boss, the first time her thoughts kept backtracking to a woman, and the first time she wanted to know more about a woman. Much more.

Brady pushed the distracting thoughts out of her head. She wasn't ready to deal with this. As a matter of fact she was never going to deal with this, because it stood in the way of her ultimate goal.

"I heard she had a tough time, but I guess anyone would."

"Of course they would. I can't even imagine how much pain she must have been in."

"I heard her girlfriend couldn't take it and walked."

"Bitch."

"You got that right. I mean, you may be all burned and scarred up and everything, but you're still the same person inside." Dig's compassion was one of the things Brady loved about him. The oil industry was comprised mostly of tough, hard, redneck men who wouldn't show an emotion, let alone talk about one. But Dig was different. He had a solid sense of right and wrong and was more honest than anyone Brady had ever met. In the three years she'd known him she'd never heard a derogatory statement come out of his mouth. His teeth might be crooked and his cheek full of chew, but in Brady's mind he was as good as they came.

"I guess she didn't think so." Brady wondered how anyone could be so cold and heartless. But what did she know? She didn't have a front-row seat to their life.

"Nothing or nobody would ever make me stop loving Sara."

Brady smiled at his statement. If it were only that simple, she thought.

"When are you going to find the right girl and settle down, Bond?"

An image of Nicole flashed in her head and she grew warm all over. *What the hell?* "Now why would I want to settle down with just one, Dig, when there are hundreds and thousands I could meet?" She hadn't confided in Dig about her plans. He wouldn't understand, and it wasn't anyone's business anyway. She just let everyone go along with the image she allowed them to see. She didn't let anyone, not even Dig, get close enough to see what was inside.

"Yeah, but don't that get old? I mean having someone new all the time is exciting and everything, but nothing beats having a wonderful woman to come home to. I mean, Sara knows what I like to eat and how I like my clothes folded, and she never fusses at me 'cuz I left the seat up."

"Jesus, Dig, she sounds like your maid, not the love of your life." And there was no way she was going to be anyone's maid.

"You don't get it, Bond. I mean it's like she knows what I want or what I'm going to say before I even say it. It's like she's inside me, and I'm telling you it feels really good."

"I'm really happy for you, buddy. Maybe someday I'll find that person and feel like you do. Who knows, maybe she'll even catch Sara's bouquet at your wedding."

Dig laughed. "I doubt it. Other than you we don't know anyone who's a lesbian."

"Well, then I guess I'll just have to keep looking. Turn out the light. We've got a fire to kill tomorrow."

CHAPTER ELEVEN

"Come on, Dig. How much further? I'm roasting in here." No one could hear Brady, the roar of the fire at this distance almost deafening. She was operating the crane carrying the explosives, and Dig was signaling her to keep inching forward. The boom of the crane jutting out almost parallel to the ground swayed as she moved the drum of C4 explosive over the flame.

Dig signaled her to stop, and she quickly set the brake and turned off the engine. Swinging the door of the cab open, she was almost knocked off the platform by the force of the heat. The thermodynamics of heat radiating off the fire were always unpredictable.

Snuffing the fire was one of the most dangerous jobs. Not only was she the closest to the fire, the C4 could explode anytime, and the inside of the cab wasn't the safest place to be. Brady grabbed hold of the handrail, jumped to the ground, and hustled to the rear of the rig. Dropping to her knees she turned away from the fire and ducked her head. She counted silently. The longest it had taken any C4 she'd dropped on a fire was ten seconds, the shortest, two.

A loud explosion cracked and the air sucked out of her lungs. The first time it'd happened on her first fire she'd fought down panic, unable to do anything other than pray she didn't die from suffocation. When the C4 detonated, the oxygen was sucked from the air for a split second. If luck was on their side, the fire was extinguished and all that was left was the oil.

A chorus of whoops, hollers, and whistles replaced the screaming voice of the fire. It could mean only one thing. The fire was out.

The replacement wellhead dangled from the end of the boom on another rig, and Brady, Couch, and Anchor donned their protective gear, grabbed their tool bags, and headed to the well. Once the fire was out, the first job was to remove the damaged wellhead, and as Brady approached she could see this wouldn't be an easy task.

Shards of metal bent at odd angles looked like petals of a flower opening in the morning sunshine. They'd have to be extremely careful not only that their tools didn't reignite the oil but that they didn't get cut or lose a finger on the sharp metal.

Unlike conventional tools that were found in just about every garage in America, theirs were specially designed and coated with a spark-resistant coating. Even though the wellhead was covered in oil that had hardened into an almost impenetrable hard sludge, any type of metal-on-metal contact could cause a spark unseen to the human eye but sought after by the highly flammable liquid.

Brady made a complete three-hundred-sixty-degree tour around the wellhead, planning their attack. The noise from the pressure of the oil escaping wasn't nearly as deafening as the flames, but communication was still difficult. She had worked with these guys for years, and with a few signals, pointing, and nods of understanding, they began the deconstruction of the damaged head.

It wasn't long before Brady was covered in thick crude oil and an hour later had made substantial headway in removing the hard sludge from the area where they needed to work. She stepped back and into a stream of water to remove as much of the oil as possible and to cool down. A few minutes later, mission accomplished, they pulled out their wrenches and began unscrewing the bolts that held the head to the well piping.

The bolts had initially been tightened with a torque wrench, but due to the dangerously flammable conditions they couldn't be removed in the same way. It took all three of them and a specially designed tool to release the hundreds of pounds of pressure on each bolt. For the next hour they released each bolt, and by noon the damaged head was ready to be removed.

When the fire was extinguished the flume pipe remained to enable them to remove the damaged head. Without it, as soon as they untightened the first bolts on the head, the oil coming out of the head would start leaking between the head and the shaft, exerting massive amounts of pressure and making it impossible to unscrew the rest of the bolts.

Brady and her crew completed another walk around the head, double- and triple-checking that everything was ready for the head to be removed.

They retreated, and she signaled Dig that the site was ready. He had replaced the bucket on the arm of the digger with what Brady often referred to as a gigantic pair of tweezers, when in fact it was a demolition tool used for crushing.

Dig moved forward slowly, the pinchers open, ready to grab the pipe and damaged head from the well. Brady watched as Dig skillfully maneuvered the pinchers around the piping. As soon as he grabbed the pipe and started to reverse, oil shot out of the flange that connected the damaged head to the well almost parallel to the ground. It often reminded Brady what it would be like if you removed a sprinkler head off the end of a hose without turning off the water.

Dig backed away from the site carrying his cargo and deposited it on the ground about fifty yards away. Another worker came forward, driving the crane Brady had driven this morning to extinguish the flame, but this time it didn't carry explosives. It carried the new wellhead. Brady, and her crew, moved forward and was quickly covered with oil, grateful for the goggles that protected her eyes.

She and the men directed the new wellhead in place. This time the reverse was true in trying to put on a sprinkler head without turning off the water. Brady lowered her full-face shield to protect her exposed skin.

The new head secured, it took all three of them to turn the control valve to shut down the flow of oil. When the last drop stopped, Brady leaned against the well completely exhausted. This was one of the most physical aspects of the job that most women couldn't do. Hell, even some men couldn't do it. But she'd worked in the field so long she'd built up her strength and learned a few tricks to make her successful.

Her legs felt like lead, and she dragged herself into the stream of one of the remaining fire hoses. Standing with her back to the water for a minute or so before turning slowly, she let the water wash off at least the top layer of oil and grime from her suit. Slipping off her helmet she dipped her head, soaking it in the cool, clean water.

Fairly certain she was as clean as she was going to be at this point, she waved her thanks to the nozzleman and headed toward the crew quarters. The mop-up crew had been on standby all day and quickly moved in as the McMillan crew left the area around the repaired wellhead.

Hanging her protective gear on a knob screwed into the side of the crew trailer, Brady ran her hand over her head and through her short hair to get as much water out as possible. Then she unzipped her jumpsuit to her waist, pulled her arms out of the sleeves, and stepped inside. She wanted a cold drink, a hot shower, and a soft bed, but not necessarily in that order.

The first two accomplished, Brady lifted the sheet separating her cot from the others, lay down, and fell instantly asleep.

❖

Nicole's phone rang on her desk and she glanced at her watch. She hoped it was Operations, reporting on Brady's well. They had called earlier in the day, letting her know that the fire was out and they were making final preparations to cap the well. Normally she didn't worry and hadn't when Flick's crew was out on previous jobs. But that was before she'd met Brady. She wondered if she'd feel this way every time Flick's crew was out on a site.

"Nicole McMillan."

"Hey, Boss." The voice she'd been waiting all day to hear came through loud and clear over the speaker.

"She's out. Everyone's safe and secure. No problems."

Nicole didn't try to stifle her sigh of relief. These last two stages of killing a fire were dangerous and always concerned her when any of her crew was at that stage. But Brady was on the crew of this fire. Even though Nicole didn't know what role she played in these steps, from Brady's reputation and the performance information in her personnel file, Nicole wouldn't have been surprised if she'd singlehandedly snuffed the fire and replaced the head.

She flashed back to the last well she'd capped. It was scorching hot, the intense heat from the Kuwaiti sun adding to the challenge. She'd been on site for over two weeks, and twice they'd tried and failed to secure the wellhead. Both times they couldn't get the bolts aligned, the pressure of the shooting oil too high.

Nicole was on point this time and signaled the crane operator to swing the head a little to her right. A little turned out to be a lot and the two pieces of metal sparked. She saw it coming but couldn't get out of the way fast enough. The well reignited in a thunderous roar. She didn't remember anything, but, according to the reports she read well after the fact, the force of the ignition threw her more than thirty feet, where she landed unconscious in a pool of burning oil. By the time the other members of her crew were able to get her out of the fire she had burns over sixty-five percent of her body.

The room spun, and Nicole couldn't breathe. Her heart raced. She trembled. She had to get out. She practically ran by Ann, ignoring her calls of concern. Sprinting down the hall she took the stairs two at a time, slamming the exit door against the outside wall in her haste to escape. She was in a full-blown panic attack. Couldn't stop it. The faster she ran, the closer it got to catching her, and she didn't know if she could deal with that again.

Nicole felt like she was crawling out of her skin. She ran until she couldn't run any more, then fell to her knees, heaving in great gasps of air. Her heart was still beating faster than normal, but now it was due to the exertion and not the fight-or-flight endorphins that had kicked in at the onset of this attack.

This was one of the worst attacks she'd had in years. She hadn't seen it coming. Other than when she woke from her nightmares already in a panic, she had learned to recognize the symptoms and, by using the tricks and techniques her shrink had taught her, was able to keep most of them at bay. But this one had snuck up on her like cotton balls in the wind.

She didn't want to think about it. She wanted to put it away, get it out of her mind, out of her life. But she needed to know what had caused it so it would never happen again. She always felt the need to run, to get away, even though she knew she wasn't running away from anything. The attacks were in her brain and in her body, and it didn't matter how fast or how far she ran; she could never escape them.

Her breathing slowly returned to normal. Looking around she saw nothing familiar. Where in the hell am I, she thought. The street signs weren't familiar, nor were the buildings, the quickie mart on the corner or the gas station to her left.

"Fuck." Now what was she going to do? She rummaged around in her pockets and found a couple of bills and loose change from lunch. She had left her cell phone on her desk. Now all she needed to do was find a phone booth. But nowadays, finding a pay phone would be like finding one on the moon.

Rising from her knees, she looked around again, this time a little calmer. She glanced to her left, then right and didn't see a phone anywhere. The grocery store a block away was probably her best bet. Straightening her clothes and wiping the sweat from her forehead, she began walking, focusing on putting one foot in front of the other.

As Nicole walked she backtracked in her mind to what might have caused this attack. She'd had a good, productive day, even if it was accompanied by the nagging at the back of her mind about Brady's crew capping their well. When the phone call came from Operations with the news that Brady was safe it was like the cork popping off a champagne bottle. She must have exploded from the pent-up pressure she'd been under all day waiting for the news.

She'd obviously relived her accident vicariously through Brady. She needed to get back on the medication her shrink had prescribed. He had told her more than a few times that taking the anti-anxiety drug wasn't a sign of weakness. "On the contrary," he'd said, "panic attacks are a chemical reaction in the brain." Treating them with medication was no different than treating any other imbalance in the body. He likened it to someone with diabetes. In some cases it could be controlled with diet and exercise, in others only controlled with daily doses of insulin.

Nicole understood what he'd said but didn't like it. She didn't want to take anything to control her brain. Goddamnit, she was strong enough to control her own actions, the things she thought about, for God's sake. She was determined that she would conquer this weakness with mind over drugs. Seeing a pay phone in front of the store she increased her pace.

"Fuck," she said, standing in front of the phone. The cord from the receiver had been cut.

She walked inside, up to the service desk, and asked if there was a phone she could use, informing the clerk behind the counter that the one outside was out of order. She knew she looked a mess, and he looked at her as if she'd just come off the street, which she had. Her clothes were rumpled, the knees of her pants were dirty, and she was sweating. If she wasn't so fucked up it might have been funny.

The clerk finally relented and pulled a phone from behind the counter and set it on the ledge in front of her. Whether he was a nice guy or just wanted to get her out of her store, it didn't matter. She picked up the receiver and dialed.

❖

Nicole had to say something. She couldn't sit in Charlotte's car while she drove back to her office and not say anything. She was ashamed at her weakness, embarrassed, and felt like a failure. She was also exhausted from the adrenaline that had raced through her during her panic.

Charlotte Sonnier was sixty-eight years old and had been her father's assistant for over thirty years. Charlotte had seen Nicole grow up in her daddy's office. Charlotte had babysat and later kept her busy when he was in a meeting or had to get something done and the constant questions from her were preventing him. As a result Nicole had confided in Charlotte instead of her mother.

Nicole's mother Theresa had always wanted her to be something she wasn't, whereas Charlotte accepted her as she was. Theresa wanted her to dress a certain way; Charlotte just made sure her face and hands were clean. Theresa never made it a secret that she thought it was appalling for Nicole to follow in her father's footsteps; Charlotte supported her completely. Even to this day as the president of McMillan, leading a global company with millions of dollars of revenue and hundreds of employees, Nicole was still not what her mother would approve of.

Other than asking their destination, Charlotte hadn't said a word, just pulled up in front of the store in her pickup and waited patiently for Nicole to climb in.

"Thank you, Charlotte," Nicole said, looking at her hands clasped tightly in her lap.

"No need," Charlotte said simply, brushing a strand of her still-red hair from her face.

"I hope I didn't interrupt anything important."

"Nothing more important than helping a friend."

"I had another attack." Nicole said it so quietly she wasn't sure Charlotte heard her.

"I know."

Even though Nicole hadn't lifted her gaze from her lap, she could see out of the corner of her eye that Charlotte had yet to take her eyes off the road. This wasn't the first time Charlotte had heard about her panic attacks. When Nicole had stopped seeing the shrink, she'd turned to Charlotte in a moment of weakness.

She had been out to dinner with Charlotte, catching up on the latest in their lives, exchanging light gossip and talking about people they both knew. It had been ages since Nicole had gone out and she was enjoying herself, laughing and generally having a great time, when a waiter carrying a tray of sizzling fajitas passed their table.

Nicole had jumped from her chair and practically run into the ladies' room. Charlotte had followed her and waited quietly for her to explain. Nicole didn't want to explain then anymore than she wanted to now. But she'd forced herself to talk in quick succinct sentences, and it was never mentioned again.

She had had other attacks when she was with Charlotte, but they were mild and she was able to work through them with Charlotte none the wiser. The severity of this one and the fact she'd run what she now estimated to be five or six miles frightened her.

"I owe you an explanation."

"You don't owe me anything, sweetheart."

The endearment meant more to Nicole than anything else Charlotte could have said. Her mother never called her that or anything other than her name. Her mother would have peppered her with questions from the minute Nicole called and asked her if she could pick her up until the minute she was finally able to flee her car. Her mother loved her but for Nicole's entire life had made it very clear that Nicole was not the daughter she'd signed up for, and this was one more way she would drill it into her head.

Nicole knew she looked a fright and must have looked ridiculous running down the street in her work clothes and loafers. At least she didn't have heels on, which would have added to her humiliation and probably caused a broken ankle.

Charlotte stopped in front of her office building and put the truck into park. It was a subtle invitation for her to talk, and Nicole knew Charlotte wouldn't be hurt if she chose not to. Too afraid to face the former, she took the easy way out and chose the latter. She reached for the door handle.

"I hope I didn't inconvenience you too much. Thanks for the ride." Before she had a chance to open the door Charlotte touched her thigh. Nicole still couldn't look at her.

"I love you, Nicole. Take care of yourself."

"You too," Nicole replied. She opened the door and walked faster than she wanted to back to the office.

CHAPTER TWELVE

The stiff collar scratched Brady's neck. It had been rubbing since she buttoned it this morning. By now it probably looked like a fresh hickey. That wouldn't be a bad thing because it meant she was getting some, but Dig's wedding wasn't the place for that. The rented tuxedo shirt wasn't too small; she just wasn't used to having something wrapped around her neck, and Sara, Dig's girl, had insisted on formal tuxedos for the men and Brady.

Months ago when Dig had asked her to be his best man at his wedding, Brady was flattered, then tried to convince him he really should have a guy, like his brother.

"My brother's an asshole. He's not even invited, but with my luck he'll show up," Dig said, his accent thick.

"But, dude," Brady said, "your best man is supposed to be just that—a man—and usually your best friend. And you're Catholic." Brady added that as if it trumped everything else.

"Come on, Bond, you are my best friend, and do I look like I follow convention?" The silver cap on Dig's front tooth glinted under the fluorescent light. They were in the crew trailer, winding down after a long shift. The last remaining dregs in the coffee pot were burned, the smell permeating the small space. Brady was too keyed up to go to sleep, even though she was bone tired.

"I've known you for three years, Bond, and I don't trust anybody more than you. I spend more time with you than I do with anyone else. Hell, even Sara likes you. And you know she don't like hardly any of my friends."

"She likes me because I'm a lesbian. I'm not a threat to her or a temptation to you."

"I don't care. I'm making the biggest step in my life, and I have to tell you, I'm scared shitless. I need you there beside me."

"So I can do what, hold your hand? Say 'I do' for you? Keep you from running out of the church? Now if you want me to stand in for you on the wedding night…" Brady loved to tease him.

So here she was in Sara's hometown of Lafayette standing at the altar of a little country church beside the tall, skinny kid from some podunk town in southern Alabama watching the first of five bridesmaids walk down the aisle. She let her eyes drift around the church, noticing the bride's side was packed, whereas Dig's had plenty of elbow room.

A woman wearing a large blue hat shifted and Brady's heart skipped a beat. She glanced at bridesmaid number two and back at the woman seated in the last row. What was Nicole McMillan doing here? Surely she didn't attend all of her employees' weddings. How weird would that be?

From where she stood, Brady couldn't see anything more than Nicole's immaculately styled hair and the top of a navy jacket over a pale-blue blouse. Nicole was watching bridesmaid number four, and Brady took the opportunity to watch her as she did. She had a small smile on her face, and Brady realized that, in the few hours they'd spent together two weeks ago, Nicole had rarely smiled. She was beautiful. The woman passed, blocking Brady's view of Nicole, and Dig inhaled sharply. Sara had entered the room, and Brady turned her attention away from Nicole.

Nicole slid into the pew a few minutes before the processional began. She'd been running late all day, and a flat tire on her truck didn't help. She glanced at the program and still couldn't believe that Sara, her best friend's daughter, was getting married. Nicole had met Barbara in the rehab center, where she was recovering from a stroke in the room across the hall from Nicole. They had the same physical therapist and would commiserate together over the afternoon snack. Sado Mado, they called him. His real name was Jeff Madoplin, but Barbara gave him the label after one particularly tough session. "He must be a sadomasochist because I swear he gets some sort of perverse pleasure in hurting me," she said in explanation.

Nicole subtly looked around the church. It was old, with all the characteristics of a solid Catholic church. The center aisle was worn from thousands of pairs of feet entering and leaving the majestic building. A large woman concentrated on the sheet music propped up on the top of the pipe organ as she played a prelude to the big event.

A door to the right of the altar opened and Sara's fiancé Mark stepped through, followed by his four groomsmen. Nicole's pulse fluttered when she recognized Brady standing beside Mark. Barbara had told Nicole that Mark's best man was a buddy of his from work, but Brady wasn't who she expected. Nicole knew Mark worked for McMillan, but had no idea he and Brady were friends. Then again, why would she? She didn't keep track of the best friends of every one of her employees.

Nicole's mouth went dry when Brady faced the front of the church. In a black peak-lapel cutaway with charcoal-gray, striped, pleated trousers, Brady was absolutely stunning. Her hair was shorter, just touching the wing collar of the white shirt barely visible under a full vest and striped ascot tie. Brady stood almost as tall as Mark, and Nicole thought she was much more handsome than the groom. But then again she'd always had a thing for androgynous women.

A bridesmaid crossed in front of her, cutting off her view of Brady, and Nicole stood with the rest of the guests when the organist began the first strains of the wedding processional. All eyes in the room except hers focused on Sara slowly walking down the aisle. She saw Brady again and couldn't take her eyes off her. The longer she looked the more her insides churned. She hadn't felt this pure raw desire for anyone since the fire, and her body's reaction was disconcerting.

Nicole thought that part of her body had died with most of her nerve endings. Sure, she felt arousal and climaxed under Katherine's skillful hands, but that was business. She was relieved she wasn't attracted to anyone, even if it meant she would spend the rest of her life alone. So what did her reaction to Brady mean?

She didn't pay attention to the ceremony or the priest's words. She watched Brady's every move and every breath. She looked at the broad expanse of her back, the perfect length of her trousers, and the way she had her hands clasped behind her back. From where she sat, the angle was perfect to see Brady smile and say something when she handed Mark the ring. Nicole's stomach fluttered again, like it was full of butterflies.

Nicole listened as Sara and Mark recited their vows. She tried not to be jaded. Everyone she knew was either divorced or their relationship was on the rocks. It was hard not to be cynical when two people recited the vows that had been said for hundreds of years and then several years later were at each other's throats and calling each other every name imaginable. Maybe these two would be different. She hoped so. She would definitely give them the benefit of the doubt. She wouldn't be saying those words ever again though. She had once, and look where that had gotten her.

The priest's words drew Nicole's attention back to the ceremony. "Ladies and gentlemen, I present to you Mr. and Mrs. Mark Phillips." Sara and her new husband turned to face the guests, practically beaming with joy and the life they were going to share.

Brady turned and her eyes immediately locked with Nicole's, whose heart jumped under Brady's penetrating stare. Brady was smiling, clearly happy for Mark and his bride, and Nicole thought she detected a slight nod acknowledging her presence.

Nicole returned the smile just before Brady's attention was drawn back to the maid of honor she escorted down the aisle. Brady kept her eyes straight ahead until she got almost even with Nicole, when she turned her head slightly and looked at her and again gave a slight nod before she passed. The rest of the bridal party filed down the aisle, followed by the family of the bride and groom, the rest of the guests leaving in an orderly manner, starting with the second row.

The receiving line was outside in the courtyard between the church and the fellowship hall, and Nicole made her way through the slowly moving procession to congratulate Sara and her new husband. After that, Nicole found Barbara standing with her husband off to the side, enjoying the happiness of their daughter. "Nicole, I'm so glad you could make it."

"I wouldn't have missed it for the world. You know that. Sara's beautiful."

Both Barbara and her husband blushed with pride. "The reception, cake, and dancing are in the fellowship hall." Barbara pointed to the doors of the building about forty feet away. Please eat, drink, and enjoy yourself. There's plenty to go around. And please stop by and chat with Sara for a few minutes. I know she'd love it."

Nicole greeted a few more friendly faces and after ten or fifteen minutes wandered into the hall with several mutual friends. The room was decorated in typical wedding motif. Streamers hung from the ceiling, balloons saying CONGRATULATIONS and JUST MARRIED hung from the lights, and a DJ had two computers open on the table in front of him, flanked by speakers on either side.

Nicole glanced at the guests milling around waiting for the bride and groom to enter the festivities, then meandered to one of the four bars placed around the room and ordered a beer. She was dressed in one of her better suits, and holding a beer in her hand probably looked out of place, but she didn't care. She liked beer. Cocktails hit her too hard, and wine sometimes gave her a headache.

She tipped the bartender just as the crowd broke into applause, and she turned as the bride and groom made their way to the bridal table. Sitting to Mark's left was Brady, then a couple that Nicole assumed were his parents. Sara's side of the family was equally represented on the opposite side.

Nicole sat at a table near the back of the room and settled down with several guests. They introduced themselves as a waiter came around and filled their champagne glasses about half full. Nicole watched as Brady stood and tapped her glass with a fork.

Tink, tink, tink. "Ladies and gentlemen," Brady said into the microphone, her voice strong and clear coming through the speakers. "Ladies and gentlemen. I understand it's my role to propose a toast to the bride and groom. But first I have the responsibility of telling an embarrassing story about these two."

Nicole watched as Brady regaled the guests with a funny story about Mark and Sara and a particular episode involving a floodlight, the back of a pickup truck, and a cold winter night. Nicole saw a very different Brady than the one who was in her office a little more than two weeks ago. This Brady was engaging, entertaining, funny, and obviously very fond of Mark.

She couldn't get over how attractive Brady was, and the saying that the clothes made the man obviously didn't quite fit in this instance, but they definitely fit Brady. But there was something about her now that kept drawing Nicole's eyes back to her. The words *dapper*, *handsome*, and *striking* came to mind. She looked strong and powerful and confident, and Nicole felt a surge of unfamiliar desire.

Brady looked like she could handle anything, like she would take charge, but she looked confident enough to let go. Nicole flushed with heat when she thought what it would be like to have Brady take control of her. Her hands itched to touch what she suspected was a tight, firm body under the formal clothes.

"So in closing, ladies and gentlemen," Brady said, "I propose a toast. To Mark and his beautiful bride Sara. May you have all the happiness and never-ending love that will create the pack of kids I know you're going to have. A toast. Congratulations."

Mark pulled Brady into a hug, slapping her on the back several times before finally releasing her. Brady leaned over and kissed Sara on the cheek. Nicole wondered what it would feel like to have Brady kiss her on the cheek, on the mouth, and in other places.

Brady took a sip of champagne and her eyes scanned the room and found hers. More than fifty feet separated them, but Nicole felt like Brady could see inside her and know what she was feeling. The heat rose to Nicole's face and Brady raised her eyebrows slightly.

The DJ clicked a few keys and music came over the speakers. Mark and Sara moved to the dance floor for the traditional first dance of the bride and groom. Brady danced with the maid of honor, and if people didn't know they probably couldn't tell she was a woman. But Nicole knew, and her body definitely knew.

An hour later Nicole was talking with Barbara and several of her friends when a voice behind her said, "Wanna dance?" She turned to look at the man beside her. He wore a slightly rumpled suit, his tie and the first button on his collar were undone, and a cocktail jostled in his chubby hand.

"No, thank you," Nicole replied politely. "I'm not really in the mood to dance right now," she said, trying to soften her decline. It didn't work.

"Come on, dance with me. I'm in the mood."

"I said no, thank you."

"You know, you don't have to be so snooty."

"I'm sorry if I sounded that way to you. I don't mean to be. I just don't want to dance right now."

"You must be related to the bride," the man said, his words slightly slurred. "My family knows how to be polite."

Nicole didn't say anything. She didn't want to encourage any further conversation with this man.

"Robbie, please," Barbara said. The words didn't deter him.

"You think that just because you've got on fancy clothes and probably drive a fancy car you're too good for the likes of me. Well, let me tell you—"

"Robbie, there you are," a welcome, familiar voice said just before Brady came into view. She stepped close to the man and put her arm around his shoulder. "Sorry to interrupt, ladies," Brady said to Nicole and the other women. She turned her attention back to the man. "Mark's looking for you, buddy. He asked me to find you."

Robbie turned his attention away from Nicole and looked at Brady. "Who the hell are you?"

Brady didn't hesitate. "Brady, I work with Mark."

Robbie looked at Brady. "What the hell?" Before Brady got a chance to say anything he added, "You're a fucking dyke."

Brady didn't miss a beat. "You're a smart guy, Robbie. Come on, man, let's go. Mark wants to talk with you," Brady said, putting her arm around Robbie's shoulder, effectively turning him away from Nicole. "If you'll excuse us," Brady said, and directed Robbie away from them and across the room.

"Thank God," Barbara said, a look of relief on her face.

"Sorry about that," Nicole said.

"Good grief, Nicole, you didn't do anything to encourage him. That was Mark's brother. He didn't want him here but was afraid he'd drop in. No one in the family wants to have anything to do with him, but obviously somehow he found out."

"Brady will take care of him. She'll get him out of here."

"She's a wonderful person," Barbara said to Brady's retreating back. "Mark talks about her all the time. When he first said he wanted her to be his best man I threw a fit. But the more he talked about her the more I realized he could have whoever he wants. It's his wedding too."

A few of the ladies nodded in agreement. "If my daughter trusts Mark and Mark trusts Brady, then I trust Brady. It's as simple as that. His brother on the other hand…" Barbara didn't need to describe him any further.

"Get your hand off me, bitch." Robbie tried to squirm away, but Brady tightened her grip on him.

"Come on, Robbie. Keep walking."

"Where's Mark? You said he wanted to talk to me."

"I lied," Brady said simply after they were outside. "You need to go home. I'll get you a cab."

"I don't wanna go home. I wanna see my brother," he said, his words slurring.

"He's gone. He left with Sara about ten minutes ago." Brady lied again. No way was she going to say anything to give Robbie any ideas of staying. "Now you need to go home."

"What are you doing here? Who are you anyway?" Robbie repeated himself.

"I'm your brother's friend and I look out for him, and because I'm his friend, I look out for you too." Brady said, keeping Robbie walking.

"That babe I was talking to, she was hot. I could get into her pants without batting an eye."

"That babe you were talking to is a lady, and she didn't seem interested to me."

"She just needed to warm up, that's all."

"Well, I tell you what, Robbie. Why don't you go home and try another day."

Brady escorted Rob to the front of the church where several cabs were waiting for just this purpose. She poured him into one, listened while Robbie recited his address, and flipped the driver a twenty to get him home. Brady stood with her hands on her hips as the cab drove away. Mark was right. The guy was an asshole.

She'd been keeping her eye on Nicole since she saw her in the church. She'd watched her mingle and make polite conversation but not stay too long with any group of people. Brady had seen her at the bar only twice, each time coming away with a bottle of Michelob Ultra in her hand. Brady thought that was pretty brassy: a fine woman drinking beer at a fancy wedding. Brady didn't like women who drank too much. They reminded her of her mother, and that was the last thing she wanted to think about when she was with an attractive woman.

She'd watched as Mark's brother circled Nicole, his eyes reflecting that dangerous look drunk men have when they're looking for trouble. She'd stood in the wings close enough to hear when he talked to Nicole. Nicole could hold her own, but everyone could use a little help now and then, and when Robbie had started getting out of line, she'd stepped in.

The look of relief on Nicole's face told her she'd done the right thing. Somehow she'd gotten him away from Nicole without making a scene and was going to reward herself with another cold beer.

Brady was counting out her cash at the bar when a voice behind her said, "Let me get that." Brady turned around and gazed into the bluest eyes she'd ever seen.

"For rescuing me," she said. "It's the least I can do."

"I didn't rescue you."

"Yes, you did. Don't argue with me."

"Let's just say I was at the right place at the right time."

Nicole seemed to think about that and finally answered, "I can live with that."

"And you don't have to buy me a beer."

"I know," Nicole said, and did anyway.

Brady tapped the neck of her bottle to Nicole's in acknowledgement of the gesture and took a sip. The cold liquid felt good on her suddenly parched throat.

"Would you like to sit for a few minutes?" Nicole asked.

"Sure," Brady said, and indicated an empty table nearby.

She held Nicole's chair as she sat, and when she sat down in the chair next to her she couldn't help but smile when Nicole said, "You're very gallant."

"No, just polite."

"Do you make it a habit to save damsels in distress?"

Brady liked Nicole's sense of humor and chuckled. "You may be a damsel, but I seriously doubt you're ever in distress." Brady's fingers tingled when Nicole laughed.

"Well, then I suppose I shouldn't call you my knight in shining armor. However, that suit is very becoming."

Brady looked down at her clothes, and for the first time since she'd put on the stifling formal wear, she liked it. And she definitely liked the way Nicole's eyes traveled down her body.

"This old thing? It was in my knapsack. I just pulled it out."

Nicole smiled again. "Good planning. You never know when you might need one."

"Did you have that in your knapsack?" Brady asked, referencing Nicole's outfit and mimicking the trail Nicole's eyes had taken over her body. She had to force herself not to lick her lips.

Nicole laughed. "No, it was in the front of my closet. The shoes, however, were another story altogether."

Brady settled back into the chair, wanting this relaxed conversation to continue. "Do tell."

"Some other time. So how long have you known Mark?"

"About three years, off and on. How long have you known Sara?"

"About six years. Actually I know her mother. She's one of my good friends, therefore..." Nicole gestured as if saying "here I am."

"They make a cute couple, don't they?" Brady tipped her head in the direction of Sara and Mark on the dance floor.

"Yes, they do."

Several minutes passed with no conversation. "I don't mean to keep you if you have best-man things to do," Nicole finally said.

"No, for the most part my job is done. I was responsible for getting Mark to the church and making sure he didn't collapse at the altar, the ring, and the toast. Oh, and the bachelor party. That was a couple nights ago. We're all still recovering from that."

"Do tell." She mimicked Brady's words back to her.

"I don't think so."

"Oh, come on."

"Nope, you're not getting it out of me." Brady crossed her arms across her chest.

"Is it because I'm the boss?"

"No, not at all. It's because you're a lady."

Nicole quickly covered her look of surprise at her answer.

"What about you," Brady asked. "Do you have any particular job as the friend of the mother of the bride?"

"Not today. Up to this point it was listening to Barbara complain, glow, think out loud, plan, change plans, Sara change plans again— you know, those kinds of friend things."

"And tomorrow?"

"Tomorrow it's listening to her recant everything that happened today. And about a month from now I'll be listening to her bitch when the credit-card bills come."

Brady laughed. "So that tradition of the parents of the bride funding the wedding is still alive, huh?"

"At least in that household it is."

"How about you?" Brady asked. "It's not a tradition, but do you have any bad habits you'd like to break?"

Nicole thought for a minute. "I don't think I'd call them bad habits."

"What would you call them then?" Brady asked, very interested in Nicole's answer.

"Things I'd like to maybe do differently."

"That's a politically correct phrase. And what would those be, give me an example."

"Well, I'd like to not drink as much coffee as I do."

Brady thought about that for a few seconds. "Give me another one."

"Um, not make as many trips to the Dairy Queen."

This time Brady ran her eyes over Nicole's body. "From what I see it doesn't look like you've taken too many trips."

Nicole blushed a very nice shade of pink. Brady wanted to see it again. "Give me another one."

"Try to have a little more work-life balance."

"What do you do for fun?"

Nicole stopped and thought about the answer to that question. Did she tell Brady the truth? She didn't remember the last time she had fun. "I paint," she said, the first lie that came to mind. No one had asked her that question, or any personal question, in a long time.

As a matter of fact she hadn't made social small talk with anyone in a long time.

"As in artist or walls?'

"Walls."

"Do you have a painting business on the side?"

Nicole didn't want to continue the lie but had no choice. "No. I bought a house several months ago that needs a lot of work, and it seems as though all I've been doing lately is paint."

"Are you any good?"

"Well, it doesn't take much skill to paint a flat wall." At least that was an honest answer.

"Sure it does. What about edges, trim, cutting in, and trying not to drip on the carpet?"

"Okay, I get your point, but I'm still convinced it doesn't take a lot of skill to paint a wall."

"So what else?' Brady asked.

"No, no, no." Nicole shook her head. "I've given you three. It's your turn. Give me one bad habit you'd like to break."

"Women."

Nicole choked on her beer. She coughed, patting herself on the chest several times. "Women?" she managed to squeak out.

"Yeah, you know, ones that aren't good for me."

Nicole had no idea how to follow up on that subject so she stayed away from it. "How about another one?"

"I really don't have any more."

"You don't have any more?" Nicole was surprised. "You have one bad habit and that's it? What are you, some kind of saint?"

Brady laughed until she could barely breathe. "Not hardly. I do what I want to do when I want to do it, and if it's not good for me, I either do it or I don't."

"I see," Nicole said, even though she really didn't. "Pretty sure of yourself, aren't you?"

"No, well, I guess if that's what you want to call it. I had to live somebody else's life for so long that when I got my own, I promised myself it would be my own."

Nicole thought for a moment. "So there's no one?" she asked hesitantly.

"Nope."

"Ever been anyone?" *Why am I asking this?*

"Well, I don't want to sound like a cad, but there's been a lot of *someones* but not any *one*." Brady emphasized the word *one*.

"Do you see one in your future?" *Stop asking questions.*

"Nope."

"You seem pretty confident of that." Nicole felt a pang of disappointment.

"Yep." Brady looked at her, obviously waiting for Nicole to say something. When she didn't she said, "It's not a bad thing, it's just my thing. How about you? Anyone?"

"No."

"Had anyone?"

"I thought I did."

"I'm sorry," Brady replied, surprising Nicole. "Looking for another one?"

"No." Judging by Brady's reaction Nicole knew that her answer was more forceful than she meant it to be. She didn't know why she was having this conversation. They weren't flirting or trying to get to know each other, just having general idle conversation. So why did she feel like they were? Why did she want to continue to hear Brady talk, to hear the sound of her deep, smooth voice, wondering what it sounded like in the dark?

"So," Brady said, "if you don't have anyone and aren't looking, and I don't have anyone and am certainly not looking, would you like to, uh…"

Nicole held her breath. Certainly Brady wouldn't be so bold to suggest what she thought she would suggest. Nicole admired her confidence to go after what she wanted.

"Dance?"

"Excuse me?"

"Dance. Would you like to dance?"

"Here?"

"No. I was thinking maybe on the dance floor."

"Um," Nicole replied, trying to get her bearings back.

"Look, it's okay. If you don't want to, that's okay. I can take rejection. I can even take rejection by a beautiful woman."

Nicole couldn't help but laugh at Brady's lightening of the mood. "Something tells me you don't have much experience in that area."

"No comment." Brady's eyes twinkled.

"All right, I'll dance with you." No harm in just one dance, Nicole thought.

Brady stood and extended her hand. Nicole took it, and Brady escorted her to the crowded dance floor.

The DJ was playing a good mix of fast, slow, and in-between music. Some guests were a respectable, chaste distance apart, and others clinched so tight Brady thought they needed a hose to get them to part.

She turned and pulled Nicole gently into her arms, instinctively knowing a compromise distance was in order. Nicole was a good dancer, and they moved like they'd been together for years.

She was about half a head taller than Nicole, and the distinct combination of Nicole's shampoo and perfume was intoxicating. Nicole's hand in hers felt right and even better to have her other hand on her shoulder. If Nicole would only wrap her hand around her neck—well, that would probably never happen.

The DJ obviously sensed the mood of the crowd and kept his selections with a slow tempo. Dance after dance Brady held Nicole in her arms, drawing her closer and closer. Actually, she wasn't sure who was doing it, and it really didn't matter as their bodies finally touched. Brady shivered as Nicole's hand grazed the hair at the back of her neck.

"Are you okay?" Nicole lifted her head and looked at her.

"Yeah, fine," Brady lied. She wanted so much for that touch to be a caress, but more than likely Nicole was probably just shifting her hand to get more comfortable.

They spoke very little while they danced. A variety of wonderful thoughts crossed Brady's mind while holding Nicole. They were completely inappropriate thoughts because it was Nicole. She didn't give a shit what people thought, and if by some absolute miracle she had a chance to sleep with Nicole, she would—without thinking twice. She didn't worry about getting attached because she never did. She viewed sex as simply two women being attracted to each other and following through on it. It was no different than two people in the mood for Chinese food going out and satisfying that craving. Nothing more complicated than that.

Emotions usually didn't sway Brady. She'd learned early on that emotions got in the way. Even when she left her worthless parents and the shit hole of a trailer they'd lived in, she didn't bat an eye. That was one of her easier decisions, based on cold, hard facts and the will to survive.

She'd been raising herself anyway. Her parents were never there. They were either too drunk to care or not drunk enough and showed her how much they cared by beating the shit out of her. She'd sold almost everything she had piece by piece and her parents never had a clue. The day she turned eighteen she left. The only thing that remained to indicate she had ever lived there was a neatly made bed against a wall in an empty bedroom. Hell, it had probably been days before they even realized she was gone.

CHAPTER THIRTEEN

Dancing in Brady's arms felt too good, and Nicole forced herself to put some distance between them. She hadn't been aware of what was happening, the slow-burning desire coming to a boil before she knew what hit her. She did know, however, that she hadn't felt like this in far too long. She didn't want it to end, and her body knew it too. Her body needed this. She needed to touch and be touched, to connect with another human being in more than a clinical sense. More precisely a beautiful woman who desired her, and it was obvious Brady did.

Nicole was astute enough to recognize the signs in Brady. Her breathing became more shallow and quick, and by the way Brady was holding her hand against her chest, Nicole could feel her heart beating faster. Nicole felt Brady's neck flush as they drew close.

In Nicole's mind, dancing was one of the most sensuous things two people could do without actually having sex. Bodies fit together, and when they didn't, unconscious subtle shifts in positioning made it work. From the moment she accepted Brady's hand, the people and activity around her disappeared. The noise, the clinking of china, the celebratory laughter faded into the background until her entire focus was on the woman holding her.

What if she were to allow this to run its natural course? She knew where they would end up—in her hotel room. However, it didn't take a genius to know that Brady would immediately lose interest when she realized Nicole wouldn't be taking off her clothes. No way would she subject herself to that humiliation. Not again.

Nicole stiffened and stepped out of Brady's arms, feeling guilty.

"Nicole?" Brady asked, obviously confused by her change of mood.

It was the first time Brady had called her by her first name, and the sound of it made her stomach quiver. "I think it's time for me to go."

"Nicole, wait," Brady said, reaching for her.

Nicole didn't want to create a scene, even though two women dancing together was probably scene enough, so she waited for Brady to catch up and then, as calmly as she could, walked off the dance floor.

However, Brady wasn't so easily dissuaded. She grabbed Nicole's hand, slowing her escape, and pulled her through the door and out into the empty atrium. It was dark now, the sun having dipped below the horizon during the festivities. The sky was cloudless, and the twinkling stars surrounding the half-moon added to the recessed lighting in the area.

Brady kept hold of her hand and didn't let go even when she led them to a nearby wooden bench and sat down. Brady unclasped their fingers and laid Nicole's palm on her hard leg and covered it with her own. Nicole didn't pull away. Brady's fingers lightly caressed the top of her hand, and Nicole had to force herself to concentrate and not be swept away in the wonderful feeling.

"I thought we were having a pretty good time," Brady said, not looking at her. "At least I was."

"We were," Nicole replied shakily. She didn't want to have this conversation. She owed Brady an explanation and struggled to find the words that would explain her abrupt turnaround without completely humiliating herself. "I'm sorry if I gave you the wrong impression," she said weakly.

"You didn't give me the wrong impression, Nicole. Something changed your mind."

Despite how confused and mixed up she felt, Nicole nervously chuckled. "I just don't think it's a good idea." Nicole felt Brady stiffen under her hand.

"Why? Because I work for you?" Brady asked, more than a hint of irritation in her voice.

"No, that's got nothing to do with it. I don't care about stuff like that."

"Surely you don't think I'm going to try to—"

"No," Nicole said quickly. "I said that had nothing to do with it." It was important to her that Brady didn't think it had anything to do with her.

"Well, then what does?"

"I just don't think it's a good idea."

"You said that already."

"Brady, please. I'm having a hard-enough time with this. Please don't make it any harder." Nicole hated that it sounded like she was pleading, but if she had to in order to get out of this she would.

"All right," Brady said. "Are you really leaving or did you just use that as an excuse?"

Nicole's anger flared. "Do you think this is easy for me? Do you think I enjoy being held by a beautiful, sexy woman and then leaving to go home alone?"

"I don't know what you think, Nicole. You won't talk to me."

"I talked to you all night."

"No, we made conversation, polite small talk. But you won't talk to me about this."

"This," Nicole said, waving her hand back and forth between them, "is not going to happen." Nicole raised her voice.

"Nicole."

"Jesus, I can't believe this is happening." The thin thread that was holding Nicole together snapped. She pulled her hand off Brady's thigh and stood and faced her. "Do you think this is easy for me?" she repeated. "Well, it's not." She started pacing back and forth in front of Brady, barely able to meet her eyes.

"All right," she said, spinning around and looking directly at Brady. "I'll admit it. Fine. You want to hear it. Here it is. Yes, I want you. I want to have sex with you. All night. Maybe even all day tomorrow. I might've even called in sick on Monday if you were as good as I think you'd be. But it's not going to happen." Nicole emphasized each word. "I don't owe you an explanation, and I don't want to talk about it."

"Well, I do."

"Too bad," Nicole said forcefully. She took a deep breath to gather herself again. "Look, Brady, I'm sorry. I didn't expect this and I won't deny it happened. I was afraid it might when you asked me to dance, and against my better judgment it did. I'm sorry I misled you and I don't know how many times I can say it. I'm done saying it. So think whatever you want of me. I'm sure you're mature enough to know what to do with this conversation, this entire evening, but I need to say my good-byes to Barbara, and then I'm leaving."

The expression on Brady's face almost made Nicole change her mind. She saw anger, hurt, confusion, and lingering desire, but she couldn't do this, wouldn't do this, and she certainly wouldn't do it with Brady.

Brady stood. "I'll walk you to your car."

"That's not necessary."

"I don't care. I'll respect your decision about what did or didn't happen here. I don't understand it, I don't agree with it, but I will respect it. And you will respect my decision about walking you to your car."

Nicole didn't reply, simply turned and strode back into the reception hall.

Brady stood beside her as they waited for the valet to bring her car around. The tension was thick, and she wished she could think of something to say to retrieve the easy camaraderie they'd shared before she lost herself in Brady's arms. She could feel the heat of Brady's body beside her; the chill in the air was like a crevasse that couldn't be crossed.

Nicole stared straight ahead, occasionally looking to her left as if she could will her truck to arrive sooner. She heard the distinctive *clackety-clack* of a diesel engine and held her sigh of relief when the big blue truck pulled into view.

"Nice rig," Brady said.

"Thanks."

"You know, first you surprised me by being here, then you surprised me by drinking beer, and now you surprise me by stepping into a big beefy truck."

Nicole smiled. "It's practical and, well, I just like big trucks."

Brady escorted Nicole around the front of her truck. She tipped the valet before Nicole had a chance and the man stepped away, clearly understanding Brady would be the one assisting Nicole into the vehicle.

Brady held open the door as Nicole stepped up into the tall truck. She waited for her to fasten her seatbelt and adjust the steering wheel before she said, "I'm glad we had the chance to spend some time together this evening."

"I am too," Nicole said, surprising Brady and herself.

"Drive safe," Brady said as she closed the door and stepped back.

Nicole waited until she was out of the parking lot before she slammed her fists into the steering wheel. "God damn it, God damn it, God damn it. What the fuck am I doing?"

She drove on autopilot back to her hotel, talking out loud and trying to make sense of the last several hours. She'd almost lost control. And worse, she wanted to. She knew what was happening, she knew she should stop it, but she didn't want to. God help her she didn't want to. But when common sense and reasoning kicked in, stepping out of Brady's arms was the hardest thing she'd ever done. Leaving her standing on the curb as she drove away was equally hard. She kept telling herself, *don't turn around, don't turn around, don't look in the mirror. Just drive.* And she did.

She tried to make sense of what had happened. She hadn't felt even remotely attracted to anyone since the accident. That part of her life had shut down, ceased to exist. Shut down just as much out of self-preservation as her body's healing took priority. But why now? She didn't want this. She didn't want to have to deal with this. People lived celibate lives everywhere, and she expected she'd be one of them. After this evening she reaffirmed she would too.

Brady drove back to her apartment completely baffled. One minute Nicole had melted into her arms, and the next she was as rigid as stone. Brady thought back over every minute of their time together, trying to determine when the change occurred. She couldn't put her finger on it. She had no idea and it bothered her. All she knew was that Nicole had done a complete about-face for reasons of her own. Sure, she'd tried to explain herself, but all she was able to say was that it just wasn't going to work. And why the hell not? Their bodies fit together perfectly. Brady had been with enough women to know that Nicole's body was exhibiting the same signs of desire as hers. Whereas she would have acted on it, Nicole had stepped away.

She pulled her truck into the drive and parked it next to her landlord's 1972 Ford LTD. Sam and Helen Coughlin were in their late seventies and charged her an obscenely small amount for rent, their justification being that she was hardly there. She argued that she should pay for the value of the space, not how much she used it. Finally after two years she'd given up and sent the meager check every month.

Sam and Helen had been married for over sixty years and were still very much in love. Brady had seen older couples who had been together for years bicker about everything and absolutely nothing. Sam and Helen were nothing like that. He still held the door for her, held her chair and her hand. And she in return looked at him like he was the only man on earth.

Whenever she was in town Brady usually had dinner with the couple. The inside of their house had dated furniture but was spotless. Even though Brady didn't have any experience living in a well-kept home, Mrs. C's pride in her house was evident.

"How was the shindig?" Mrs. C asked as Brady locked her truck. She must have been waiting for her to come home.

"Good, a lot of fun," Brady replied, suddenly very tired. It had been a long day, and the hour drive back to her apartment had seemed twice as long.

"Come on in and tell me all about it. You know I don't get out much anymore, and I can live my life vicariously through yours."

Brady didn't have the heart to deny Mrs. C this simple pleasure, and she steeled herself for a few more hours of entertaining.

CHAPTER FOURTEEN

"Nicole McMillan."

A rush of excitement shot through Brady's body when she heard Nicole's voice on the other end of the line, and she completely forgot what she'd planned to say. She'd debated for hours whether to call. Half the time she thought Nicole was just being polite when she told her to call the next time she was in town. Brady wanted her to have meant it just for her.

"Hello?"

Brady cleared her throat. "Good morning, it's Brady Stewart." She paused, and the silence was awkward.

"Brady," Nicole replied, excitement in her voice. "How are you?"

Brady relaxed a little. "I'm well, thanks. Um…you said if I was ever back in town to give you a call. Since you bought lunch the first time, I thought I'd return the favor. If you're available," Brady said, much too fast. God, she sounded like a teenager asking for her first date. When Nicole didn't answer immediately Brady said, "I know it's short notice and you're probably…"

"No, I was just looking at my calendar. When were you thinking?"

"Today? Tomorrow? I know it's short notice," she said again.

"I'm sorry, I can't make lunch."

Brady interrupted Nicole to save her the embarrassment of turning her down. "That's okay, I knew it was a long shot." Brady wanted to get off the phone and crawl into a hole. What had she been thinking? She'd never done anything so stupid in her life.

"I can do dinner…tonight," she heard Nicole say. "It doesn't have to be any place special."

Brady was caught completely off guard. "Dinner's great." She tried to tamp down her excitement. "How about Marshalls?" It was a nice but not too nice restaurant.

"Sounds great."

"What time are you through for the day?"

Nicole laughed. "Well, if this were a normal day I'd say eight, but I know the boss, and I think she'll let me knock off early."

Brady could hear Nicole's smile in her voice. She liked her sense of humor and teased back. "If you're sure. I don't want you to get in trouble, and I certainly don't want to be responsible for you losing your job."

"I'll take the risk."

"How about I pick you up in front of the building, say six?"

"Make it six thirty."

"Perfect. I'll see you then."

"Looking forward to it," Nicole said just before Brady hung up.

She dropped into the chair by the window, her legs suddenly feeling weak. A small shaft of sun forced its way through the clouds that had filled the sky for the past few days, and Brady smiled.

❖

"'I can do dinner.' Jesus, Nicole, what the hell were you thinking?"

The call had surprised her. She was in the middle of proofing a contract and didn't even wait for Ann to answer. She just picked up. When she heard Brady's voice on the speaker the papers she was holding fell out of her hand and scattered across her desk. The wedding had been less than a week ago, and it was good to hear Brady's voice. She hadn't expected to hear from her again.

She had meetings all week over lunch, so dinner was the only option if she wanted to see Brady. Actually, saying she just couldn't make it was an option, and by suggesting dinner, obviously one she didn't consider seriously. Her remark had come out spontaneously. Now what was she going to do?

Marshalls was a step above casual, and as she glanced at her clothes she sighed. They would have to do. She didn't have time to go home and change. And if she did, that would make it more like a date than a business dinner. Which was it? What did Brady think it was? She refused to consider it anything other than the latter.

The rest of the day dragged by. Nicole had several meetings, but they didn't hold her attention, and several times she had to ask someone to repeat what they'd just said. Buck looked at her questioningly. She was never anything but totally focused.

Finally it was time to go, and Nicole's pulse raced when she looked out the window and saw Brady waiting at the curb. She was pacing back and forth in front of a car, fidgeting with her clothes. Was she nervous? Why would she be? Brady had appeared so calm and self-assured the two other times they'd been together. What would she have to be nervous about?

"Get real, Nicole. You're the boss, for crying out loud. You sign her paycheck." Yeah, that had to be it. It certainly couldn't be because this was a date.

❖

Brady was still pacing when Nicole exited the building but stopped and smiled when she saw her. Nicole's throat suddenly became very dry.

"You're early." Brady looked at her clunky black watch.

"The boss told me to get out." Brady didn't need to know she hadn't been able to concentrate and get any work done since her call earlier this morning.

"She sounds like a great boss."

"She tries. Sometimes she has to be a hard-ass, but I know for a fact she hates doing that."

"Is that so?" Brady held open the passenger door for her to get in.

"Yes, and I'm starving," she said, sliding into the leather seat. She told herself to calm down as Brady hurried around the front of the car and slid into her own seat. What had gotten into her? She was simply having a meal with an employee. No big deal. Then why did it feel like it was?

She'd had more important dinners before. Just last week she'd eaten with the CEO of Shell Oil, and a few months ago the President of BP and the King of Rolfim, the largest oil producer in the Middle East. But those meetings didn't make her heart pound, her palms sweat, her mouth dry, and her brain stop working.

They pulled into the parking lot of the restaurant fifteen minutes later. The conversation on the ride over was relaxed, even if she wasn't. She kept waiting for Brady to bring up what had happened at the wedding. And what would she say if she did? *Sorry, I got carried away by the romance of the entire event? I lost my mind when you took me in your arms?* She'd think of something if the subject came up, but the more she thought about it the more she realized Brady was too polite to bring it up.

Nicole opened her door before Brady had a chance to get around and do it for her, if that was her intent. Nicole had to regain control, and the door was a small yet important step in that direction.

"Reservation for Stewart," Brady said as they approached the hostess stand.

Nicole couldn't miss the unmistakable reaction of the hostess, who obviously thought they were on a date. Was she the only one who didn't? Did Brady?

Their table was in the far corner of the room, and Nicole felt eyes on them as they walked across the crowded dining room. Even though her scars were hidden underneath expensive, perfectly tailored clothes, she hadn't yet gotten over the feeling that everyone was staring at her. She wondered if she ever would.

Brady held her chair as she sat, and Nicole cursed herself for not thinking about that. She put her napkin in her lap and noticed her hands were shaking. She made a mental note to keep them there unless she was holding something.

The waiter took their drink order and Nicole surveyed the menu. She settled on a petite filet, hoping she'd be able to swallow the tender meat because her mouth was so dry.

"I'm glad you could make it," Brady said as the waiter returned with their drinks and took their order.

"I am too."

"I have to admit I wasn't sure if you were being polite or meant it when you said to call," Brady said, just before she took a sip of her beer.

"No, I was serious. I don't get out to the field as much as I'd like, and it's a good way to keep in touch with what's happening." There, she thought. That established this as a business dinner.

"I don't know half of what it takes to run a company like McMillan. Do you like working in a comfortable, clean office, away from the dirt, grime, and filth at a fire?"

Nicole took a rather large swallow of her drink to dislodge the sudden lump of longing in her throat. "Actually, I miss it," she said honestly. "I loved being out there. The challenge, the camaraderie of the crew, the unbelievable sense of accomplishment when the well is capped. Talk about making a difference in the world."

She stopped, shocked at what she'd just said and the conviction with which she'd said it. She hadn't talked about how she felt to anyone. Everyone believed, like Brady, that she was happier out of harm's way. That was the furthest thing from the truth. She was afraid to make eye contact with Brady for fear she'd see how desperately she did miss it. When she finally did look at her, Nicole saw Brady actually did understand.

"I'd be miserable sitting behind a desk. I know everyone has a job and hopefully they're doing what they like. But I couldn't do it."

"And you love killing fires," Nicole said. It was an observation more than a question.

"Yes, I do. At first I did it for the money, and I suppose that's still a part of it. But I agree with what you said. There's nothing like the rush of knocking it down and killing it."

"Is that really why you got into the business? For the money?" Nicole heard herself asking.

"Yes. I didn't have much as a kid, and I didn't want to stay that way as an adult."

"Do you have siblings?"

"Not that I know of."

Nicole tried to hide her surprise.

"My parents were a bit out there," Brady said, waving her hand in the air to help make her point.

"Out there like hippie or…" Nicole struggled to find the right set of words.

Brady blanched, apparently realizing she'd probably said too much. "Well, let's just say I'm pretty sure you and I had very different childhoods." Brady's expression clearly said that was the end of that discussion. However, Nicole was curious. Her childhood had made her who she was now, and she was very interested in learning about the adult Brady. But she let it drop, for now.

"How about you?" Brady said, shifting the subject.

"Nope, only child, same as you. But I'm a little more confident that I am an only child."

"How is your dad?" Brady asked.

DD McMillan was highly known in the industry, akin to Red Adair in the oil-fire suppression business.

"I heard he was ill," Brady said carefully.

"Yes, Parkinson's." After several years Nicole still was uncomfortable saying the word. "He's doing as well as expected. Thank you for asking. Every time I see him he insists on getting the rundown on what's going on, the state of the business. You know, who's who, where we are, what we've killed."

"I can imagine." Brady nodded. "He started the company. It's his baby."

"Yes. It was his baby, and as with any baby growing up, it's hard to let go when it's time."

"Does he live nearby?"

"About fifteen minutes from me."

"And your mother?"

"Same." Nicole reflected back on her last conversation with her mother. It was like all the others lately. They stayed on safe topics such as the weather or current events. They never talked about the company or Nicole's personal life. She didn't approve of Nicole being a lesbian and still held out hope that she'd marry an oilman and give her half a dozen grandchildren. By mutual agreement neither of them spoke about it. Her father was the only thing they had in common, and even then they disagreed about his condition more often than not. Theresa thought he was doing fine whereas Nicole saw him deteriorate more each time she saw him.

"How's the painting coming along?"

"Painting?" Nicole had no idea what Brady was talking about.

"Your house," Brady replied, sipping her beer.

Nicole hoped her face didn't betray her complete lack of understanding of what in the hell she was supposed to be painting.

"At Dig's wedding you said you were painting your house."

"Oh, that painting," Nicole said, remembering the lie she'd come up with. "It's still a work in progress." She hoped her answer was vague enough so as not to draw any follow-up questions.

"So what else do you do in your spare time?"

"Spare time?" Nicole asked.

"Yeah, you know the time after work and before you go to bed?"

"Oh, that spare time," Nicole responded, trying to give herself a few seconds. Was this going to be twenty questions and twenty lies? "I guess normal stuff. You know, make the coffee, pack my briefcase, take the dog out, set the alarm. You know, regular stuff." Nicole rattled off her activities six out of seven nights of the week.

"Is that all you do?" Brady asked, then blushed. "I'm sorry. It's really none of my business."

Nicole shrugged. "That's okay. I'm pretty much known as a workaholic. Work takes up the majority of my time. My father spent his life building a solid, reputable company, and it's my responsibility to continue that and make it grow. Even after all this time I still have so much to learn and do, I don't have much free time." Nicole hoped her answer was acceptable.

"At the expense of your personal life?"

Brady had no way of knowing that she didn't have much of a personal life. She had a few close friends who periodically would drag her out; she didn't do much other than work.

"I don't consider it at the expense of," Nicole said, using Brady's words. "I'm happy with my life."

"That's really all that matters, isn't it? That you're happy?"

"Yes, it is," Nicole replied, stabbing a piece of her salad. "How about you?"

"Can't complain. Got a great job, some money in the bank."

Nicole looked at her and waved her fork at her to draw more information out. When Brady didn't say more she said, "And...?"

"And that's all."

"Then let me ask you what you do in your spare time, between working and going to sleep?"

Brady looked at her with a peculiar expression. Nicole felt herself blush when she realized how that question could be interpreted, especially with a woman as dangerously attractive as Brady. "I mean, what do you do when you're not working?"

Brady's smile was sly, clearly telling Nicole she knew what she meant. "Read, do some yard stuff, visit friends, take care of my landlords. You know, normal stuff."

Nicole was relieved that the topic had moved away from a very uncomfortable subject. "How do you take care of them? Are they ill?"

Brady took a sip of her beer. "No, Mr. and Mrs. C, Coughlin, are elderly and can't get around very well. I rent an apartment over their garage. You know, nothing special—keep an eye on them, keep the yard trimmed, do some weeding. Right now I'm painting the exterior."

"Painting?"

"Yeah, it probably hasn't been done in over twenty years. It was starting to blister and peel in some places, and they couldn't possibly do it themselves or even pay someone to paint it for them. So I'm doing it."

Nicole looked at Brady's hands, intending to envision how they held a paintbrush, but instead she wondered how they would feel holding her. She put the fork down before she dropped it and took a swallow of her tea.

"That's awful nice of you."

"Nice doesn't really have anything to do with it. It needed to be done and I'm capable of doing it, so I just do."

"Are you related to them?"

"Nope, not in the slightest. I've lived there four or five years, and I guess they're like the grandparents I never had. Their children live in Maine and they're just a sweet old couple. Somebody's got to look out for them."

The waiter brought their steaks and Nicole was amazed that she enjoyed every bite. They chatted about innocuous topics, and when coffee was served she realized she was quite relaxed and was enjoying herself immensely. Though she went out to dinner with friends, that was different. She hadn't enjoyed the company of another woman in a long, long time.

Nicole was sipping her coffee when she glanced over Brady's left shoulder and froze. Walking to a table was Gina, wearing a low-cut, very short red dress and followed by a stunningly beautiful blonde. Her dress was even shorter, and she was balanced confidently on come-fuck-me pumps.

Nicole's heart lodged somewhere in her throat. She couldn't breathe, she couldn't move. It was as if time stopped and she was back there in their bedroom all those years ago.

She hadn't seen Gina since she walked out on her. She had made it a point to not be home when Gina came to collect her things. Now here she was. Nicole had known she might eventually run into Gina but that it was improbable because she didn't go out much, they didn't frequent the same grocery stores, and they no longer had the same circle of friends.

The woman was obviously Gina's date and showed more skin than not, and the places that did show were the places on Nicole's body that were scarred. Gina had always been a bit superficial, and after Nicole had thrown her out she'd realized just how superficial she was. It should have been no surprise to see her sitting at a table with one of the most beautiful women Nicole had ever seen.

"Nicole?" She heard her name, but it sounded like it was coming through a thick fog. She heard it again, this time more clearly, her attention drawn away from Gina to Brady. Brady wore a look of concern on her face.

"Nicole, are you all right?"

Nicole's mouth opened and closed a few times, like a fish gasping for air. But that was exactly what she felt like; she too was gasping for air. "I need to go," she said quickly, and started looking around for their waiter. "Please take me back to the office."

Brady saw the instantaneous change in Nicole. At the risk of being rude she looked over her shoulder at whatever had caught Nicole's attention. She didn't recognize anyone at any of the tables, but behind her sat two women, obviously lovers or would be soon, their heads bent in intimate conversation. She turned back around, and Nicole was again mesmerized by the women.

What in the hell is going on, she thought to herself. "Nicole?"

"I'm fine. Sorry. What were we talking about?"

Brady thought it odd that one moment she wanted to leave, and now it appeared she wanted to continue their conversation. She risked another look over her shoulder at the women, then back at Nicole. She was still as pale as she was when she first saw them. Nicole must know one of them.

Then it clicked. The rumor around the job was that the girlfriend had left her on her sickbed. At Dig's wedding she had said that she *had* someone. Was one of those women her? It had to be. What else would cause such a reaction in Nicole?

That was it, she thought. The accident, the burns, the scars. Brady was instantly furious. What an ass. Nicole was a beautiful, charming woman. So her body wasn't perfect. Whose was? Brady had scars, some from fire, but not as extensive as Nicole's. Some from the craziness of youth. Most from the belt buckle wielded by her father.

Brady tamped down her anger and focused on Nicole instead. She stood and held out her hand. "Dance with me?"

"What?" Nicole replied, her coffee cup rattling on the saucer as she set it down.

"Dance with me?" Brady indicated the dance floor on the opposite side of the room. For some reason it was important to her that Nicole felt good about herself again. They'd been having a wonderful time. She'd been smiling and laughing and completely radiant. Now Nicole was a mere shell of who she'd been just minutes ago.

Nicole studied her hand as if deciding if she wanted to call attention to herself on the unoccupied dance floor. She glanced at the women then at Brady. Finally she squared her shoulders and took her hand.

As they walked to the dance floor Brady was glad she'd bought new clothes for the occasion. When she'd been in the store, however, she'd felt ridiculous. It wasn't a date, but then again maybe it was. She wanted it to be and had finally settled on a pair of navy silk trousers and a royal-blue, long-sleeved, tailored silk blouse. She didn't want to overdress because she knew Nicole would be coming from the office, but she also didn't think her standard khakis were appropriate.

Brady stopped in the middle of the dance floor and pulled Nicole into her arms. She was stiff, almost wooden, and moved like she'd never danced in her life. Brady slid her arm around her, pulling her closer, their bodies intimately touching. Brady leaned closer and whispered into her ear, "She's an idiot. I think you're beautiful."

Nicole stumbled and moved her head back to look Brady in the eyes. Brady didn't flinch or blink, just cocked her head as if to say, "Yeah, I figured it out."

Nicole stared at her for several seconds, and Brady wondered how much longer they could stand there in the middle of the dance floor without drawing more attention to themselves than they already were. Nicole was searching for something in her eyes. She didn't move but let Nicole find it. Finally, Brady felt her relax and step back into her arms.

"You've been practicing," Brady said after they'd been dancing a few minutes.

Nicole put a little space between them and looked up at her. "Very funny."

"No, honest," Brady replied, relieved to see the tension in Nicole start to dissipate.

"That's the second time tonight you've lied to me."

Brady was confused. "What are you talking about?"

"Telling me I'm a good dancer."

"You are, and if that's the second time, when was the first?"

"When you said I was beautiful.'

Brady cocked her head again. "I wasn't lying."

"Yeah, right."

Brady swung her around so the women at the table were at Nicole's back. "I wasn't lying," she said firmly

"So you make that judgment based on the little of me that you see."

"No, I make that judgment on what I see about you, the person, not how you look. How kind you are to people, how thoughtful, how smart."

"And that makes me beautiful?"

"Yes, Nicole, it does."

"But you haven't seen what I look like under my clothes."

"Is that an invitation?"

"No. You'll think differently then."

"No, Nicole, I won't."

"How can you say that? You have no idea."

"No, I don't, and I don't need to. Your skin or the shape of your body doesn't make you a beautiful woman."

"You say that so simply."

"It is that simple."

"No, Brady, it's not that simple. I had third-degree burns over sixty percent of my body. I will never be beautiful. I will never have skin that's soft to the touch. I'll always be puckered and rippled and scarred."

"So what?" Brady replied. "I don't care. Do you think my body's perfect? I have scars. Not like yours, but I do. I can't even imagine what you went through, and I won't even pretend I can understand what you think or what you see when you look in the mirror. But I can tell you what I see when I look at you, and that is beautiful. I've been with a lot of physically beautiful women who were very unattractive inside. And that woman over there," Brady said, tipping her head in the direction of the women at the table, "she's an idiot if she let you go. Because fifty years from now, her outside isn't going to be pretty, and then where's she going to be?"

"Thank you," Nicole said, so quietly Brady wasn't sure she'd said it at all. She put a little distance between her and Nicole.

"Nothing to thank me for. I just spoke the truth. I wanted to dance with you again."

Nicole's eyes narrowed as if she was looking for any sign of lying in her eyes. Not sure if Nicole was satisfied, Brady pulled her tighter, their feet barely moving, Brady making sure the women were behind Nicole's back where she couldn't see them. But Brady could. And she didn't like what she saw. She didn't know which one of them had hurt Nicole. But it didn't matter. She certainly didn't know the extent of the betrayal, but anyone could hazard a guess and probably be pretty damn close. How anyone could do something so cruel to a woman like Nicole was beyond her.

Brady didn't know if it was the first, the fifth, or the tenth song that ended when Nicole stepped out of her arms. She didn't look at her.

"Would you take me back to the office now?"

Brady searched Nicole's face and saw she wasn't as upset as when they'd started dancing but still in no mood for an argument. "Certainly." She took Nicole's hand and walked off the dance floor and back to their table.

The bill had arrived while they were dancing, and Brady quickly put five twenty-dollar bills in the pad, keeping one eye on Nicole. Nicole was doing a good job keeping her eyes focused on something on the table, and Brady suspected she was struggling with an inner battle not to look over at the women again.

"Shall we?" Brady asked, moving to block Nicole's view of the women. She held out her hand again, and this time Nicole took it without hesitation. Nicole's hand tightened in hers as they walked out of the restaurant. They had to pass the women's table, but at the risk of looking like a jigsaw puzzle, Brady took a circuitous route between the tables and out the front door.

Neither one of them spoke as they walked to Brady's car, the chirp of the security alarm breaking the sound of the still evening.

Nicole reached for the handle of the door at the same time Brady did, trapping her hand on the handle. Brady was close behind her and Nicole felt the heat radiating off her body. She was tempted to lean back into those warm, strong arms that had saved her from complete humiliation and given her the strength to see the evening through to its natural end. Brady's arms were strong and confident when they held her, and Nicole inhaled sharply when she realized she wanted them to hold her again. This time, all night.

"I meant what I said. You are very beautiful," Brady whispered in her ear.

A shiver of excitement ran down Nicole's spine. She felt her mouth open and close a few times, no words coming out. She couldn't have said anything even if she'd wanted to. No one had called her beautiful since the accident except her parents, and they didn't count.

"Someday you'll believe me when I say that," Brady said.

Brady pulled on the door handle, and the dome light inside the BMW was shockingly harsh. As she slid into the car for the second time that night, Nicole told herself to calm down and this time get a tighter grip on what was happening. No way could she lose control with a woman, especially one as compelling as Brady.

They drove back to Nicole's office in silence, for which Nicole was grateful. First she'd invited Brady to dinner and enjoyed herself thoroughly. Then Gina walked in, and everything Nicole had worked for and rebuilt in the past six years had come crashing down around her. All her thoughts about the past had shot across her mind again as if on a teleprompter. All the feelings she'd gone through had been magnified, all because Gina had walked in on the arm of a half-naked beautiful woman.

And then Brady had rescued her. Had asked her to dance. Had taken her mind and eyes off the women behind them. Brady had whispered in her ear that she was beautiful. And she had said it again just before they got in the car.

Nicole looked at her hands clasped in her lap. The sleeves of her blouse came down and covered her wrists. She never rolled them up. To do so would be to expose what she kept carefully hidden beneath. If she hated what she saw, others would as well. And she wouldn't subject them to it.

"Four dollars for your thoughts," Brady said.

"Four dollars?"

"Yeah. Inflation, you know."

"You mean I'm not worth five dollars? No, don't answer that. I'm not fishing for a compliment."

Brady chuckled softly and Nicole's stomach jumped a little.

"Don't worry about it. I don't bite."

Nicole couldn't help but smile at Brady's quick wit. She had a way of breaking through the tension and setting Nicole at ease, of making her feel like she was just an ordinary person.

Nicole's office building came into view, and she didn't know if she was relieved to be able to escape the small confines of the car with Brady or sorry that she had to.

"Where are you parked?"

"In the garage. You can just let me off here."

Brady's head snapped around as if she'd just uttered the eleventh commandment. "Are you nuts? I'm not leaving you here to walk to your car by yourself."

"I need to go back upstairs and get my briefcase."

Brady glanced at the clock on the dashboard, then back to her. "It's ten thirty. You don't need to do any work. You need to get in your car and go home. Do you have your keys?"

Nicole nodded and realized just how exhausted she really was. It had been an incredibly emotional day. She rummaged around in her purse and pulled out her card key and handed it to Brady. Their fingers touched as Brady took the piece of plastic no bigger than a credit card. A surge of something Nicole didn't want to identify shot through her.

Brady maintained contact with her fingers for longer than necessary before she pulled the card from her fingers, then rolled down the window and waved the white card in front of the reader and the red-striped arm of the security gate rose silently.

Brady didn't immediately return the card but kept it in her hand as they pulled into the garage.

"Still driving the big blue truck?" Brady glanced over at her.

"Yes, I'm on the third floor."

"What? No reserved parking space?"

"Nope, 'fraid not."

"Well, you need to talk to your boss about that."

"And why is that?"

"Because you work late. All the time, if what you said earlier was true. You should have a parking spot close to the door. It's a safety feature, for crying out loud, and McMillan is very safety conscious. You tell her I said so."

"I'll do that," Nicole replied as the headlights of Brady's car illuminated her truck. When Brady pulled into the space next to her, Nicole said, "Thank you for dinner."

Brady turned off the engine and Nicole's heart sped up. She didn't know what Brady was going to do. Anyone else would have dropped her off at her truck and driven away. But Brady was different.

Brady unbuckled her seatbelt and turned to face her. "My pleasure. I had a great time." Brady's voice was strong and smooth.

Nicole's heart beat even faster because she thought Brady might lean over and kiss her. What the fuck would she do then? She wanted to kiss her back, but that couldn't happen. She wouldn't let that happen. She reached for the door handle to make her escape, but Brady was faster and covered her trembling hand with hers.

"Don't move," Brady said, her voice husky.

Like she could with Brady this close to her. Brady's mouth was mere inches from hers, and if Nicole turned her head just slightly they'd be in the perfect position to kiss. And God, she wanted to kiss Brady. She wanted to feel the thrill and rush of desire. She couldn't help how her body reacted as she looked at Brady's mouth. Her breath stuck somewhere in her throat when Brady's tongue snaked out and wet her lips.

"My daddy taught me to never let a woman open her own door," Brady said, her breath fanning across Nicole's face.

"Far be it from me to get you into trouble," Nicole managed to squeak out. She hoped her voice didn't betray the jumble of emotions bouncing through her.

"I knew you were more than just a pretty face," Brady said just before she opened her door and hustled around to open hers. Nicole admired the graceful, smooth movements of Brady's stride as she rounded the front of the car.

Before she had a chance to react, Brady's hand was palm up in front of her, offering assistance. Of course she had to take it. It would be rude not to. When she stood, she was just as close to Brady as they'd been on the dance floor. Nicole's nipples tightened, her breathing became shallow, and her fingers longed to touch the taut body in front of her.

It had been a long time since Nicole had felt like this. The nerves under her skin were firing on all cylinders, and she was scared to death. She sensed Brady was holding herself back, and for that she was grateful. If Brady had made one move, one slight tip of her head, Nicole would be in her arms. But she couldn't do that. If that dam were to burst she wouldn't be able to turn back. And like a wooden shack downstream she'd be destroyed in the aftermath. She'd worked too hard to put her life back together again to have it come crashing down around her in the arms of Brady Stewart.

Nicole stepped to the side before her body overruled her brain. "Thank you for seeing me safely to my truck." She choked out the words as she dug her keys out of her bag. "Your daddy would be very proud."

Brady chuckled. "No, he'd box my ears and say I was stupid for not kissing you when I had the chance."

Nicole dropped her keys, her hands shaking again. She knew Brady had wanted to kiss her, but to hear her verbalize it so honestly was almost more than she could bear.

Brady bent down, picked up her keys, then held them by the tip of one key, allowing Nicole to retrieve them without their fingers touching. Thank God. She didn't know what she'd have done if their skin had touched again.

"Good night," Brady said, dropping the garage entrance card key into her open palm.

Nicole unlocked her truck and climbed in. Brady backed out of the space far enough for Nicole to do the same and exit the garage. She fumbled with her keys, dropping them to the floor twice before she was able to get them in the ignition.

The halogen blue of Brady's headlights filled her rearview mirror, giving Nicole a sense of security she hadn't felt in some time as she drove out of the garage. She wasn't afraid for her life or of getting mugged, but she always felt exposed.

❖

Brady drove home, a string of obscenities flowing freely out of her mouth. *What in the fuck were you doing? For God's sake, Brady, get your shit together. You made a pass at your boss, for Christ sake.* A variety of other self-deprecating comments filled the interior of the car.

She did congratulate herself for not following through on what her body was very clearly telling her to. She wanted to kiss Nicole. Hell, she wanted do more than kiss her, and Nicole wouldn't have stopped her, but she wasn't ready. This wasn't the time or the place and certainly not the circumstances for their first kiss. And she wasn't going to take advantage of her weakened defenses just to steal a kiss or cop a feel.

Nicole had been through a lot. The burn Brady had suffered while rescuing that idiot Steckman had been excruciating, and that was nothing compared to what Nicole must have experienced.

The scuttlebutt in the field was that Nicole wasn't the woman she was before the accident. Brady had always thought that was one of the stupidest things she'd ever heard. Those kinds of injuries would change anyone. Everyone would have lingering scars, not only physically but emotionally. And based on Nicole's reaction to the woman in the restaurant, they were deeper than most.

What had the sex life of Nicole and the woman in the restaurant been like before her accident? What was it like after? Some women had difficulty baring their bodies while performing one of the most intimate acts two people could do. However, Brady believed baring your soul was more intimate than standing naked in front of someone.

What had happened between them? Had the woman been repulsed by Nicole's body? Had Nicole herself not been able to make love with her again? It could have been any number of things, but if Brady were Nicole's lover, she wouldn't have turned her back on her whatever the reason.

Whether Nicole liked it or not, her body had reacted when they were together. It had surged against her when they danced, and she had felt Nicole's restraint by her truck in the parking lot.

How would she react if she saw Nicole's body? She truly did believe that what was inside a woman made her beautiful and that Nicole's scars wouldn't bother her. But Brady was honest with herself. She really didn't know how she'd react, what she'd do, and to be completely honest, she was scared shitless that she would do or say the wrong thing.

"Brady, is that you?" Mrs. C's voice interrupted her thoughts as she locked the car door.

"Yes, Mrs. C. It's me."

"Well, come in out of the cold, girl. Have some coffee and some breakfast."

"I'm really not up for it, Mrs. C." She'd pulled off in a rest stop sometime during her three-hour drive back to Moss Bluff and caught a quick nap before she finished her drive. It was close to six when she parked the BMW behind her truck and turned off the engine.

"Nonsense, don't be ridiculous. Come on in. You need to put some meat on your bones."

Brady knew Mrs. C wouldn't take no for an answer, so she retraced her steps down the driveway and followed her inside.

With a heavy sigh Brady sat down at the kitchen table as Mrs. C filled the cup in front of her and started to crack some eggs.

"So tell me about your evening," Mrs. C asked.

"Nothing special. Just went out to dinner."

"With who?" Mrs. C whipped the eggs in a glass bowl.

Nothing would make her happier than for Brady to find a good woman and settle down, and she'd voiced that opinion on more than one occasion.

"Nobody special," Brady replied in her "don't get your hopes up" tone.

"A woman?"

"Yes." Brady answered before she took a swallow of the hot coffee.

"What's her name?"

"Nicole."

"What does she do?"

Brady couldn't help but smile. The twenty questions had begun. Actually it would probably be more like forty before Brady could manage to change the subject. She was tired and wanted to go to bed so she told Mrs. C about her evening with Nicole.

After Brady finished eating, Mrs. C sat back in her chair and crossed her arms over her ample bosom. Mrs. C didn't have breasts. She was one of those women who had a bosom.

"Sounds pretty special to me."

"Mrs. C. It was dinner. That's all."

"So you say. But you obviously stayed out all night with her. You're just now coming in."

"She lives in Morgan City. We had dinner, I took her home, and then I came home. I got sleepy about halfway and stopped at a rest area near New Iberia to take a power nap and now here I am."

"Sounds like a date to me."

"It wasn't a date."

Mrs. C pointed a gnarly, arthritic finger at Brady and shook her head. "You couldn't have picked someone to date who was a little more geographically desirable?"

"It wasn't a date. It was two people having a meal together."

"Bullshit."

Brady choked on her coffee and it dribbled down her chin. She reached for her napkin. "What did you say?"

"You heard me. I didn't stutter. I see the look in your eyes. I know you better than that. You like this girl."

Brady wiped her chin. "Of course I like her. I wouldn't have had dinner with her if I didn't."

"That's not what I meant and you know it."

"There's nothing going on."

"Not yet, there isn't."

"Since when have you become so interested in my love life?"

"When you stopped having one."

"And how do you know I don't have one?'

"Because if you're not on a job your truck is parked in the driveway every night all night. And what's with that fancy car you're driving?"

"What about it?"

"Where did you get it? Did you buy it?"

"No, it's a rental."

"A rental? You rent a fancy car and drive all the way to Morgan City to take this woman out to dinner, and you still mean to tell me it's nothing special."

"I couldn't pick her up in my truck."

"Why not? It's been good enough for all your other women."

"Well, she's not like all the other women."

"I knew it." Mrs. C slapped her hand on the Formica tabletop. "I knew it. You haven't been yourself since you got back from that safety award. Is that where you met her?"

"Yes," Brady said patiently.

"Well, it's good that you two have something in common. Other than the fact that you both like girls."

Brady didn't try to hold in her laughter. At seventy-eight Mrs. C was more liberal and un-homophobic than women half her age. She wasn't shy. She'd asked Brady all kinds of personal questions about lesbians when she first moved in because "it's just something I don't know anything about." Mrs. C was very concerned about keeping her mind active in her retirement years.

"Did you kiss her?"

"No." Even though her landlady had asked her the same question on more than one occasion, this time Brady was ready.

"Why not?"

"Because I didn't."

"Did she kiss you?"

"No, she didn't."

"Why not? You didn't eat garlic at dinner, did you? I told you never to do that on a date, no matter how much you love it." To her it was that simple.

Brady laughed again. "No, I didn't eat garlic."

"Then why didn't you kiss her?"

"She wasn't ready to be kissed."

"What does that mean?'

"Just what it means. She wasn't ready."

"Isn't that what foreplay's for? I mean, it's been a while but I do remember that part."

"Yes, that's what foreplay is. But that's not what this was about."

"Why doesn't she like you? Did you say something stupid?"

"I don't think so."

"Did you insult her?"

"Of course not."

"Then why didn't you kiss her?"

"Mrs. C, it wasn't the time or the place. It started out looking promising, but by the end of the evening everything had changed."

"What happened?"

Brady refilled both of their cups and divulged the evening's events. Mrs. C wouldn't let her up from the table until she did. Brady never talked about personal things with anyone, but she felt comfortable with Mrs. C.

"So you think one of those women dumped her?"

"That's the conclusion I came to."

"But that's just stupid."

"Actually I called the woman an ass."

"Very astute." Mrs. C shook her head disapprovingly. Gingerly she got up from the table and took Brady's empty plate. "I can see your point about not kissing her. I guess that wasn't the time. She probably would have slapped your face. You're a pretty smart girl, Brady."

"Thank you, Mrs. C. It's important to me what you think about me."

"As it should be. Now you have to leave. I have things to do today. And I need to think about what your next move needs to be."

"My next move?"

"Yeah. What you need to do so it is the right time, place, and circumstances to kiss her."

Brady laughed. Over the years she'd come to love Mr. and Mrs. C, and it really didn't bother her when they pried into her personal life. "Be sure to let me know what you come up with." Brady kissed her on the cheek and walked up the steps to her apartment.

CHAPTER FIFTEEN

Tears threatened to spill out of her eyes as Nicole looked in the mirror. Seeing Gina last night had thrown her back to a place she didn't want to be. She didn't like what she saw. Where was the woman she'd been? The confident hell-raiser. The emotionally strong kick-ass-take-no-names woman. According to Brady she still was, underneath her maimed exterior, but she wasn't so sure. Other than work and the obligatory social occasions she couldn't get out of, she had no life. And when she did go out she always felt on the fringe of the activity, never fully engaging as those around her did. She put the mirror away and walked back to her desk.

"Excuse me, Nicole," Ann said, walking into her office. "There's a President Charsea on the phone for you. He says it's quite important."

"Thanks, Ann. I think I know what he wants. Would you see if Buck's available?" Nicole found her pen, pulled out a fresh tablet of paper, and picked up the receiver. "Nicole McMillan."

"Ms. McMillan, this is President Charsea," the man said with a heavy accent. "I am in need of your services."

"Yes, Mr. President, I've been watching the news reports. How can I help you?" Greslikstan was a small but oil-rich country to the east of Turkey. The country had been invaded seven months ago by their not-so-friendly neighbors to the east. The news told of massive casualties as Greslikstan defended itself from attack.

"By doing what you do best. I am in need of McMillan Suppression to save my country from environmental disaster. When the rebels retreated three days ago they sabotaged our wellheads. Eight wells are burning."

Nicole was taking notes as the president spoke and thinking of what she would need to do in response to his request. As the president continued to outline the extent of the damage to the oil fields in his country, Nicole wrote quickly and asked questions to fill in the gaps.

"Of course we'll help you, Mr. President. I'll send five of my best teams to your country within the week." Nicole was transferred to the minister of affairs and provided the man with a list of items and material the crews would need. Forty minutes later she hung up and Buck was sitting across from her.

"We've been called to Greslikstan," Nicole said, moving to the large map on the wall of her office. "Where in the hell is it?" It took her and Buck a few minutes before they found the dot of a country on the wall map. "They have eight wells sabotaged by rebels and all are on fire."

"Eight? Holy God," Buck replied, almost in reference of the powers of the fire.

"Yes, and we need our best crews. Who's available?"

Buck rattled off the names of five crews, and when he named Brady's, Nicole's heart lurched. This would be a very dangerous situation. Not only were the fires hot, but rebels might still be in the area and would shoot anyone trying to help the government. Nicole always worried when she sent a crew out, but she would doubly so now. There was no such thing as a routine oil-well fire. The mere fact that oil and flame were mixed together…well, enough said.

"The crews?"

Nicole had never hesitated before sending any of the crews out. They were well trained and could do the job. So why was she hesitating now? Because Brady was on one of those crews. Even though Brady had been on one of the crews dozens of other times, this time it was different. This time it was personal.

"Send them."

❖

Brady's phone buzzed while she was in the chair getting her hair cut. She ignored it, but the third time in five minutes it buzzed, she reached in her pocket and answered.

"Brady, I'm glad I got you," Flick said hurriedly. "We're going out. It's a big one. Expect to be gone for a while."

"When?"

"Tonight. We've been called to Greslikstan."

"Where?" She'd never heard of the country but it didn't matter.

"Greslikstan," Flick repeated. "They have eight wells sabotaged by rebels."

"Eight?" Brady tried to imagine the destruction. "What a mess."

"I'll say. It's like a mini Kuwait."

The environmental disaster could be astronomical if the wells weren't capped quickly. In early 1991 Iraqi forces had set fire to more than six hundred Kuwaiti oil wells, creating huge columns of smoke that turned the day into night. Suppression teams from around the world arrived and worked together to extinguish the burning wells within nine months of the original callout. McMillan, including Nicole's father, was one of the US teams called to support Kuwait's firefighting efforts. Even though eight wells weren't near the magnitude of the fires in Kuwait, this could still be bad.

"Bring your A+ game, Brady. This one's going to be a son of a bitch."

CHAPTER SIXTEEN

Nicole, President Charsea is on the line," Buck said, stepping into her office two weeks later. "He's insistent that you come, and even though he hasn't said directly, he may pull our crews if you don't."

"Oh, for God's sake," Nicole barked, tossing her pen on her desk. She pushed her chair back, stood, and faced the window. "What does he want me there for? It's not like I'm going to put out his goddamn fire. I don't do that anymore." Judging by Buck's silence, Nicole realized she'd reacted badly. President Charsea had called her the day before, insisting on her presence, and she'd gotten off the line with some excuse. In a much softer tone she said, "Fine. Book me on a flight the day after tomorrow."

When Buck closed the door behind him she rested her forehead against the cool glass. One, two, three, breathe, one, two, three, breathe. She was having a full-blown panic attack. No way could she make the trip. Merely discussing it had brought on the attack. No way would she be able to sit in the confines of an airplane for twenty hours. They'd have to take her out in a strait jacket, or she'd be so highly medicated she'd be a zombie. Then what was the point?

Nicole paced around her office in a nice, neat little square reciting all the calming techniques her shrink had taught her. She walked behind her desk, up the left side, across the front, and down the other side. She did six laps in that direction before turning and repeating the sequence in the opposite. Eventually she started to calm down. Her hands still shook albeit much less than before.

"I can't do this. I can't do this. I can't do this. I cannot do this anymore." Nicole grabbed her keys and headed out the office door, pausing long enough to tell Ann something had come up and to clear her calendar for the rest of the afternoon. As she pulled out of the parking garage of McMillan Suppression she couldn't get away fast enough.

❖

"What does he expect me to do?" Nicole repeated the question she'd asked Buck yesterday, but this time in the confines of her psychologist's office. She'd called Dr. Craig after she left her office, and he was able to squeeze her in before his first patient this morning.

"Personally put out his goddamn fire. I don't do that anymore. I can't do it anymore," Nicole said, her voice cracking. Tears burned behind her eyes.

She reached for a tissue from the box on the table between her and Dr. Craig. Other than in the complete privacy of her house, this was the only place and he was the only person who had ever seen her cry.

She'd first gone to talk to him as part of her rehab therapy. He specialized in burn victims, and she'd seen him twice a week the first year, then weekly for the second, tapering off during the third and visiting occasionally after that.

"What's it been now? Eight months since I've seen you, Nicole?"

"Longer than that," she answered. He knew full well how long it had been. Nicole was sure he'd consulted her file before she got here.

"Why don't you fill me in on what's been going on in your life."

Nicole dabbed at her eye when a lone tear escaped. "Dad is hanging in there. Gets tired easily. My mother's the same, maybe a bit worse. My biological clock is ticking loudly in her head, but not mine."

"Is she still pressuring you to get married?"

"Yes."

"Quit your job?"

"That goes without saying."

"What are you doing besides work?" Nicole didn't answer. "When was the last time you went out with friends or someone special?"

"You know I don't date."

"All right," he said calmly. "When was the last time you went out with friends?"

"I went to my BFF's daughter's wedding."

"Tell me about it."

Brady flashed across her mind. The way she looked in her tuxedo with her black round-toe shoes, black-and-white cufflinks and button studs when she stood beside Mark. The way her smile lit up her face. The way it felt to be in her arms.

"It was nice," she answered benignly.

"Nicole, you're wasting my time and your money."

She had tried several counselors before selecting Dr. Craig. She felt more comfortable with a man, which surprised her. She thought it had something to do with the fact that she couldn't bring herself to admit any amount of weakness in front of a woman. She also liked his no-nonsense style and that he didn't put up with any bullshit.

"All right, I enjoyed myself a lot."

"Talk to anyone new?"

"Yes." He wouldn't stop until she told him what he wanted to know.

"The groom's best man also works at McMillan. Actually it was more like his best woman. She's his best friend. I was surprised when she walked in with Mark. I saw her later when she ran interference with an asshole who wouldn't take no for an answer."

"And?"

"And..." Nicole hesitated. "We talked...and danced."

"I didn't see that coming," Dr. Craig said, clearly surprised.

"Neither did I." Nicole remembered how safe she'd felt in Brady's arms.

"How did you react to that?"

"Fine."

"Don't lie to yourself, Nicole."

"I'm not."

"Uh-huh." Dr. Craig frowned. "What did you feel?"

"Nothing." *Okay, now I'm lying.*

"What did she do?"

Nicole was surprised he let her comment drop without challenge. "What do you mean?"

"Was she attracted to you?"

"I don't know."

"Yes, you do."

Nicole fell back in the plush chair. "Yes, she was."

"Were you attracted to her?"

Her body reacted as it had that night weeks ago. Heat coursed through her middle and her pulse beat faster.

"Are you going to see her again?"

"Of course not."

"Why not?"

"You know why not."

"We've talked about this, Nicole."

"We talked about a lot of things and then moved on."

"No, Nicole, you moved on because you didn't want to talk about it."

"No, I moved on because I'd come to terms with it. Isn't that your favorite phrase?"

"But your terms aren't good for you, Nicole."

"So you think it's *good for me* to get involved with a woman to the point of getting naked, which in case you're not up on today's dating rules, happens very quickly, and subject myself to the embarrassment and humiliation of her turning away in disgust?" She was angry now.

"I think you have higher standards than to choose a woman who would be so shallow to treat you like that."

"Didn't look that way with Gina."

"From what you've told me there wasn't really much to your relationship with Gina other than sex. At least from her perspective."

They'd talked about this, but Nicole didn't believe it. Or didn't want to. She'd planned to spend the rest of her life with Gina.

"Gina was a diversion."

"Excuse me?" Nicole asked incredulously.

"A diversion. You and Gina just happened to be in the same place at the right time. You two fell into each other because you didn't have anything better to do. When it got tough, she bailed."

"We loved each other." The look on Dr. Craig's face said he believed anything but. "I loved her."

"And you can love again."

"No, I can't."

"It's not that you can't, Nicole. It's that you won't let yourself."

❖

"I can't do this anymore, Charlotte."

"What can't you do?" She had called Charlotte after leaving Dr. Craig's office to see if she was free for lunch. Charlotte was sitting across from her in a beat-up coffee shop frequented by roughnecks, drillers, and other assorted riff-raff that happened to wander in.

Nicole looked into kind green eyes. Charlotte was looking at her, obviously expecting an answer. She never let Nicole give her any grief, guff, or bullshit. But she never overstepped her bounds unless Nicole asked her to.

"Be the head of McMillan," Nicole said, choking out the few words.

"Start from the beginning and tell me what's going on." Charlotte settled back in her chair and sipped her coffee.

"We're doing a job and the president of the country insists I go and make sure everything is being done." Charlotte sat patiently. "I can't do it."

"Why not?"

"I haven't been to a job site since the accident."

"I know," she said softly.

Nicole jerked her eyes up from her cup of coffee and looked at her. She saw nothing but concern and love.

"I still have my sources, young lady, so don't even think about doing anything your daddy wouldn't approve of," Charlotte said. "Tell me."

"I have nightmares, of the accident," Nicole added, to be more specific. "I wake up and can't breathe, my heart is racing, and I'm shaking like a twig. I need to run, get out, and get away."

"Isn't that to be expected after what you went through?"

"That's what my shrink said. Kind of like post-traumatic stress disorder."

"What are you doing about it?" Charlotte never let Nicole look at a problem without also searching for a solution.

"I have relaxation techniques."

"Do they work?"

"Most of the time."

"But not when it comes to this."

"No."

"Do you have medication? I understand there are all kinds of things to help with this kind of anxiety."

"Yes."

"But?"

Charlotte knew her too well. "But I don't want to take it."

"Why not?"

Nicole suppressed her sigh of exasperation. Charlotte had to be on question number eighteen by now. Who knew when she'd stop? "Because I don't want to."

"Why not?"

"Because I don't want a chemical to control my brain." She'd had this conversation with her shrink this afternoon and was at the end of her rope with the topic.

Nicole preempted any further questions. "Don't ask anything else about this, Charlotte. The subject is closed."

Charlotte held up her hands. "Okay. You don't have to bite my head off."

Nicole dropped her head and shook it. "I'm sorry. I didn't mean for that to come out as harsh as it did. Obviously I'm under a little stress. My temper is short, my anxiety high, and my patience thin. I just somehow have to get through the next three days."

CHAPTER SEVENTEEN

Nicole stared at the two little blue pills in her hand. One would make her drowsy so she could sleep. Two would knock her out. If she put them back in the bottle the twenty-hour flight to Greslikstan would be unbearable.

The first time she'd tried to go to a site, she'd actually landed and made it all the way to baggage claim but turned around and booked the next flight out to anywhere. She'd tried on several occasions after that but never got any farther than boarding the plane. No one was expecting her so it wasn't a big deal that she didn't. But to Nicole it was one more strike against her as being an effective CEO of McMillan Suppression.

Her father had always made periodic visits to the sites. Of course he couldn't make it to every one, but he went out enough that the crews knew he continued to understand what they were up against and was supporting them every way necessary. Nicole believed the same way, and not being able to go made her reevaluate her position every time she tried.

The Qatar Airlines lounge for the flight to Greslikstan was crowded with eager travelers mixed in with a few obviously road-weary travelers. Nicole spent a few seconds looking at each one and imagining their story. Why were they going to Greslikstan? Work, personal? Were they transferring planes in Turkey like she was? She doubted it. None of them looked like oil workers or had anything to do with oil production. She was hoping she could spot one and strike up a conversation to distract her for the next fifty-five minutes until the flight was scheduled to board. Instead she checked her carry-on at the concierge desk and went for a walk through the international terminal.

The exercise helped calm her nerves. She was able to move around and shake the restlessness from her limbs. Nothing in the extensive bookstore caught her attention more than the book she'd brought to read. She also had work to do. If she could get lost in a good book, or plow through the pile of work that had piled up in the last few weeks, or watch one of the mindless on-demand comedy movies on the transatlantic flight she could keep her mind busy. Nervously looking at her watch she reversed her steps, retrieved her bag from a different concierge, and waited for the gate agent to call her row.

Nicole took a deep breath and walked down the jetway. It was new and didn't have the musty smells of the older units. Even though it was about six feet wide, to her it felt like walking down a tunnel into the abyss. The fabricated walls started to close in on her and she was breathing too fast. She moved off to the side, letting other passengers pass, and closed her eyes tight. She was running through her list of mind games to help her relax when Brady's face flashed in front of her eyes. Nicole saw her smile, the one she used when they saw each other for the first time at Mark's wedding. The one she used when she laughed out loud. The smile that lit up her entire face and Nicole's blood pressure. Nicole opened her eyes and, fortified by memories of Brady, took a deep breath and walked onto the plane.

Stowing her bag in the large bin above her seat, she glanced around the large seating area. She had elected to fly business class instead of coach for this trip, something she normally didn't do when traveling on company business. But with this trip the last thing she needed was to feel claustrophobic with fellow travelers crushed in front of and beside her. She needed the extra space and freedom the section allowed.

"Can I help you with anything, Ms. McMillan?" the flight attendant asked. She was a short woman, no more than five feet tall. Nicole recognized her accent as British, her eyes blue and hair blond and cascading over her shoulders in soft waves.

Nicole's heart jumped for just one beat. That was what her hair had looked like—before.

"No, thank you," she replied, glad to hear her voice didn't betray her emotions. She didn't want anyone to think she had a fear of flying. On the contrary, she loved flying, traveling around the world. It was simply the destination on this trip that scared the ever-living holy shit out of her.

"Just standing for as long as I can. I'll be sitting for hours," Nicole replied, coming up with the first excuse she could think of why she hadn't yet taken her seat. The flight attendant nodded.

"Yes, that is true, and I completely understand. If I can do anything for you, please let me know. My name is Clarice."

"Thank you, Clarice," Nicole said as Clarice moved down the aisle.

When it appeared the final passenger had boarded and everything had been stored, Nicole finally sat down in her seat. She had chosen the aisle seat in her row, and luckily the window seat next to her was empty. Thank God for small favors, she said to herself, buckling her seatbelt.

As the safety-procedure video played on the small screen in front of her, Nicole took out her disinfectant wipes and scoured the area around her. If she stopped long enough to think about the number of hands that had touched her seatbelt, the arms of her chair, the controls for the video, her tray table, and everything else within arm's length, she would become a Howard Hughes germ phobic. She followed this routine every time she flew, sometimes to the shock of her seatmate, though others asked if she had an extra wipe they could use.

This particular aircraft offered the option of watching the takeoff from the view of the cockpit. The image was displayed on the screen in front of her, and Nicole took full advantage of it. Another thing to keep her mind occupied.

The flight was long and she was unable to concentrate on anything she was doing, her mind drifting off to places she didn't want to go. Four or five times the beginning sensations of a panic attack tickled the back of her brain, and between walking up and down the aisles and utilizing the coping skills her shrink had taught her, she managed to keep them at bay. She spent some time chatting with Clarice, who was friendly enough to convey to Nicole that she was interested but not enough to offend if she wasn't.

Two meals, two movies, eight financial reports, and thirty-two e-mails later the wheels of the big plane touched the ground in Turkey. Nicole had been to this airport many times, it being the transfer point to many countries where she'd been dispatched to kill fires. She'd loved her job fighting fires, doing what she'd always wanted to do. She loved to travel to new places, meet new people, test her body and mind to the max on every job. No two jobs were alike and none was easy.

Forcing herself to relax, she slowed her pace and made herself enjoy the familiar surroundings. She had shopped in the duty-free shops, had spent many hours in the airline lounge, and dined at almost every restaurant in this corridor. Her bags would automatically be checked to her final destination so she didn't have to worry about a stop in customs at this point.

Nostalgia washed over her, taking the place of the overwhelming current of anxiety that had accompanied her since the day she'd agreed to make this trip. She could do this, she told herself, trying to keep a positive attitude. She had to. The reputation of McMillan was at stake and her own sense of self-respect was on the line. Squaring her shoulders she entered the gate area for the flight that would take her to her biggest fear. And to Brady.

CHAPTER EIGHTEEN

Ann had arranged a driver for Nicole in Greslikstan, and he would be waiting for her outside customs. Her first stop was the hotel to drop off her bags, and then out to the site. Tomorrow she'd meet with President Charsea and soothe his ruffled feathers. Hopefully she'd need only one trip to the site, then be able to get the hell out of here.

The line in customs crawled and Nicole shifted her weight from foot to foot, more nervous and anxious now that she was on the ground. Taking stock of her surroundings she noticed eight military guards, each carrying very big, ugly looking weapons. Their expressions were hard and serious.

The soldier to her left touched the radio earpiece in his right ear, stopped scanning the crowd, and zeroed in directly on her. He stood a little straighter, his hand tightening on his gun. Trying to appear calm she glanced around and saw that two other soldiers had the same level of interest.

She tensed, her heart racing even faster. Why were they paying attention to her? Sure, she clearly wasn't a national, with her blond hair and fair complexion, but she'd always been out of place in most of the countries where she worked. Never to this extent, though. What about her had drawn their attention?

She moved her backpack from her left shoulder to her right, and all three of the soldiers took a step forward. Of course! That was it! She was so nervous and anxious she couldn't stand still or stop fidgeting. Telling herself to calm down, she looked at the soldier closest to her and smiled. No terrorists wanted to call attention to themselves, and making eye contact was one sure way to be remembered. All McMillan employees had extensive training in how to identify potential threats to their personal safety and security. Rarely did they go to a country that hadn't been affected by some type of armed conflict. She knew what to do and, most important, what not to do, and she turned her focus away from herself to the current situation.

Careful not to make any sudden moves, or any moves for that matter, Nicole repeated the same acknowledgement to one of the other two soldiers. To do all three would show that she knew they were watching her, and that in and of itself could be construed as a signal that she was up to no good.

Finally she was at the counter with her bags open and two of the three guards somewhere behind her, the third in her peripheral vision to her right. Her bags were searched more thoroughly than those of the travelers in front of her, which told Nicole the customs agent was instructed to do so. Finally after her bags had been searched like they were looking for a microchip, Nicole slung her backpack over her shoulder and headed toward the exit.

She frowned when she didn't see the driver waiting for her. He should have been just outside the exit holding a sign with her name on it. And looking around, she didn't see anyone that fit that description. Then she heard her name.

"Brady?" she said aloud. What was Brady doing here? When she got close enough she asked.

"I needed to come into town for a few supplies and volunteered to pick you up."

Nicole was surprised to see her, and it took her a few moments to catch up. When she did she immediately felt the comfort of a friendly face. "You didn't have to do that."

"I wanted to," Brady said seriously.

Nicole's stomach tingled. She studied Brady's eyes to detect… what? She had no idea. She had to stop second-guessing everyone's motives for wanting to spend time with her. Brady was waiting for her to say something. "Okay, after you."

Brady's smile was genuine and Nicole's heart did a little pitter-patter. Brady took her bags and Nicole followed her out of the airport.

"How have you been?" Brady asked cautiously after they were buckled inside the truck. Brady had expected Nicole to be surprised to see her, but she seemed to be on edge instead of happy.

"Good, keeping busy. There's always something to do."

"I'll bet. How long are you here for?"

"Not long. I'll go out to the site after I check in, and tomorrow I have a few meetings with government people, then probably back out the day after that."

Brady was disappointed that Nicole wouldn't be staying longer. When Flick had mentioned she'd be in the country Brady had hoped she could spend some time with her. But then again when in the hell would she do that? In the twelve hours between her shift? Where would they go? To the chow hall? *Get a grip, Stewart.*

Brady tossed out a few more softball questions, and it was obvious Nicole didn't want to talk. Was she embarrassed about what had happened at the wedding or at dinner? Or maybe she didn't want to say anything for fear Brady might bring those situations up. They rode in silence the remaining ten minutes to her hotel.

"Are you my driver to the site?" Nicole asked, breaking the quiet.

"Unless you want someone else."

"No, not at all." Nicole replied quickly, the first emotion Brady had seen from her since she picked her up.

Brady pulled into the circle drive of the hotel. "Great, I'll wait for you in the lobby. Take your time."

Brady nursed a Coke while waiting for Nicole to return from her room. God, it was good to see her again. She looked better than Brady remembered, and she remembered a lot. Especially when her head hit the pillow. Nicole's voice, her scent, the feel of her body against hers.

Someone stopped in front of her. Brady looked up from a pair of scuffed work boots, well-worn jeans covering long legs, a dark long-sleeved work shirt with a McMillan logo over the left breast pocket, and into Nicole's eyes. She held a hard hat in one hand and a pair of safety goggles in the other. Brady had seen Nicole dressed for work and dressed up for the wedding, but standing in front of her in work gear she was just plain hot. She jumped up and tried not to stammer—or drool.

"Ready?"

"As I'll ever be, I guess."

Brady detected more than a little trepidation in Nicole's voice and wondered why. She risked a glance at her sitting in the passenger seat and saw her hands clenched in her lap so tight it looked like the circulation had stopped. She looked terrified. She was about to ask if she was all right when they entered the well site.

Brady stopped the truck in front of the office and turned off the engine. "Here we are." Duh, that was pretty obvious. "The crew quarters are over there." Brady pointed out the windshield. "The chow hall is to the right and the equipment corral behind that." Nicole didn't seem to be interested and hadn't moved since the truck came to a stop.

Brady touched Nicole's hands, which were as cold as ice. "Nicole?"

Hearing her name seemed to break whatever trance she was in because Nicole turned to her. "Thanks. I'll check in with Flick, then take a look around."

❖

Something was wrong with Nicole. Brady knew it. She could sense it. She'd been watching Nicole since she exited the office two hours ago wearing a pair of McMillan coveralls. She walked next to Flick and checked every piece of equipment and talked to whoever was manning it. She was asking questions and nodding her satisfaction with the answers, but her body language said otherwise. No one else seemed to be picking up on it, but for some reason Brady was attuned to Nicole and knew that something just wasn't right and wasn't getting better.

Brady walked over to her and stopped just behind Nicole's left shoulder. "Done any more dancing?" she asked. Flick had stepped away to answer a question and Nicole was standing by herself.

She saw Nicole jump, then relax a little.

"No. Have you?"

"Now where would I have an opportunity to go to a fine establishment and dance with someone as charming and witty and beautiful as you?"

"Not much night life here, huh?"

"Not the kind I'm interested in. But that's okay. For some reason it's not the same anymore."

Brady kept up the benign conversation, keeping it light. The more they talked, the more Nicole seemed to relax, but she still seemed on edge. The stiffness in her shoulders subsided but didn't completely go away, and her hands remained in her pockets but not tightly fisted like they were before.

When Flick returned, Brady said, "Whenever you're ready to head back, Ms. McMillan, just let me know." That gave Nicole an out if she wanted to leave and the information that Brady would return her to her hotel.

An hour later back at the hotel Brady turned to Nicole. Fear flashed in her eyes for an instant before it disappeared. What was she afraid of? Was she afraid Brady would run back to her crew and tell all? Could be. Then it hit her and Brady felt like an idiot. Nicole was afraid to be alone. No shit, she'd been in a horrible accident and had figuratively come back to the scene of the crime. Who wouldn't be freaked? She couldn't leave her like this.

"Would you like to grab a bite? The hotel has a pretty good restaurant and more than a few Western dishes."

"That would be great," Nicole answered quickly.

Brady heard the relief in her voice. "Just don't order the burger," Brady said, trying to release some of the tension. Nicole's attempt at a smile increased Brady's determination to make it real.

"I'm glad you suggested this," Nicole said after the waiter served their after-dinner coffee.

"I was afraid you'd say no."

"Why would I?"

"I don't know. Don't want to hang with the help." Hang with the help? Where in the hell had that come from? The expression on Nicole's face said she was asking the same question. "I meant you might have wanted to be alone and relax," Brady said quickly, trying to cover her inane statement.

"Not at all. This is just what I needed. It's been a long time since I've been to a site. I've forgotten how intense it is."

"When I go home I don't turn on the TV or radio for days. After months with all the noise and no privacy, sometimes I just sit in my living room and do absolutely nothing."

"You don't have someone back home to spend your time with?"

"No. I have some friends, but you know how it is. It's hard to keep connected with people when you're gone so much."

"Most of the people I knew were on the job or related to the job."

The conversation had shied away from being personal, and Brady wanted to know what was behind the sadness in Nicole's eyes. She leaped. "What about a girlfriend?"

Nicole's eyes shot up and Brady felt like she'd crashed and burned. She didn't give up, even though this could be a career-limiting move. "It's common knowledge you had a girlfriend."

"And is it common knowledge that she walked out on me?" Nicole asked angrily.

"I don't follow or believe gossip."

"She was one of the few that wasn't connected to the business."

"What does she do?" Brady treaded lightly with her questions. She wanted to spend more time with Nicole, and the last thing she wanted was to piss her off and have her cut the evening short.

Nicole corrected her. "Did. She's an architect, but I don't know what she does anymore, and frankly I don't care. The rumors are true, and I haven't kept up with her since I threw her ass out." Nicole sipped at her coffee.

"So who's waiting at home for you now that worthless piece of humanity is out of your life, good riddance?" Brady hoped Nicole's answer was no one. Nicole answered and she wasn't disappointed.

"I've got other more important things on my plate right now than a social life."

Brady took note how Nicole was trying to steer their conversation away from her personal life. She wasn't going to let her.

"What do you do for…" Brady was about to say entertainment, but the look in Nicole's eyes told her she expected her to say sex. Brady wondered what would happen if she did. Nicole didn't give her the chance.

"Thank you for dinner, Brady." Nicole picked up the credit-card receipt and stood. Brady quickly did as well.

Brady was angry at herself for pushing Nicole too far. They had shared amusing stories of people they knew and laughed till tears came. Nicole had a wonderful laugh and a breathtaking smile, and Brady wanted to see it more often.

Nicole stopped in the lobby and turned to her. "Thanks again for the ride and the company, Brady."

"My pleasure," she said honestly. She was about to leave when she saw the same fear and look of panic flood Nicole's eyes. It seemed like she was ready to bolt out the front doors and run away. No way was she leaving her like this.

"At the risk of overstepping the bounds and my place, I think you're a bit out of sorts and it's late. Why don't we go upstairs and you crawl under the covers, and I'll just sit and read until you fall asleep."

"What?"

"Look, I know you don't know me very well and certainly not enough to trust me, but I'll say it anyway. You can trust me. I don't take advantage of people, and I don't engage in shoptalk. The events of this evening are between you and me. Nobody else."

"I can't ask you to do that." Nicole's voice was soft but still shaky.

"You didn't." Brady didn't want Nicole to say no so she didn't give her the chance. "What floor are you on?" She took Nicole's arm and walked toward the bank of elevators.

Brady followed Nicole into her room after she unlocked the door. A soft light was on in the corner of the room, the bed covers turned down. Brady dragged her gaze away from the large bed with the white sheets and a dozen pillows.

"Now go take a hot shower, climb into your jammies, and hit the sack," she said as she followed Nicole into the big room. "I'll sit over there," she pointed to the stuffed chair in the corner of the room, "and read." She held up her iPhone to show where her reading material was.

For a few seconds Nicole didn't move. Her eyes were dark and piercing, as if trying to see inside Brady's head. Brady was afraid she'd still toss her out, but finally, Nicole turned toward the dresser and a few minutes later the shower started.

The last thing Brady was capable of doing was concentrating on the words in a book, no matter how engaging it had been. If Nicole naked in the shower thirty feet away wasn't distracting enough, trying to de-code the events of the day were.

No one had noticed how her body language had changed the longer she was at the site. It was as if she were the oil well and her own internal pressure was ready to blow. Like a fire, it was just waiting for a spark. Not sure why, but acting on impulse, Brady had stepped in, and before she knew it she was driving Nicole back to her hotel. Now here she was sitting in a very uncomfortable chair while a beautiful woman was naked in the other room.

CHAPTER NINETEEN

Brady was the most beautiful woman Nicole had ever seen, and she hadn't expected to see so much of her when she opened her eyes this morning. It was just after five when the sound of the water in the shower woke her.

From the angle of the mirror on the wall at the foot of the bed Nicole could see Brady move the shower curtain and reach for the towel. Her body was magnificent and Nicole couldn't pull her eyes away. Her muscles were well defined but not so much to be too much. The water dripping down her body was like a fountain on a renowned statue. But Brady was no statue. She was a breathtaking woman and she was looking right at her.

She had no idea how long Brady stood there, but Nicole saw her nipples harden in the cool air. Even through the reflection in the mirror she couldn't miss the burning desire in Brady's eyes. Brady wrapped the towel around her and stepped from the shower, away from her reflection in the mirror.

Nicole didn't remember falling asleep, but when she had woken twice during the night Brady was there. The first time was a complete surprise, finding she was wrapped against Brady's side, Brady's arm around her. The slow, steady beat of Brady's heart pounded against her cheek. What was she still doing here and how had she ended up in her arms? Too shocked and exhausted to figure it out, she turned over and scooted back to her side of the bed.

The second time Brady was spooned against her back, her warm breath heating her skin. Or was it Brady's hard, hot body that had ignited her? Fortunately or unfortunately she couldn't slip out of Brady's arms unless she climbed out, went around the bed, and lay down on Brady's side.

Brady's side. The thought that Brady would have a side of the bed didn't help Nicole ignore the rising temperature between her legs. She tried to relax, but her body had other ideas. It hummed and beat with life. What should have made her anxious and panicked was doing just the opposite. She felt safe. Safe from her dreams, her nightmares, herself. She hadn't felt like this in a very long time. Not since before the accident, and she didn't think she ever would again. Convincing herself she'd figure it out in the morning she'd leaned back in Brady's arms. She fit perfectly. Brady would never know.

Brady stepped out of the bathroom fully dressed. Nicole wanted to pretend this moment wasn't happening. Or if it was, it was happening to somebody else. Talk about an awkward morning after.

"I didn't expect to see you this morning."

Brady lifted her hands as if to remark, "What can I say?"

"I thought you were going to leave when I fell asleep." Just the sound of the words still made her head spin with humiliation. Brady didn't say anything and looked like she didn't want to.

"Brady?"

"You had a nightmare."

The simple words were like a blow to her gut. "Fuck." Nicole fell back against the pillows and took several calming breaths. "I'm sorry."

"Don't be. I can't imagine what you've been through." Brady's voice was calm, her eyes soft.

"Well, let's just say I wouldn't wish it on my worst enemy." Nicole felt like shit because she'd put Brady in this awkward position.

Brady looked at her for a long moment. "Do you have transportation for today?"

"Yes."

"Okay, well, I'll be heading back to the site then," Brady said, hesitating before she turned around and started to walk away.

"Brady, wait." She didn't want Brady to leave like this. She'd done something special for her and she had to acknowledge it. Before she knew what she was doing she slid out of bed but froze after a half a dozen steps.

Holy mother of God. She was wearing only a pair of boxers and a short-sleeve T-shirt. The scars on her arms and legs were completely exposed. She couldn't move if she wanted to, her feet glued to the floor as she waited for Brady to look at her with disgust and pity in her eyes.

Brady's eyes stayed on hers as she waited for her to say something. "Thank you." Those simple words in no way said enough. She wanted to say thank you for caring enough to talk with me, distract me, stay with me.

Brady smiled and Nicole's heart melted. "You're welcome."

CHAPTER TWENTY

President Charsea had been a gracious host, but Nicole was tired and all she wanted to do was go home. She had fought against thinking about Brady all day and lost the battle more than once.

Nicole stopped at the hotel desk and notified the clerk she'd be leaving in the morning. She arranged for a driver to the airport and headed toward the elevators. She thought of Brady as she passed the chairs where she'd waited for her yesterday. Was it just yesterday? It felt like a lifetime. So much had happened to her in the past few weeks. Her phone rang. She stepped to the side, recognized the number, and answered.

It was Operations notifying her that Brady's crew was scheduled to kill their well tomorrow. Nicole rode the elevator to her floor. She inserted the card key and on automatic pilot pushed the door open when the green light appeared. She tossed her bag on the chair and kicked her shoes off next to it.

Brady was going to kill the fire tomorrow. Nicole shuddered, knowing how dangerous that was. And she hated it. She was so much better off not knowing too much about any of her crew who put their lives in danger every single day. She was a nervous wreck the last time Brady's crew killed a fire, and she knew she would be this time as well.

She debated whether to pick up the phone and call room service and order dinner and a six-pack of beer or call Brady. She needed to eat, she'd barely eaten all day, and the beer would give her a nice little buzz to calm her nerves and help her sleep. But she wanted to call Brady. But she couldn't. First of all she was at the site and cell phones didn't work. Second, what in the world would she say?

Her order confirmed with room service, Nicole stripped off her clothes and went to take a quick shower. Turning the water off she thought she heard her phone ring. She hadn't brought it into the bathroom with her because that was ridiculous and it was the middle of the night for anyone in the States.

Drying off she stepped outside the shower and caught the reflection of the perfectly made bed in the mirror just outside the door. Her heart skipped and her pulse beat faster. This is exactly what Brady had seen this morning. What did she think when she saw her in the bed? What did she think when she realized Nicole could see her?

This time she was sure her phone was ringing and grabbed the hotel robe and crossed the room, tying the belt. She didn't recognize the number.

"Nicole McMillan."

"It's Brady."

The sound of the voice and the two simple words made Nicole's knees weak. She sat down on the bed.

"Hi."

"How were your meetings?"

"They were fine."

"Get done what you needed to get done?"

"Yes, I did."

"Good."

"How was your day?" Nicole said because she wasn't able to think of anything else.

"You know, spray some water, move some mud. Typical day at the office."

Nicole wished she could take the danger of Brady's job so lightly.

"I was wondering, and I'm going to jump out on another limb here…if you're free for dinner?"

"Dinner?" Nicole thought about the order of room service that was due to arrive in the next ten minutes. "As a matter of fact, I am."

"Fifteen minutes too early?"

"Fifteen minutes? It takes over an hour to get here from the site."

"I'm not at the site."

"Where are you?" Nicole asked, even though it was really none of her business.

"In the lobby."

"My lobby?"

Brady chuckled. "Yes, your lobby. Like I said, I took a chance."

Nicole felt something she couldn't quite identify hearing that Brady had driven all this way on the chance she'd be available. "Fifteen minutes will be fine." She hung up the phone and dashed back into the bathroom.

"Jesus Christ, Nicole, you're acting like you've never gone out to dinner before." She tried to tamp down her giddiness about Brady waiting downstairs. She applied her lip gloss, made one last sweep over how she looked, grabbed her bag and door key, and closed the door behind her. Then she met the room-service waiter, signed for the check, and told him to leave the beer in her room and take the rest back to the kitchen.

Her legs were moving faster than her mind told them to. Obviously her body wanted to see Brady quicker than her brain did. She punched the down button on the elevator three times, looked at her watch twice, punched the button again, and the door finally opened.

Four other people were in the elevator, and as she stepped inside and pushed the button for the ground floor, she saw that she'd be making three stops before getting to the lobby. A hint of impatience and irritation filled her but was quickly replaced with the excitement she'd felt ever since hearing Brady's voice.

Surreptitiously she looked at herself critically in the mirrors inside the elevators doors. She was wearing a pair of tan khakis with a royal-blue long-sleeve shirt and loafers. The buckle of her belt reflected off the mirrors as the doors opened.

When she stepped into the lobby Brady had her back to her, looking at a bank of visitor brochures in front of her. Nicole slowed her pace and took Brady in without her knowledge. She looked just as good from the rear as she did from the front. Brady was dressed equally casually in a pair of pressed blue jeans and a short-sleeve green polo shirt that would bring out the color of her eyes. She had a wide belt, cowboy boots with a low heel, and a clunky watch on her left wrist. The long-dormant stirrings of desire started low in her belly.

This was not good, she told herself. She couldn't go down this path. Not with Brady, not with anyone. She wouldn't allow herself to be hurt like that again. She took a deep breath and approached.

"I hope I didn't keep you waiting too long."

Brady's eyes made a quick pass over her from head to toe, then back up again. Her eyebrows quirked, indicating that she liked what she saw. She smiled and Nicole's heart skipped. "No, not at all. Ready to go?"

Nicole shook her head. "Where are we going?"

"Just a little place not far from here one of the guys recommended. A little bit of the local cuisine but not too much that it's bizarre." Brady wrinkled her nose as if to say "too bizarre" would be awful.

Brady held the door as Nicole climbed in the passenger side of the truck. Again she noticed how clean it was. Yesterday when she was at the site everything was covered with a layer of oil, dirt, and grime so thick she could barely see the company logo on the door. This truck gleamed. The inside was equally spotless, and Nicole knew from experience that it was next to impossible to keep a vehicle onsite anywhere near clean. Brady must have made the effort to clean it.

Nicole tried to relax as they made small talk on the way to the restaurant. She waited for Brady to bring up last night and this morning, but instead she kept the conversation on inconsequential and normal topics that two people going out to dinner would. But this wasn't any normal dinner. Brady had sought her out and, knowing that, she had accepted. As much as Nicole didn't want to, she was attracted to Brady, and she had a strong suspicion that attraction went both ways. No, this was definitely not an ordinary dinner.

Brady kept up a steady stream of conversation over dinner, peppering Nicole with questions about her childhood and growing up with a world-renowned oil-well firefighter as her father. When Brady shifted topic to her experiences in the field she asked specific questions about technique, water pressure, flow arc, and cable strength, which indicated to Nicole that Brady was interested in improving her skills as a firefighter. Nicole was impressed, very impressed.

Most people when they talked to her just wanted to know the gory, exciting details about her accident. When she talked with colleagues, they avoided the subject like the plague. They avoided the subject with *her*. She knew how these conversations went. These guys talked shop at every opportunity. The work was sometimes so intense they had nothing else to talk about.

It was almost as if Brady didn't know she'd been in such a serious accident. But she knew. She couldn't have missed it this morning since she was standing less than three feet away, the results of that accident clearly visible. But Brady hadn't looked. Not once did her eyes stray from Nicole's, and she found that amazing.

"Your accident," Brady said hesitantly. "Would you tell me about it?"

For an instant Nicole frowned and thought, yep, she's just like all the others. She looked at Brady critically, but what she saw on her face was very different than everyone else's. It wasn't morbid curiosity. It was a combination of interest in knowing what happened from the professional side in order to prevent something like that from happening again and interest in an event that she had experienced.

Nicole weighed her choices. She could give her standard flippant, short answer. "We were capping the well, something happened, and it exploded." And usually because of her no-nonsense tone when she delivered those few words, she rarely had to say anything more. But Brady wouldn't accept that answer, and Nicole wouldn't insult her by giving it.

For the first time ever she wanted to talk about it. In every single excruciating detail. She wanted to share exactly what happened with Brady. She wanted to tell her everything she heard, everything she saw, everything she felt, and when she thought she was going to die. She hadn't even told the story she relived in her nightmares to her therapist.

Nicole owed her an explanation, but Brady didn't ask in order for her to pay up. She wanted to describe the sounds and the searing pain, the months of hazy fog under sedation and how tears slid silently down her cheeks as she endured the excruciating pain as dead skin was peeled off her body, and the emotional effects of the scars left behind.

She'd never wanted to tell anyone any of this before. Her shrink had practically demanded she talk about it—to face it and put it behind her. She didn't need to face it and put it behind her. It was in her face every day when she looked in the mirror. But she wanted to tell Brady. No, that wasn't quite right. She wanted to share it with Brady. Brady would get it.

Brady sat across from her, her expression not changing as she waited for her to make her decision. What was it about this woman that made her want to do things she either didn't want to or couldn't't? Ever since the accident Nicole had held her emotions strictly in check. She knew she was the subject of gossip, that everyone looked at her knowing what had happened. She saw people look at her face, her hands, her neck, searching for any evidence of the scars that covered her body.

When she'd started to recover and was out from under the effects of the heavy narcotics, she decided that what people saw would be what she wanted them to see, and that was the woman she'd been before her life changed in the flash of a flame. For six years she'd accomplished that successfully. And she was tired, tired of living behind the mask.

"We were bringing in the new head," Nicole said, her voice unsteady. Brady touched the top of her hand, and she looked up into soft, understanding, caring eyes. They gave her the strength to continue.

Brady sat quietly as she described the actions she and her fellow crewmembers had taken in their attempt to secure the new wellhead. When she was about to talk about the well flashing, Brady asked her a question.

"I'm sorry, what did you ask?" While she'd been talking she'd been back at the site. Feeling the heat, smelling the oil, the weight of the oil coating her clothes, the sting of the oil hitting her body.

Brady repeated the question and brought her back to the present. She answered it without hesitation. Then Brady asked a second and a third, then a series of other technical questions, again focusing on the specifics of what happened so she could understand.

"Do you know what I want to do?" Brady asked, suddenly changing the topic.

"What's that?"

"Dance with you again."

"Excuse me?" It took Nicole a minute to shift her train of thought from the serious topic.

"I'd like to dance with you again."

Nicole couldn't help but laugh. The way Brady released the tension with just one statement shocked her. "Look around, Brady. I think we'd probably be stoned."

"It would be worth it."

"You can't be serious." Nicole was suddenly uncomfortable with the tingling between her legs that had instantly turned to throbbing.

"Dead serious. To hold you in my arms again. To feel your body pressed against mine. To smell your hair, feel the way you fit perfectly against me."

Nicole's body hummed at each descriptor Brady ticked off. The woman was dead serious. No doubt remained in her mind of Brady's attraction to her. The way she spoke was so matter-of-fact. She was sitting across the table with one hand in her lap, the other holding her half-empty coffee cup, the tone of her voice slightly husky.

Holy crap, Nicole thought. Actually this was more like a holy-shit moment. She couldn't think of anything else to say except, "I do too." And before she could stop herself the words drifted across the table.

Other than the slight rising of Brady's eyebrows, no one looking at them would have any idea of the verbal seduction happening at their table. But then again Nicole could hardly believe it herself. This was the last thing she'd expected when Brady asked her to dinner. *Come on, Nicole, admit it. This is exactly what you expected.*

"Are you surprised by my comment?" Nicole asked.

Brady quirked a little smile that Nicole found endearing. "Yes and no."

It was Nicole's turn to quirk her eyebrows.

"No, I wasn't surprised because obviously something is going on here."

"And the *yes* part," Nicole prompted, anxious to hear more.

"The *yes* is that I'm surprised you actually did."

"Am I that aloof?" Nicole asked, feeling her back begin to stiffen in defense.

"No, not at all," Brady said quickly. It's just that you seem…"
Brady hesitated, apparently searching for the right word, "careful
about who you let inside."

"Inside?" Nicole wondered if Brady intended the double entendre.

"Yes, inside you, who you are inside. Not what you make certain
everybody sees."

Nicole was amazed at Brady's insight. "How did you get to be
so smart?"

"I read a lot."

"What, *Psychology Today*?"

Brady fidgeted in her seat. "As a matter of fact, yes."

"You read *Psychology Today*." Nicole was flabbergasted.

"You don't have to act like I'm too far down the food chain to
do that."

"No, not at all. That's not at all what I meant." It was Nicole's
turn to clarify her statement. "It's just that I've never known anyone
who's not in the mental-health field that reads it."

"I read all kinds of things."

"Like what?"

"*National Geographic*."

"Uh-huh."

"I do read the articles. But sometimes I do look at the naked
people." Brady winked, and Nicole's heart took a tumble.

"Good thing. I was beginning to think you were too good to
be true. What are your other literary pursuits?" This side of Brady
fascinated Nicole. It was amazing how well rounded she was.

"Whatever I can get my hands on. I have standard subscriptions.
You know, *Time*, *U.S. News and World Report*, the *Wall Street Journal*.
Yes, the *Journal*," Brady said, obviously amused at her reaction. "It
comes to my iPad every morning."

"Well, what do you know. We have something in common."

"I think we have more than that in common," Brady added
confidently. "But my favorite magazine is *Field and Stream*."

"*Field and Stream*? That's a pretty significant shift from the
Journal."

"I read a lot of things to learn, and I read a lot of different things
for enjoyment."

"You like to fish?'

"I love to fish."

A small bubble of laughter escaped from Nicole's lips.

"What's so funny?" Brady asked, pretending to be perturbed.

"You love to fish and you work in the middle of nowhere where water is scarce."

"I know." Brady sighed and sat back in her chair. "Sometimes I think I should work on an offshore oil rig. That way I could fish every day. I even have a tattoo of a blue marlin. Looking at it is my daily fix when I can't drop my line in the water."

"Really? Where?" Nicole asked, suddenly very interested in tattoos.

Brady thought for a moment. "Well, I could tell you or you could find out."

"Why don't you just tell me?"

Brady looked at her as if sizing up her reaction. "I'd rather not," Brady said with the cutest attitude Nicole had ever seen. "I'll wait for you to find it."

Nicole's stomach dropped and something very big got stuck in her throat. Was that an opening? An invitation? A challenge? A dare? She wasn't ready for this. She glanced nervously at her watch. "It's late, Brady, and you need to get back. Aren't you killing the fire tomorrow?" Brady's face showed surprise. "It's my job to know everything that's going on in my company."

After several moments Brady replied, "I suppose you're right."

❖

"I'll walk you to your door." Brady followed Nicole into the hotel lobby.

"You don't have to do that," Nicole said out of force of habit.

Brady stopped. "I know. I want to."

The simplicity of her statement was overwhelming.

Brady walked close beside her through the large lobby. Nicole was still a little unnerved by being with Brady and the direction the conversation had taken after dinner. Yet, she felt more comfortable with her at the same time. She wanted to feel the reassurance of

Brady's hand at the small of her back or her elbow as Brady had done while going to and from the dance floor at Mark's wedding. But they couldn't do that here. It might even be dangerous for them to be walking as close as they were. Nicole toyed with the idea of increasing the distance between them but didn't want to.

The elevator was empty and Nicole pushed the button for her floor, her hand trembling slightly. The doors closed and she looked at Brady's reflection in the mirror. She typically hated mirrored elevator doors, but right now she wouldn't have it any other way.

They'd gravitated toward each other again, and Nicole felt the heat radiating off Brady's body. Brady was looking back at her, and the longer she did the warmer she got. There was no mistaking the expression on Brady's face, the fire in her eyes.

Brady's gaze moved over her body, hesitating at her breasts, and a quick glance at herself in the mirror confirmed the flush she felt on her face and neck. She was breathing faster, the rapid up and down of her chest drawing Brady's attention. Brady licked her lips and Nicole's mouth grew dry.

"Stop it," Nicole said, her voice weak and holding absolutely no conviction.

Brady quirked an eyebrow and broke into a grin but continued her lazy observation of Nicole. Her eyes stopped again, just below her belt buckle. Nicole's legs threatened to give out on her. Brady was making love to her with just her eyes.

The mechanical voice in the elevator notified them they had arrived at her floor. When the doors silently slid open Nicole didn't know if she was angry or relieved that she had the opportunity to escape from the confining box. They had been in the elevator for only a short time, but during the climb from ground level to her room on the forty-first floor, everything else in her had risen with it. Her breathing was quick, her pulse and heart rate up, and the pulsing in her groin had increased to an almost painful point. Somehow she managed to make it to the door to her room, and her hand trembled so badly she had difficulty fitting the card key into the lock. Without a word Brady reached around from behind her and steadied her hand. Brady slowly slid the card in and out of the lock.

Nicole almost sagged back against Brady, the simple, mechanical movement of the card in the slot seductive. Nicole didn't miss the symbolism of other things sliding in and out.

The door clicked open and Nicole couldn't move. She didn't want to move. She wanted this moment to go on for a very long time. Brady was touching her, the length of Brady's body not even a respectable distance.

"Do you know what that reminded me of?" Brady's voice was low and very close to her ear.

Nicole knew the answer. Brady was leading her down that slippery slope, and she was almost powerless to stop their progress. She knew she could, or at least she hoped she could. But at this moment in time, after the evening spent with Brady, she didn't want to. She shook her head and whispered. "No."

"The way the card slid into the slot perfectly just like it was designed to. It was made for it. It reminded me of other things that are made for sliding into each other. Fingers, tongues, and other things."

The world started to swim and Nicole found it difficult to breathe. Brady's soft, seductive voice, her warm breath on her neck, the fire she ignited on her skin was overwhelming. She felt light-headed and put her hand on the doorjamb in front of her to steady herself. Thankfully Brady didn't say anything else or she might have melted into a puddle in front of her door.

Suddenly the heat of Brady's body dissipated, and it took a few moments for Nicole to realize she had stepped back a few steps. Becoming aware of other voices in the hall she rubbed her hands over her face to try to pull herself together and to not look like she'd almost been completely mind-fucked in the hallway of this elegant hotel.

Somehow she managed to swing the door open and step inside. She'd left the light next to the bed on, and it cast the room into comforting shadows. She turned around and Brady was standing not quite in the doorway. She was waiting for Nicole to make a decision.

Nicole wanted Brady more than she'd wanted any woman in her life. But her mind and her heart screamed in conflict. She wasn't ready to expose herself, but she'd always believed that in order to conquer your fears you needed to face them. Without a word Nicole stepped to the side and Brady crossed the threshold.

CHAPTER TWENTY-ONE

Nicole closed the door and turned the dead-bolt lock. The loud click of the bolt into the jamb signaled more than just their guaranteed privacy. Brady must have sensed her nervousness, because in less than a second Brady pressed against her again. Brady touched her shoulders lightly and slid down her arms to grasp her hands.

"You're in charge here, Nicole," Brady said, her voice tight and controlled. "We don't have to do anything you don't want to."

Nicole turned, and when Brady didn't move their breasts touched. She inhaled sharply and was afraid of what she'd see in Brady's eyes. She focused on the floor instead. "I'm worried about you."

"Me, why?" Brady responded.

"I'm worried about you getting hurt tomorrow."

"I know. I'll be extra careful."

Brady's response surprised her. Nicole had expected her to brush off her concern with words like "I won't," or "nothing will happen," all of which would have been condescending. She finally looked at Brady, and instead of finding smug satisfaction at having seduced her way into the boss's room, she saw Brady's eyes were warm and understanding.

"It's uh…" Nicole tried to laugh, but it came out more of a *harrumph* than anything else. "It's been a long time since I've done this."

"This?"

"Yeah, you and me getting naked." Nicole used her hands back and forth to indicate each of them.

"Who says we have to get naked?' Brady's quirky smile was sweet.

She studied Brady's eyes, and they didn't look any different than they did a few moments ago. "You're not serious?"

"Why not? Nothing says we have to get naked."

"I know I'm a little out of practice, but isn't that how it works?"

"There's lots of ways to make it work that don't involve taking your clothes off."

"You mean like the mind-fuck you gave me in the elevator?"

Brady laughed. "Is that what that was?"

"You know damn good and well that's what it was."

Brady leaned toward her and Nicole thought she was going to kiss her, but at the last minute Brady diverted her lips to nuzzle her neck. Her warm breath tickled. "Was it good for you?"

"If you do it right you shouldn't have to ask."

Nicole breathed in Brady's cologne. The scent had drifted across the table and the cab of the truck, and she found it alluring. Nicole clenched her fists and squeezed them against the side of her legs. She was afraid to touch Brady. Afraid of what she might do, might not be able to stop doing.

"Why are we standing here having this conversation?"

"Because you haven't done anything but stand close and make me crazy."

"And what exactly am I supposed to do?"

Brady lifted her head and shifted it to the other side of her neck. "Anything you want."

"Without getting naked?"

"It's up to you. Naked, not naked, I don't have a preference. No, I take that back. My preference is naked, but as long as you just please do something, I can go with it."

"And what would you like me to do?" Nicole asked, terrified at what Brady's answer might be.

"You can start by unclenching your fists," Brady said softly, sliding her hands down Nicole's arms and holding her hands.

❖

Oh my God, Nicole thought, her chest still heaving as she attempted to fill her lungs with air. Brady was equally breathless beneath her. What just happened? One kiss and she'd absolutely lost control. She was driven to feel Brady, touch every inch of her, smell her, taste her. Her need to make love to Brady was overwhelming.

Brady started to stir. Fuck. Nicole wanted to run, escape. She didn't want to face her. She felt completely humiliated and embarrassed by the way she'd treated her. She hadn't let Brady touch her except that when she was tasting her she clasped Brady's hand. They stayed that way until Brady came in her mouth. The second time, when her fingers were exploring and brought Brady to orgasm, she let Brady wrap her arms around her.

Nicole couldn't risk Brady's touch, afraid it would crumble her weakening defenses. She didn't know how she felt. She'd used Brady for her own needs. She needed to feel the soft skin of a woman, trace soft curves and hard muscles over soft skin. Inhale her scent. Hear her gasps of pleasure in the dark. Feel her tremble in her arms. And Brady had.

Thinking Brady had fallen asleep, Nicole started to remove her fingers from inside her. Surprising her, Brady reached down and held her hand in place.

"Just a few more minutes."

Nicole's mouth went dry with the overwhelming desire to take her again. The thought shot out of her mind and she stiffened as Brady rolled her onto her back.

"Shh," Brady said, simply snuggling Nicole beside her, settling her head in the crook of her neck.

Realizing Brady wasn't going to try to do something she wasn't ready for, Nicole relaxed. She was amazed at Brady's self-control, or maybe she was just exhausted. Nicole was. She had no idea what time it was, and when she started to move to look at the clock, Brady spoke again.

"Shh, be still." Brady pulled Nicole closer. After a few minutes Brady was asleep, her breathing deep and even.

How did this happen, Nicole asked herself. Three weeks ago I was happy and content with my life. Loved my job, had a few friends, and had rebuilt my life. How did I find myself with this woman in my arms?

The scent of her on my hands, the taste of her on my lips, the feel of her next to me. How did she get here? How did I let her get here?

This couldn't happen again. Nicole's confusion turned into resolve. This wouldn't happen again. She would go home today, Brady would go back to her job, and Nicole would make it a point that they never saw each other again. Nothing could come of this, so why even try? Brady deserved more. Nicole couldn't give it to her. She relaxed as her action plan formed in her mind and her thoughts drifted to the woman holding her.

Nicole woke, stretched her arms above her head, and opened her eyes. She was a little groggy and didn't understand why she was still dressed. Like a shot, the events of the evening and most of the night bounced through her head. She quickly sat up, looking around the room for any signs Brady was still there. She listened for any sound of her in the bathroom. When she was certain Brady was gone she flopped back on the bed, throwing one arm over her eyes.

"Oh, my God," she groaned. "What in the hell did I do?" She knew exactly what she'd done and what had happened, and either fortunately or unfortunately she didn't have anyone to blame but herself.

She rolled over and the scent of Brady lingered on the pillow and her hands. Heat flushed through her as she remembered how Brady had done exactly what she said she would, and that was absolutely nothing unless Nicole asked her to. She'd told Nicole she was in charge and she'd kept her word.

Nicole remembered a few times when Brady had started to reach for her and then stopped. How did Brady know that if she made a move, however slight, Nicole would probably freak and throw her out? What an amazing woman. She didn't know if she could have been as strong if the roles were reversed. It was one thing to be made love to and another thing to be made love to and not be able to respond as a woman would naturally do. Brady hadn't grabbed her hair while her tongue was in intimate places; she hadn't tried to sneak her hand under her shirt or unbuckle her pants. She hadn't done anything but lie back and let Nicole take her.

Nicole glanced at the clock, noticing how late it was, then got up and headed to the shower. Propped up against the sink faucet was a note obviously written in Brady's bold handwriting. Her hand shook as she picked it up.

Nicole,
Last night was magnificent and so are you.
Take care,
B

"That's it? That's all you have to say. It was magnificent, I'm magnificent? No request to see me again? No phone number? What the fuck, Brady? Obviously you got what you were after."

Nicole tossed the note onto the counter and started to unbutton her shirt but stopped when she caught her reflection in the mirror. Her wig was slightly askew, her lips swollen from Brady's kisses. Her clothes were rumpled from sleeping in them.

She looked at herself with disgust now. "Isn't this what you expected? Why are you so upset?" she asked to the serious woman reflected back at her. "This is what you want. You don't want a relationship with her. You don't want a relationship with anyone. What kind of relationship would that be? Having sex when she's completely naked and you're completely dressed. What does she get out of that? Do you really think that's what she wants? Someone like Brady wants a complete woman...and you're not it."

Nicole wheeled her bag through the lobby and took her place in line at the front desk. She'd been angry when she packed, throwing her clothes into her suitcase with no sign of order. The note from Brady, however, was tucked securely in her backpack.

The line moved slowly and Nicole couldn't think about anything other than Brady. She should be thinking of all the work that had piled up on her desk while she was gone, the contacts she had to solidify after her meeting with President Charsea. But none of those things held her attention. Not anymore.

"May I help you, ma'am?" A heavily accented voice repeated itself before Nicole realized the desk clerk was talking to her. Everyone in front of her was gone and it was obviously her turn at the counter.

"Checking out, ma'am?" the young man asked politely as she approached.

"No, I'm not," Nicole said, surprised at the words that tumbled from her mouth.

CHAPTER TWENTY-TWO

Nicole hired a driver and gave him instructions to the well site and told him to step on it. Brady was there. Her crew was going to be capping the well today. Nicole didn't want to be there, but she was going nonetheless. She didn't want to be there if a problem occurred, but she had to be there with Brady if there was a problem. Brady was a professional, and judging by the way she'd quizzed her last night about procedures and the nuances of fire, Nicole knew she was well prepared for this job. But shit happens, as they say, and if something happened and Brady was injured she wouldn't fly to a strange hospital in a strange country alone like she had.

The sky held less smoke than two days ago, indicating the fire was out. She hoped she wasn't too late. She started to fidget, feeling the panic begin to set in, but pushed it away. She couldn't think about Brady, couldn't think about what could happen to her.

Suddenly, without warning, she felt completely calm. Her hands weren't shaking, her breathing was normal, and she didn't feel like she was about to crawl out of her skin. She had a job to do today and that was to support Brady and her crew during this very dangerous step.

Brady checked and double-checked the cables holding the barrels of C4. She would be driving the crane that would place the explosives over the fire. If the barrels came loose for any reason while they were suspended above the ground they could explode and destroy everything around it.

She climbed into the cab and double-checked that everything she needed was in place. She surveyed the path she would take to the fire to ensure nothing would cause the big rig to move any more than it had to. Carrying the extra weight with the boom extended exaggerated any dip or pothole, which made controlling the machine challenging. Brady was the best at this, which is why Flick had given her the job today.

Brady took a deep breath and made a visual check with her spotters. Dig was to her left and would be giving her directions. Couch and Crank would give directions to Dig to pass on to Brady to center the explosives over the fire. Mast and Anchor were manning the water hoses. It was time. She fired up the engine and gripped the controls.

The rig moved slowly toward the fire. Brady kept her eyes on Dig, who kept his eyes on Couch and Crank. For the first few hundred yards the pace was slow and Brady concentrated on keeping the explosives calm. She adjusted the controls to increase her speed when Dig signaled her.

The heat intensified as she moved closer. Only the front of the cab was protected with a heat shield, a section cut out for her to see through. There was no protection on the sides, which allowed her to escape from either exit if the need arose.

Sweat dripped down the side of her face and between her breasts. Her mind flashed to Nicole licking the sweat from the same place last night and the rig lurched. "Shit!" she shouted, but no one could hear her, the distance and the roar of the fire her silent partner. Focusing her attention back on Dig where it belonged, she regained control. She had never lost her focus on the job and couldn't afford to now.

Closer and closer she steered the barrels to the fire until Dig gave the signal they were in place. She set the brake, turned off the engine, and jumped out of the cab. Scrambling to her safety zone behind the rig she waited for the results of her handiwork.

The deafening sound of the C4 exploding was what Brady was waiting for. She carefully peered around the rig and saw Dig give the signal for the new wellhead to be brought in.

For this step Couch would be driving a different crane carrying the new head. Her job was to secure the new head to the well. She grabbed her tool bag and, along with Dig, stepped forward. Pulling down her face shield she began to get to work.

The last bolt in place, Dig turned the valve and the uncontrolled flow of oil started slowing until it stopped completely. The silence after the constant roar of the fire was eerie. Dig slapped Brady on the back. "Another one bites the dust," he said, removing his hard hat and wiping his brow before putting it back on.

"Yep," Brady replied. "No one got hurt. That's the most important thing." They peeled off what they dubbed the oil coat, the layer of protective gear designed to help keep the oil from soaking their clothes.

"I'm gonna hose off, take a hot shower, and head into town. What do you say, Bond? You in?"

Yes was on the tip of Brady's tongue when she pulled off her helmet and wiped the oil from her facemask with a clean rag he handed her. When she turned she looked right at Nicole.

Dig didn't notice that Brady had stopped, too shocked at seeing Nicole to go any farther. She didn't expect her here. Flick had said she'd gone home. Her exhausted body immediately responded on autopilot to how Nicole had made her feel last night.

Brady had rarely had sex without the ability to reciprocate. But it was far more than that with Nicole. She had wanted to touch her so badly, not in a sexual way but to make a connection. She'd had sex with a lot of women, and most, if not all, episodes were strictly physical. And next to what she'd felt with Nicole, almost mechanical. Insert tab A into slot B. Push, then release. Rub vigorously until climax, then soothe.

It hadn't been like that with Nicole. For the first time she felt something. Not physically. Hell, she felt that every time. No, it was something else she couldn't put her finger on. And when Nicole put her fingers on her and in her, Brady had gone somewhere else. Her senses had never been so alive. Every nerve ending was hypersensitive, so all Nicole had needed to do was lightly blow on her and she came unglued.

Brady broke into a smile and started toward Nicole but stopped again when the look on her face shattered her euphoria. Nicole was terrified.

❖

Brady hurried over to where Nicole stood as if she were frozen in time. Nicole didn't look at her or give any indication she realized Brady was there. Her eyes were glazed, and if Brady didn't know any better she'd think she'd fallen into some kind of trance or seizure. But she did know better. She'd heard her scream in her nightmares that first night she'd stayed with her. She knew what post-traumatic-stress syndrome was.

PTSD often caused flashbacks to the original event as if it were happening that very second. Every sight, sound, and smell captured forever in time. Some sufferers reenacted the event up to and including hurting themselves or someone else they believed were the enemy. Others ran from the hurricane, tornado, or physical attack as they had tried to escape the first time. While others, like Nicole, simply relived it all in the screams in her head.

Brady approached her cautiously. "Nicole?" she asked softly. She didn't know how Nicole would react if she was startled so she repeated her name and touched her lightly on the arm. The others were busy with their own jobs, and most of them probably didn't even realize Nicole was on site again.

"Nicole, it's Brady," she said, stepping closer and into her direct line of sight. "Nicole, today is June 12th and we're here in Greslikstan. You are the big boss at McMillan and I'm just a peon worker way down on the food chain." Brady tried to lighten the conversation, hoping that her light tone and unthreatening words would cut through to wherever Nicole was.

"Nicole, we had dinner together last night, remember? We went to that dive Mast recommended. You had some mystery chicken thing, and I have no idea exactly what was in my rice. Remember laughing and naming far too many things we thought it might be and hoped it wasn't?"

Finally Nicole turned and looked at her with a gradual awareness of her surroundings. Brady thought it looked like what coming through a thick fog would be like.

"Brady?" Nicole asked, a confused expression on her face. She glanced around and Brady recognized Nicole's comprehension on her face.

"I'm fine," Brady said quickly. "Not a scratch on me, or anyone else for that matter. We did everything by the book and we're finished. The mop-up crew will be here tomorrow and then we can all go home." Brady allowed Nicole to get her bearings a little better. It was clear she was still a little fuzzy.

"I'm glad," Nicole finally said, glancing around her and more alert every passing minute. "What time is it?"

"A little past four thirty."

"Four thirty?" Nicole repeated the time, shock on her face. "I left the hotel this morning a little after eleven."

Brady saw Nicole bite back her words when she realized what had happened. The color drained from her cheeks and her jaw sagged.

"I don't know what time you got here, but everybody was so busy and concentrating on their job I don't think anyone even knew you were here. Most probably still don't." Brady hoped her words gave Nicole the comfort of anonymity.

She heard Flick calling Nicole's name and knew he'd expect her to come by and at least say something.

"Nicole?" Brady asked.

"I'm okay."

Nicole's response did nothing to assure Brady that she was ready for her conversation with Flick.

Nicole recognized Flick coming toward her and forced a smile. Out of the corner of her eye she saw Brady slowly step back to a more professional distance.

"Ms. McMillan, I didn't expect to see you today."

"Last-minute decision," she said, forcing the words out of her throat so they didn't sound as weak as she felt. "I haven't had the chance to see a well killed in some time. My meetings were finished so I jumped at the opportunity."

She reached out to shake Flick's hand and grasped it tight to mask how bad hers were shaking. However, one quick glance at Brady calmed her significantly. "Excellent job, Flick. You and your crew should be very proud."

"We appreciate that, ma'am. Not too often we get the boss out here to see what we do two days in a row."

"All your guys coming in?" Nicole asked, looking at the workers scattered around the site.

"Yes, ma'am, I'll round them up. I know they'd love to hear from you," Flick said hopefully.

"Of course," she replied. The last thing she wanted to do was stay and chat with a dozen other people. She could barely hold it together with Flick. But it was the first thing she had to do as the boss.

"How about we meet you in the chow hall in ten?" Brady suggested.

"Perfect," Flick said, just before he gave Nicole a mock salute, turned, and whistled.

Nicole turned to Brady and couldn't read the expression on her face. It didn't look like anything out of the ordinary, but if this was what a woman looked like when she threw a lifeline, she was beautiful. Because that's exactly what Brady had done. Her suggestion to meet in the chow hall gave her a few more minutes to pull herself together. And getting something to drink and holding it in her hand would mask any lingering jitters.

Brady looked at her as if she could read her thoughts and again waited for her to respond. "Lead the way," she replied, and indicated for Brady to do just that.

Brady was silent as they walked the fifty yards or so to the meal trailer. Nicole was grateful Brady didn't need to fill the silence with conversation. Especially about what had just happened or last night. She was quite remarkable in that respect, Nicole thought. Other women might have gloated about getting the boss in bed or try to finagle round two. But Brady simply walked beside her, unzipping her coveralls, pulling her arms out of the sleeves, and tying them around her waist.

Brady held the door for her to step inside. Only one man was inside and he was headed toward the bathroom. Brady walked over to the sink and started washing her hands.

"You know," Brady said. "I wish someone would invent some sort of sealant you could just peel off your hand when you're done. This is the one thing I hate about this job. It's so damn hard to get this shit off your hands. It soaks into your pores, and no matter how hard I scrub I can't seem to get it all off."

The creaking of the bathroom door saved Nicole from responding, and a man walked out. He wore a blue shirt with the McMillan logo above the left pocket and a sewn-on name badge that said Stevens above the right and was wiping his hands on a crackling paper towel.

"Bond, you kicked ass today," he said before realizing Nicole was also in the room.

"Oh, shit, I didn't know we had company." A blush filled his face. "Shit, I'm sorry for my language, ma'am."

Nicole smiled effortlessly at the man's discomfort in using profanity while apologizing for his profanity.

"Mast, this is Nicole McMillan. Ms. McMillan, this guy with the mouth of a sailor is Mast. He's our heavy-explosives guy."

The man in front of her paled but then must have remembered the good manners his mother had probably drilled into him and extended his hand. "Pleased to meet you, ma'am."

"My pleasure, Mast. Good work out there today." Before she had a chance to say anything else the outer door opened and the noise in the room increased as ten more men stepped in. Each of them grabbed something from the fridge and settled down around the large table.

Nicole shook hands with each man as he introduced himself, her discomfort decreasing with each one. By the time she greeted the last man her nerves had settled and she almost felt normal again.

She glanced around the trailer, and other than a few updates over the years, this one looked like the countless ones she'd spent time in while in the field. The basic elements were still the same: two refrigerators, a microwave, and cases of bottled water. The only thing different was the neat stack of magazines on the corner of the counter.

Nicole thanked them for the job they did, and when the men started in on the good-natured one-upmanship that all the crews shared, she looked at Brady. She wasn't participating in the banter but looking at her intently, as if to judge how she was holding up. Nicole's confidence grew as her nerves disappeared. Taking a risk, Nicole looked a little longer, not able to drag her eyes away. She smiled and was rewarded with Brady's smile, but this time when her pulse started to race it wasn't because of nerves; it was because of Brady.

Nicole fought down an overwhelming desire to unzip Brady's coveralls the rest of the way, unbutton Brady's McMillan shirt, and drag her pants and everything under them to the floor. Instead, she turned her attention back to her crew and chatted easily with them for another twenty or thirty minutes.

"I don't mean to rush you, Ms. McMillan, but whenever you're ready to go back, Bond will take you," Flick said.

She looked at Brady for what, confirmation? Brady nodded. "Sure, no problem. Just give me a chance to clean up." Brady rose, pushed her chair in, and dashed out the door.

The men remained, an expectant look on their faces.

"You don't have to stay. I know you all want to shower and get cleaned up."

The men looked at Flick more out of respect than for permission. Flick nodded slightly, and they all got up and pushed their chairs under the table before leaving.

Nicole turned to Flick. "You've trained these guys well," she said, indicating the neatness of the chairs around the table.

"Yes, ma'am. We may be out in the middle of nowhere doing the dirtiest job in the world, but that's no excuse to be a slob."

Nicole's smile felt genuine and not forced. "You've done a wonderful job with this crew, Flick."

"Thanks, they're a good group of guys."

Nicole found it interesting that he didn't specifically single out Brady on his crew. When she was on a crew she hated it when a foreman did. She didn't care if she was referred to as one of the guys. In her mind, and especially in this situation, the term was generic, like Kleenex. When they didn't single her out one way or the other, Nicole knew she'd been accepted as an equal, and Brady had obviously achieved that same status. Nicole was proud of her.

While she waited for Brady, Nicole chatted with Flick about work-related things and noticed that her level of anxiety increased the longer Brady was gone. She forced herself to concentrate on the conversation as she waited for Brady.

It felt like an eternity before the door creaked open and Brady stepped inside. She was breathing fast, as if she'd run all the way from the crew quarters. What Nicole would describe as a joyous expression on Brady's face quickly sobered when she saw Nicole wasn't alone.

Flick stood and shook Nicole's hand again. "Thanks again for coming out. I know the guys appreciated it. Have a safe trip back."

❖

Nicole and Brady followed Flick out the door, and Brady pointed to the truck parked at the end of the trailer. "I'm sorry it's not clean." Brady opened the passenger door for her. "It's the one I had last night so hopefully it's not too trashed inside."

"Where to?" Brady asked as she maneuvered the truck onto the hard main road. Conversation had been next to impossible while driving around the site, the potholes and mounds of congealed oil making the trip rough and noisy.

Nicole laughed.

"What's so funny?" Brady looked at her for the first time since entering the truck.

"I'd ask you to dinner, but I have absolutely no idea where to go." Nicole felt like a complete idiot.

"I accept," Brady said quickly. "We could go back to one of the places where we've been, or we can live life on the edge and try something different."

Nicole thought for a minute. "How about the hotel restaurant? It was pretty good, and I think I've been on the edge enough for one day." Nicole hoped her voice sounded as flippant as she wanted it to.

"Sounds good," Brady said, without acknowledging her comment about what had happened today.

Forty minutes later, seated at the table, Nicole studied Brady over the top of her menu. Brady was quite a remarkable woman. She knew exactly what to say and when to say it. She also knew what not to say. Two very important attributes, in Nicole's book.

"What are you going to have?" Brady asked, interrupting her thoughts.

"I have no idea. I haven't even looked."

"What have you been doing over there? Daydreaming?"

"Looking at you." She waited for Brady's reaction.

Brady looked up from her menu. "What are you looking for?"

"Some indication you're not what you appear to be."

Brady's eyebrows rose and she cocked her head. "Have you found anything?"

"Not yet." Nicole answered honestly.

"Sounds like you're expecting to."

"Maybe. I don't know."

Brady looked a little disappointed. "Well, at least you're honest."

"You deserve at least that." Actually, Nicole thought, you deserve much more than that.

"I appreciate that," Brady said, with a hint of sarcasm. "And if you don't find what you're looking for? Will that be a bad thing?"

That was the question Nicole had been asking herself since she met Brady. There was something unique about her, and Nicole was trying not to attribute it to the fact that Brady was the first woman she'd felt any attraction to. That could be very dangerous.

But Brady was unlike any woman she'd met before. Her stunningly cute butchness was one thing, but it was her attitude, the way she approached life, the way she smiled, the way she thought, and how smart she was.

"I'm not sure," Nicole replied. "The more time I spend with you, the more layers that peel back and reveal something new." As soon as the words were out of her mouth, the memory of peeling off the layers of Brady's clothes flashed through her mind. Heat shot through her as she remembered what she'd discovered.

Brady put her menu down on the table. She leaned forward, her forearms resting on the table, her hands around her bottle of beer. Her eyes were piercing and serious. "I don't think you will and I hope you don't. But go ahead and keep looking." Brady leaned back in her chair, picked her menu back up, and turned one of the pages, obviously comfortable with ending the topic.

During dinner when there was a lull in the conversation she thought she saw Brady ramp up her nerve to ask something, but she never did. Finally, after her third cup of decaf, Nicole brought it up.

"About what happened today," she said tentatively. The last thing she wanted to do was rehash how she'd frozen where she stood when she saw Brady at the wellhead. The world had stopped turning and all sound ceased. Her field of view narrowed and centered on

Brady, and she could barely breathe as she watched her move in what looked like slow motion.

Watching Brady secure the wellhead had been like watching a well-choreographed ballet. She and her crewmates worked in unison as if they knew what the other would do almost before they did it. Every action was completed flawlessly with no hesitation. Conversation was next to impossible from the noise of the oil shooting out at thousands of pounds of pressure.

Nicole saw herself, then Brady, then herself maneuvering the big head over the bolts that would secure it to the well piping. She watched Brady guide the head in and herself move the heavy piece slightly to her left. She didn't know where memories of herself stopped and Brady actually began in the scene unfolding in front of her.

She was in a daze, a spectator at a movie about her own life. Everything Brady did she had done that fateful day. Every signal, every move, every tool pulled from the pouch. Nicole waited for it to happen. She knew it would come. It always did. That one day when her life had burned up in front of her.

"Hey," Brady said in a soft voice. Nicole didn't look at her but Brady continued anyway. "Nobody knows what happened. Nobody saw anything."

"You did." Nicole's voice cracked.

"No," Brady countered easily. "I saw my boss watching over her crew. I saw a fabulous woman standing tall in the face of danger. I saw only you."

Nicole swung her eyes up from her hands and into Brady's. This could not be happening like this. She expected platitudes, expressions of empathy, or a dozen other empty, meaningless words uttered by meaningful people. Brady's face was serious, and Nicole couldn't detect a hint of pity or sympathy. On the contrary, she saw compassion, kindness, and concern reflected in Brady's eyes.

"Thank you." It was all Nicole could manage.

Several minutes passed before Nicole realized they were practically the only ones left in the restaurant. "Good grief. What time is it?" she asked, glancing at her watch. "It's late," she said, picking up her credit card from the small silver tray. "I better let you go."

Nicole stood, knowing she was rambling but for some reason couldn't stop herself. "How did you manage to get so much time off?" When on a fire the crew usually never left the site, spending their time either on shift, in the chow hall, or sleeping.

"Flick seems to have a sixth sense about when we need a break. It's dangerous if we're distracted, and we're lucky we're so close to town and can completely get away for a few hours."

"You're lucky to have a chief that thinks like that. Not many do." Nicole wished she could hire a dozen more Flicks.

"I know. I've worked for most of them and refuse to work for them again."

They arrived at a natural fork leading from the restaurant and branching to the left to the elevators and the right to the lobby. Nicole stopped, fully intent on saying good-bye to Brady. She saw a different intent on Brady's face.

"You don't need to walk me to my door."

"Don't argue with me, Nicole." Brady took her arm and led her to the left. "We've been through this before and I won. I'll win again, so save your breath and effort for something that matters."

Nicole started to argue but stopped when she realized she would have a few more minutes with Brady. But that was all it would be. They would not repeat what had happened last night. She could not and would not do that again.

The hall was empty and the thick carpet muffled any sounds of their feet hitting the ground. In far too short a time, they were at her door. This time she managed to open her own door and turned to say good night to Brady. Her voice stuck somewhere in her throat. Her brain forgot to think but her body instinctively knew how to communicate. And it was telling her what she didn't want to hear.

Brady didn't move but stood there, her eyes glued to hers. Nicole wanted to reach out, pull her into her room, and kiss her. She wanted to strip Brady naked and take her again and again. She wanted to feel Brady under her hands, her mouth, her tongue. She wanted to hear her cry out in the dark, feel her body convulse, and hold her when she climaxed. She wanted her, plain and simple. But there was nothing simple about this. And there never would be.

"Good night, Brady."

Brady's expression didn't change. She didn't blink, frown, or look surprised. She simply smiled, stepped forward, and kissed her lightly on the mouth.

"Good night. Travel safe."

Nicole watched as Brady retraced their steps to the elevator. With each step her body screamed at her to stop Brady, to call her back. But her brain was telling her something different, and Nicole knew which one would win. It always did. It had to.

Closing the door behind her sounded like the slamming of a cell door in an empty prison. It echoed in the overwhelming silence of her room and ripped her breath away. Nicole took a few steps into the room, and before she could think about what she was doing she turned around, opened the door, and ran down the hall.

CHAPTER TWENTY-THREE

Brady needed a drink. No, she needed several. This entire day had been bizarre, unsettling, and one of the most thrilling of her life. She had killed the fire, capped the head, and helped Nicole down from the ledge. She'd been examined, scrutinized, and peeled by Nicole over dinner and dismissed at her door. Brady wasn't about to go away without one more kiss, and she risked being pushed away and took it.

It was sweet, Nicole's lips tasting like coffee and peppermint, and she wanted it to go on forever. But Nicole had other ideas and Brady wasn't going to push. Sure, she wanted to be with Nicole again, feel her weight on top of her, her hands on her, in her. But she didn't want the complications it would bring. More than one or two nights was a potential complication, and getting involved with Nicole would be a big one.

After stopping at what seemed like every floor, the elevator arrived at the lobby. Brady stepped out and started for the exit but made a detour to the bar area first, her three cups of coffee needing a release.

Drying her hands on a pristine white towel, she examined herself in the mirror. She had circles under her eyes from lack of sleep and weeks of hard work. She needed a massage and about three days of nonstop sleep. As soon as she got home she'd take care of both.

Tossing the towel in the basket by the door, she stepped out and headed toward the lobby doors. They'd just opened in front of her with a swish when she heard her name called from behind her. When she turned Nicole was practically running toward her. Her heart jumped. Was something wrong? She was on full alert by the time Nicole slid to a stop in front of her.

"Nicole, what is it? Did something happen?" Nicole silenced her with a finger on her lips.

"Will you come upstairs with me?"

Of course she would, but what was going on? Was Nicole afraid to be alone again? "Of course."

"No," Nicole said quietly, scrutinizing her. "I mean will you come upstairs with me?"

It took a few moments for Nicole's words to take effect and for Brady's mind to shift from danger to...what...pleasure? Was Nicole saying what she thought she was saying, or was she just reading something into the situation? God, what a mess this woman makes of my mind, Brady thought.

"I'd like for you to come upstairs with me." Nicole's voice didn't waver.

Suddenly it was clear. Nicole was offering her the opportunity to be with her again. Would it be a repeat of last night? Would Nicole do everything while she was forced to lie back and take it? It sounded great, but she'd wanted to touch Nicole so bad it hurt. Wanted to feel her naked body against hers, their breasts touching, their legs wet with desire. She didn't know how it would turn out, but she did know that she wanted to find out.

The sexual tension in the elevator was thick. Nicole was studying something interesting on the floor, and no matter how hard Brady willed her to look at her she didn't. Brady couldn't stand it anymore. She wanted to be with a woman who wanted a joint experience, two people connecting and not just physically. Nicole had to want this as much as she did.

"You don't have to do this," Brady finally said.

"I know." Nicole's voice was more resigned than eager. She still hadn't looked up.

"Then why are you?" That got her attention and Nicole looked at her.

"Because I do want to."

"Why?"

"Why? Isn't it obvious? We're attracted to each other. This is the last time we'll see each other. Why not?"

Brady didn't comment on Nicole's statement that they'd never see each other again. Instead she said, "So this is a good-bye fuck?" Nicole squirmed, and as much as Brady wanted to be with her again, she refused to let her off the hook this easily.

"No, yes," Nicole said, exasperated, and leaned against the back of the elevator. She looked up at the ceiling this time and sighed. "I don't know what it is, Brady. All I know is that I want it to happen again."

Brady didn't push it any further, sensing how much it cost Nicole to admit that one little bit.

❖

"Please, Nicole," Brady begged, and not for the first or second time. She was in the middle of Nicole's bed, Nicole nibbling and kissing her way down her body. So far Nicole hadn't touched her where she needed it the most, preferring to spend at least the first half of eternity kissing almost every inch of her.

Nicole was driving her crazy. Her mouth licked her breast everywhere but her nipples. They were rock hard and she ached for Nicole's lips around them again. She tickled her belly with light, butterfly kisses that continued across her hips and the top of her thighs, and when Nicole spread her legs Brady knew when she kissed her in that perfect spot she would immediately explode. But Nicole had her own agenda. She licked the spot between her outer lips and the crook of her thigh. She kissed her lips but didn't venture any farther. Nicole's teasing was agony and ecstasy at the same time. She resumed her trail down her legs to her feet, then back up again.

Brady gathered Nicole close and kissed her passionately. She pulled away and looked into Nicole's eyes. "Please let me touch you."

Brady knew she'd said the wrong thing the instant it was out of her mouth. Fear replaced passion and Nicole froze. "Nicole, I'm sorry. I didn't mean to push. It's just that you're so beautiful, and it makes me crazy not to be able to touch you."

"I can't." Nicole's words were so quiet they were less than a whisper.

Brady lifted Nicole's chin but she averted her eyes. "Nicole, please look at me." Brady was ready to repeat her words when Nicole finally made eye contact. Pain filled her eyes, and Brady felt like a complete shit.

"Hey," she said silently, and stroked her cheek. "I won't do anything unless you tell me to." She repeated her promise. She didn't want to scare Nicole away. She'd never come back. It was several agonizing moments before Nicole lowered her head again.

"Cold?" Nicole asked several hours later. Brady was on her stomach and Nicole's hot breath had moved to her neck.

Brady shivered both from what Nicole was doing to her and where the cool night air hit her damp skin. "No," Brady managed to say, her throat parched from gasping and breathing too hard and fast.

"Then why are you shivering?"

"Because you're making me crazy." Nicole was taking her time, and Brady was so wired again she could explode any minute.

"In a good way, I hope."

Without thinking, Brady slid her hand under her, but before she reached her target Nicole stopped. She felt her weight shift off her.

"If you're going to do that then you don't need me."

Brady did need Nicole more than she wanted to admit and quickly removed her hand and grabbed the sheet above her head instead. She squirmed, craving Nicole's heat on her again. She didn't have to wait long.

Nicole's hand started to drift down her back and between the crack of her ass. Brady instinctively arched to get closer to her tantalizing touch. "Oh, I need you all right. But if you don't touch me soon, I'm going to spontaneously combust."

Nicole chuckled at the same time she slid a hot finger inside her. She moaned so loud she almost didn't hear Nicole say, "Aren't you lucky I used to put out fires?"

"Then do it, goddamnit." Brady was beyond asking, had long since passed begging and was now demanding release.

Nicole flicked her thumb over Brady's clit and she exploded. Her head pounded; red, blue, and white lights flashed behind her eyelids;

and she felt as if she were suspended in time. She wanted this moment to go on forever.

It almost did. Just as she was coming down, Nicole turned her over, spread her legs wide, and stared at her. Brady barely had enough strength to rise on her elbows to look at Nicole, what she saw almost making her come again.

The light from the lamp in the corner was enough for her to see pure, raw desire burning in Nicole's brilliantly blue eyes. When their eyes met it was as if they were connected by some unseen force. Brady couldn't look away, and when Nicole bent her head neither did she.

Brady watched as Nicole licked her clit gently, then harder and faster as Brady couldn't help but respond. Their eyes remained locked as Nicole loved her and Brady showed her just how good it felt.

Chapter Twenty-four

When are you leaving?" Brady asked, breaking the silence in the room. Her voice was muffled by Nicole's shoulder. "Later today." Nicole glanced at the bright-blue numbers on the clock on the nightstand. She had four hours. Brady and her crew would remain on site for another few days, tying up loose ends, making sure all the equipment was secure for transport either back to the rental company or the next job site. The eight fires McMillan was fighting in Greslikstan were out.

Nicole watched the fan blade spin in circles and felt like that was her life now. Going in circles but getting nowhere. She closed her eyes and visualized what they might look like from above.

The bed was more than a little rumpled, the sheets tangled around their legs. The pillows were on the floor scattered around the bed, except for the one under her head. Brady lay in her arms as naked as she had been the night before except Nicole had on a completely different set of clothes. How ridiculous she must look. She felt ridiculous yet couldn't do anything about it.

"Where are you going after this?" Nicole asked.

"Home. Gonna take some time off and unwind."

Nicole wanted to say something, but an overwhelming sadness filled her to the point she couldn't think. She could barely breathe. Brady must have sensed it because she untangled herself from the sheets and her arms.

"I guess I'd better go," Brady said, sitting up and looking around for her clothes.

Nicole wanted to pull her back down and keep her there, but she didn't. There was no future in this. She'd had this same conversation with herself yesterday and had reached the same conclusion. This wouldn't be enough for a woman like Brady, and she couldn't give any more. Reluctantly she let her go. Her pulse raced again at the sight of Brady's long, lean body gathering up her clothes before she closed the bathroom door behind her.

As Brady showered, Nicole got dressed, fighting the urge to join her. Wouldn't that be something? If she did she'd have to either take off her clothes or stand in the shower completely clothed and be totally humiliated.

She wanted to feel Brady's body against her, feel her skin against hers. She wanted Brady's hands on her, in her, all over her, and she'd almost let her last night. In a moment of weakness Nicole had reached for Brady's hand and was guiding it to the button on her pants before she realized what she was doing. She'd stopped herself in time, grasping Brady's hand in hers instead.

Her clothes were rumpled and she smelled like smoke. Quickly she changed into a pair of sweatpants and a long-sleeve T-shirt with the McMillan logo on the back. She ran her fingers over her face and checked her wig. As together as she could be, she turned on the light beside the bed and walked around to turn on the other one. She couldn't help but glance at the bed, and when she did memories flashed through her mind, accompanied by a hundred different emotions she couldn't identify.

Obviously passion was one, as were desire and simple, plain lust, but also tenderness, concern, and warmth. Nicole had chemistry with Brady, yet she held back at the same time. She had to, for her own self-preservation. She didn't know whether to run or to stay, whether to let Brady go or push her away or ask her to stay. But for what? Another few hours? Then what? She was leaving later today. She'd already postponed her departure once; she couldn't do it again. She had obligations, significant obligations, and she had to get back to the office.

And what happened then? She certainly wasn't going to ask to see Brady again, and she knew Brady wouldn't. Funny how after such a short time together she felt like she'd known her forever. Except she could never figure out what she was thinking.

Brady was very good at masking her emotions. If only...Nicole stopped herself. There was no *if only*. There would be no *if only*. She couldn't live on *if onlys*. She'd painfully learned to put those thoughts away, close the door, bolt it, and throw away the key. It only tore her guts out. And she wouldn't do that to herself again.

"Nicole?" Brady said, bringing her thoughts back to the present.

She looked up, embarrassed that Brady had caught her staring at the bed, the effects of their lovemaking clearly evident. Brady was freshly showered, her hair still wet. Her clothes were a bit wrinkled from where they'd been tossed on the floor. God, she looked good.

Her constant burning for Brady kicked in but she didn't let herself act on it. Instead she walked toward her, and Brady met her halfway. Brady waited for her to say something. Nicole said what she had to, not what she wanted to. "You be careful out there."

"I will."

Brady gazed at her, and Nicole suspected she'd hoped she'd say something different. If only...*No. Nicole, do not go there.*

"I know you will."

They stood there for several seconds, Brady's eyes piercing. Nicole felt as if she were being swept up into a vortex, Brady pulling out of her what she couldn't do on her own. She was very close, and if Brady gazed at her like that much longer, her resolve would ultimately crumble. She couldn't risk it.

Brady finally stepped forward, cupped her cheeks with both hands, and kissed her. Nicole was afraid she'd break with the tenderness of Brady's kiss. It was soft and sweet and light, obviously a good-bye kiss. A remember-me kiss. When Brady broke away she didn't look at her.

"Take care, Nicole," Brady said, just before she turned, crossed the room, and closed the heavy door behind her.

CHAPTER TWENTY-FIVE

If Nicole thought the flight over was torture, the flight back was sheer agony. She didn't even try to occupy her mind with work, a book, movie, or chatting with her seatmate. As soon as she was settled in, she leaned her head back, closed her eyes, and relived every moment she'd spent with Brady, only rousing when it was time to eat, use the bathroom, or simply stretch her legs.

She went through the motions of gathering her luggage, clearing customs, and driving home. She unpacked, tossed in a load of laundry, and checked her home phone for messages. Two were from friends inviting her out for a drink on Saturday, the other from her mother.

"Nicole, sweetheart, it's your mother." Why does she do that, Nicole thought irritably. Like after all these years she wouldn't recognize either the greeting or her mother's voice. "Your father and I would like you to come over for dinner Thursday night. I know it's a workday, but I'm sure you can pry yourself away at a decent time to join us." Nicole couldn't miss the dismissal-like tone of "workday" and the intentional jab at her devotion to her job. Any other parent would have simply asked her over. How was she related to this woman?

She erased the message and picked up the phone. After confirming that she would arrive as summoned, she grabbed a beer out of the fridge and headed to the patio.

The next few days Nicole felt as if she were in a fog, just a half step behind what was going on around her. She felt sluggish and irritable and attributed it to jet lag. She'd never had problems with time change, but she was six years older than the last time she flew across the world. She had trouble focusing on her work, meetings seemed to go on forever, and for the first time in her life she wanted to be out of the office more than in.

Charlotte called her on it later in the week over dinner. She'd invited Nicole over and was grilling steaks on the patio. "Are you going to tell me about it?" Charlotte asked, turning down the fire and closing the lid.

Nicole was propped against the rail of the deck, her back to her. She didn't even bother to pretend she didn't know what Charlotte was talking about. "How do you know me so well, Charlotte?"

"Because I love you and care about you."

Nicole shrugged. "I had dinner with my parents last night. My mother never stopped talking. It was as if she didn't even see me." That dinner wasn't much different from any of the other dozens of dinners, but somehow this time Nicole noticed what it had really been like. Her father had lost most of his ability to communicate and sat silently in the chair across from her. Her mother never asked about her friends, her work, or anything remotely personal. She kept reminding Nicole of the myriad of social obligations she had as both the daughter of DD McMillan and the president of McMillan Suppression. Like she needed reminding.

"You and your mother are very different."

"I used to wish you were my mother," Nicole admitted, still not turning around. She'd never told Charlotte that before, believing it was disrespectful to her mother. Now she didn't really care.

"Why has it taken me this long to see who she really is? She's more concerned with appearances and obligations than she is with my happiness."

"Are you happy?"

"I thought I was," Nicole admitted for the first time. Maybe that's what it was. Maybe that's why she felt that her life no longer revolved completely around her work.

"You met someone?"

Nicole's heart jumped and her pulse started to race just thinking about Brady. "Yes."

Charlotte put her arm around her shoulders. "Let's eat first and you can tell me about her over my best bottle of wine."

It was the best wine Nicole had ever tasted, and when Charlotte told her she'd picked it up at the grocery store, Nicole had to laugh. "And to think what Mom served last night probably cost north of a hundred dollars a bottle and gave me a headache."

"Did you expect anything different?"

Nicole shook her head. "No."

Charlotte refilled their glasses several times, neither of them speaking. Finally Nicole said, "Her name is Brady."

Charlotte didn't say anything else, her way of letting Nicole talk when she was ready to. It didn't take long. "She's the most amazing woman I've ever met. She's smart, speaks two other languages, and is incredible. Her eyes are so dark they almost glow, and her smile lights up the sky. Her laughter fills the air around her, and I swear I expect to see little butterflies flying around her head. She's strong but not overwhelming, yet she can bring me to my knees with just a whisper."

"When do I get to meet her?"

"You don't."

"Why not?" Charlotte asked with no hint of anger in her statement.

"Because it's over."

"Sounds to me like it didn't even get started."

"Oh, it got started all right." Nicole's face heated. Maybe Charlotte would think it was from the wine. No, she knew better than that.

"So why did you end it?"

Nicole looked at her friend, mentor, and the only one she trusted with this conversation. "How do you know I did?" Charlotte looked at her as if to say, "Please, I know you better than you know yourself," and she probably did.

"Because nothing could come of it."

"What does that mean?"

"We were together but…I…ugh…never took my clothes off." God, what a humiliating memory.

"I see," Charlotte said, nodding. "What did Brady say about that?"

"Nothing."

"Nothing? She said nothing?"

"Nope."

"Why?"

"Because she knew I couldn't. That's what makes her incredible."

"Did you even try?"

"No."

"And that's why you ended it?"

"Yes." The word felt like a brick in her stomach.

Charlotte didn't say anything for a few minutes, and when she did Nicole was surprised. "Nicole, I've never told you what to do or how to live your life, but I'm going to now. You cannot live without love in your life." Charlotte held up her hand, silencing Nicole. "And I'm not talking about me or your parents. I'm talking about the love of another person, the person who makes you bigger, better, and stronger than you ever thought you could be. The one who you can't stop thinking about and makes you nuts at the same time. The person who, if you didn't spend the rest of your life with, you would regret it for the rest of your life. You need that, Nicole. Some people don't, but you do, and you have to be strong enough to grab it."

Nicole stared at Charlotte. She'd never said anything remotely like this to her. She'd always been nothing but completely supportive of whatever Nicole chose to do with her life, but it was obvious she thought she'd made the wrong decision on this one.

"I will love you whatever your choices are, Nicole, you know that. But I will tell you I will not be happy if you let this slip through your fingers."

Nicole drove home feeling like she'd just received a scolding. She was a grown woman, for crying out loud, more than capable of making her own decisions. She didn't need anyone's permission or approval to live her life any damn way she wanted. Fortified with resolve to take back control of her life, she pushed the accelerator to the floor.

CHAPTER TWENTY-SIX

You've become quite the homebody, Brady."

"No, I haven't," Brady said, pushing the peas around on Mrs. C's flowered dinner plates.

"It's Friday night and you're having dinner with us."

"And what's so wrong with that?"

"Nothing, if it was once in a while, but you've spent almost every night with us since you got home."

Brady wasn't the slightest bit hungry but put a spoon of mashed potatoes in her mouth to be polite. Mrs. C did the same.

"And if you don't stop pushing your food around on your plate and eat, you're going to waste away into nothing."

"I'm just not very hungry," Brady replied. She'd been out of sorts since leaving Nicole's hotel room two weeks ago. The walk to the elevator was only a dozen yards or so but felt like a trip to the cold side of the moon. Her heart was heavy, her limbs sluggish, as if they had a mind of their own and didn't want to walk away. She certainly didn't. But what choice did she have?

She hadn't known what to expect when she finished her shower and went back to Nicole, but she'd rehearsed what she would say. However, Nicole didn't give her a chance. She obviously didn't want her to stay, but Brady couldn't leave without one last kiss. One last chance to sear the scent and taste of Nicole into her memory.

"You've changed, Brady," Mrs. C said, scrutinizing her. Her husband echoed her observation.

"No, I haven't." Brady denied it, but she had. She felt different. She was no longer driven to succeed, to make money and acquire possessions so no one could ever call her poor white trash again. She had no interest in going out or accepting every call for extra work. She roamed around her apartment, went for walks, and thought about Nicole all the time.

She was at a crossroads. She'd envisioned her life very differently than what she saw in front of her now. She'd thought she knew what she wanted until she met and fell in love with Nicole. There, she'd said it. She was in love with Nicole, and it wasn't as scary as she expected it to be. She couldn't imagine her life being anything without Nicole in it.

Brady realized she'd been burning through her life until she met Nicole. Every day she was free and easy, no encumbrances, obligations, or commitments. That had been her life since she'd walked out of that broken-down trailer fifteen years ago. If she kept up this pace she'd be worth a million dollars by the time she was forty. But she'd have absolutely nothing if she didn't have Nicole. What good was it if you were alone? If you didn't have love in your life, someone to share it with?

Brady leapt from the chair, kissing them both on the cheek. "I've got to go. Thanks for the dinner."

"Where are you going?" Mrs. C's frail old-lady voice came from behind her.

"To the rest of my life," Brady said, before flying out the door and digging her truck keys out of her pocket. She'd finally admitted to herself she loved Nicole, and she refused to let her get away.

CHAPTER TWENTY-SEVEN

Nicole rubbed her eyes. The numbers on the page had started to blur thirty minutes ago, but she kept at it. There was no point in going home when she had things to do here. All that waited for her was an empty fridge and deafening silence. Ann had left hours ago, and Nicole frowned when she heard an insistent knock on the outer doors of the office.

Careful not to be seen she cautiously crept down the hall. When she peered around the corner her stomach lurched. It was Brady. She stepped back before Brady saw her. Was something wrong? Gathering her composure, Nicole stepped toward the door.

"What are you doing here?" Nicole asked after unlocking and opening the door. Brady stepped inside and she locked it behind her.

"I wanted to talk to you."

Nicole stepped back and had a chance to get a good look at Brady. She was thinner and looked troubled. "Sit down." Nicole indicated the chairs in the lobby. "What is it? Is it Flick, one of the crew?" She would be the first one notified if there had been an accident.

"No. I want to talk about you and me."

Nicole straightened. "There is no you and me."

Brady moved to the edge of her seat. "There was and I want there to be again."

"What? No. There is no us and there won't be. What happened was a bad idea, and it won't happen again."

"Why not?"

"Why not?" Nicole repeated. She stood and started pacing back and forth in front of the reception desk. "Because I said so." That was a stupid answer but the only one she could come up with right now. Brady's words had caught her completely off guard.

"That's not a reason." Brady said calmly.

"I don't care. It's the one you're getting." Nicole was rattled. It was hard enough just to see Brady again, but this conversation was almost too much.

"You felt it too, Nicole. I know you did. We have something here and—"

"Don't tell me what I was feeling, Brady. I know what I was feeling, but I can't figure out what the fuck I was thinking." The shock on Brady's face almost broke her. She shook her head and waved her hand dismissively. "Just forget I said anything,"

"I don't think so," Brady said. "You opened that door."

"And now I've turned around, backed out, and closed it." She wished she'd never opened herself and let Brady in.

Brady shook her head. "It doesn't work that way. You can't close a door already opened."

"I have the key and I'm doing it anyway," Nicole replied metaphorically. She wasn't going to let Brady talk her into continuing their relationship.

"Coward."

"What?" This time the spark in her was anger.

"You heard me," Brady said quietly, her eyes never leaving hers.

"You think I'm a coward?"

"I could have used the word *chicken*, but it doesn't have the same impact."

"You think I'm a coward?" Nicole couldn't help repeating the question. She'd stopped pacing and stood in front of Brady.

"Yes, I do."

"I see," she said, holding her rising anger in check. "And specifically in what way do you think I'm a coward?" Every time Nicole used the word her anger ticked up a notch.

"That's not really what I meant," Brady said, obviously growing uncomfortable with the direction the conversation had taken.

"Then what did you mean?" Nicole asked, sitting down and crossing her arms across her chest defensively.

"Look, can we just go back about four minutes?"

"No. I want you to tell me why you think I'm a coward."

"It was a poor choice of words."

"A poor choice of words?" Nicole mimicked her. "So what word would you use? What does your thesaurus have that might better define it?" Nicole leaned forward, her arms on her thighs, and didn't wait for Brady to answer. "Because let me tell you, Brady, I am not a coward. You have no idea what I've been through. I've faced everything head-on. I stepped into a man's world when there was no woman in front of me. You have no idea the bullshit I had to put up with, the words and innuendos, the leers from men in this industry who thought just because I was a woman they could treat me like shit. Or their wives who thought I was the camp whore.

"I fought the biggest fires the world had ever seen. I walked right into prejudice, ridicule, and humiliation and walked out with my head held high. Everything that has stood in my way I have faced and conquered. I am not a coward." She was surprised at her fury.

"Aren't you, though?" Brady asked calmly. "Look at your life, Nicole. Other than your family, who's in your life that matters? How long are you going to hide behind your scars before you let someone in?"

"You don't have any fucking idea what you're talking about," Nicole said through clenched teeth, standing again and walking away.

"No, I don't, because you won't let me in. And that's exactly what I'm talking about." Brady's voice was close behind her as she walked down the hall to her office.

"What about the people who care about you? Care about you the person, Nicole? What's inside you, not the outside wrapper. They don't care about your scars and what they look like. But they do care about how you've been hurt, what you have to deal with every day. They care about your joys. They care about your insecurities. They care about you. And they could care less about what you look like. And I'm one of those people, Nicole."

Nicole tried to slam the door but Brady stopped it. "Get out."

Brady didn't move. "I don't know how many of those people you have in your life. I don't know how many of those people you let in, but I'm one of those people, and I'm standing right here on your doorstep, knocking on your door. It's up to you whether you let me in. And if you're as strong and as brave as you say you are," Brady hesitated for a moment before continuing, "you'll open it."

"I said get out." Nicole's voice quivered and held less conviction than the first time she said it.

"You know what the difference is between you and me, Nicole?"

"Besides the fact that your body is perfect and mine is repulsive?" Nicole shouted.

"Oh, for God's sake," Brady said, stepping farther into her office. "All you see is that the possibility of being hurt again far exceeds any amount of joy and happiness you may find on the other side. Because the last time you opened the door Gina was on the other side, and not everyone is a Gina. I am not Gina, Nicole. You need to face the fact that I'm nothing like her. If you believe I'm worth the risk you'll do it. But you won't. That's why I think you're a coward."

Brady was within arm's length. "It's up to you, Nicole. I won't like it if you don't let me in. I won't like it at all. But I will accept it and eventually come to terms that I wasn't worth it and move on."

Brady started to turn to leave but stepped even closer.

"Do you think you're the only person who has something on the line here? My entire life I've clawed and scratched and dug myself out of being thought of as trailer trash. My parents didn't give a shit about me. I had no friends. I was the subject of finger-pointing and ridicule growing up. I was teased every single day I went to school because I was on welfare and the only clothes I had to wear came out of the church rummage box that my classmates donated. And don't you think they didn't have a field day with that? The girls looked down their noses at me. The boys thought just because I lived in a trailer, I'd spread my legs for them. And the more I ignored them the more they pushed. Well, let me tell you something, Nicole. When you defended yourself," Brady pointed her finger at Nicole, "you were a grown woman. I had to defend myself when I was twelve and thirteen and fourteen years old from boys and men who thought because of where I lived they could have me."

"So you know what, Nicole? We both have scars that have deeply affected us. But it's what we do about those scars that make us who we are today. So yeah, I've got something at risk here too. Ever since I can remember I had a plan to get out, and nothing or no one was going to get in my way. And nothing has." Brady stepped away and it was her turn to pace.

"I have never compromised my principles or my goals to get where I want to be. Nothing was worth risking that. *Nothing*," Brady said, "until I sat in your goddamn conference room with your clean coffeepot and your plush carpet and you walked through the door." She pointed down the hall, where the conference room was. "That's when my plan started to fracture. That's when my scars started to heal," Brady said definitively.

"The difference between you and me, Nicole is that my door is wide open and *you* are the only person I'll let in. Because you *are* worth it. That's why I think you're a coward."

❖

Nicole dropped into her chair. What the fuck had just happened? She felt like she'd been in the middle of a hurricane. Her hands were shaking, her heart racing, and she was having trouble breathing. She hadn't lost her temper like that in years, and never as bad as this.

When Brady called her a coward, something inside her snapped. Six years of pain, suffering, frustration, and being alone had pushed its way through the scars and to the surface. Six years of covering her insecurities behind a mask of competence and indifference had worn thin. All Brady had to do was utter one word and it had ripped open.

She stood, her eyes darting around the room as if she could still see Brady in her office. "How dare you, Brady!" she shouted to the empty room. "How dare you come into my perfectly built life with your sexy smile, your pretty words, and your psychobabble. What the fuck do you know? You don't know anything about me." Nicole's voice rose as she continued.

"How dare you make me hope for something? Make me want something I can't have. Open scars that no one can see. How dare you make me fall in love with you?" Nicole's voice broke as tears slid down her cheeks.

CHAPTER TWENTY-EIGHT

B ond," Flick shouted.
Brady looked up from the water nozzle she was manning to see Flick motioning her over. She hadn't noticed Dig standing beside her to take over. Brady followed Flick into the crew quarters.

"Everything all right, Bond?" Flick asked as soon as they were seated in the two matching recliners.

"Yeah, sure, Flick." *Liar.*

"Bullshit. You're distracted, preoccupied, and not eating, and that's not good."

Okay, not so good of a liar.

Flick was far too observant for Brady to deal with right now. Since leaving Nicole's office two weeks ago she'd jumped at the slightest sound outside her apartment, hoping it was Nicole. Her heart leaped every time her phone rang. But it was never Nicole. Nicole. Even the thought of her name sent bolts of lightning heat through her. But in the last few days when she finally admitted Nicole wasn't going to come to her, the bolts had shifted to jagged shards of pain.

"Really, Flick. I'm fine." *Or I may be in about ten years.*

"I'm not going to pry into your life off the job, but something's going on and I'm sending you home."

"What?" Brady exclaimed, surprised at Flick's words. And the thought of going home to what, an empty house with nothing to do? Nothing but memories of Nicole to occupy the long nights?

"Flick, I'm fine," Brady repeated.

Flick studied her, and the longer he looked, the more Brady started to squirm. Where had her ability to separate herself from her emotions flown to? She had mastered the ability to have everyone see exactly what she wanted them to see, yet Flick could see right through her.

"Then in two weeks when I see you again, you can show me, because right now you're a danger to yourself and this crew. I don't like doing this, Bond, but the safety of this crew comes first, no exception. And right now that means you go home."

"But Flick," Brady sat forward in her chair, "I can't go home. Let me stay. I'll do paperwork, make the supply runs. Hell, I'll even clean the chow hall." To her own ears she sounded as desperate as she felt.

"No. I'll have Mast drive you to the airport."

Brady sat in stunned silence as Flick walked across the room, his heavy boots pounding on the floor echoing the pounding of her heart.

❖

"Nicole? Nicole?"

Nicole looked up and Ann was standing in her doorway. "I'm sorry, must have been daydreaming." The expression on Ann's face told her that was the wrong thing to say. She was never anything but one-hundred-percent work. She never even got a personal phone call. But that was before Brady threw down her gauntlet at her feet.

It was still there. Nicole hadn't stepped over it, nor had she picked it up. What she had done was ignore it. No, that wasn't true. She'd *tried* to ignore it. And that wasn't working. If she were able to be busy enough to keep her mind off Brady, she was reasonably okay. However, most of the time she felt in a fog, like she was a half second behind the rest of the world.

"Yes, Ann, what is it?" The woman walked forward and handed Nicole a stack of papers.

"The status reports from the crew chiefs." Ann looked at her as if she were afraid Nicole would bite her head off. No wonder there. That was exactly what she'd done several times this week.

"Thanks," Nicole said, and set the papers on the side of her desk." She glanced at the clock on her desk. It was barely after two. Another very long day.

Nicole leaned back in her chair and stared at the reports Ann had given her. There was information about Brady in that pile. Well, maybe not her specifically, but a report from Flick. After she met Brady, Nicole would read every word on every page, not wanting to miss any reference to her. Occasionally Brady's name did show up on an overtime report or some other noteworthy event. She'd barely been able to read them these last two weeks, afraid Brady's name would be mentioned somewhere.

Reluctantly she picked up the pile and started to read. One down, twelve to go. Two down, eleven to go. One by one she read each report, making a note here or there until she had two left in her hands. Flick's report was next.

Brady's name leapt off the page like it had springs. Nicole read the words surrounding it again. Then she read them again and then a third time. She reached for the phone.

"Eugene? It's Nicole McMillan. Yes, how are you? Wonderful. Eugene, can you do me a favor? I need an address."

❖

"Seven eight two five, seven eight two nine," Nicole read out loud as she craned her head to see the numbers on the houses. "There! Finally seven eight three seven." She pulled next to the curb and turned off her truck. She'd made the three-hour drive in two and a half. The sun was low in the late afternoon sky.

The big diesel engine clicked and clacked a few times as the engine cooled off. If only she could do the same. Her hands were sweaty and her stomach threatened to revolt. She opened the door, climbed out, and walked across the wide street before she could change her mind.

She remembered Brady saying she lived above the garage and that her landlords were an older couple she looked out for. That must be her landlady, Nicole thought, seeing the woman sitting on the ground pulling weeds from a colorful flowerbed.

Nicole approached the woman and called out, "Hello."

The woman looked up, her face partially shadowed by her wide-brimmed hat. "Hello."

"Does Brady Stewart live here?"

The woman frowned. "Who wants to know?"

"I'm Nicole McMillan. Brady and I—"

"You're her boss," the woman said quickly.

Nicole was surprised but took a few tentative steps forward. "Yes, I am. Is she home?" Nicole looked toward the garage for any sign that Brady was here.

It took several efforts before the woman was able to get to her feet. She walked toward Nicole. "Is she in trouble? 'Cuz if she is, I'm not letting you on my property."

Nicole grinned. This woman was spunky. And she obviously cared for Brady to protect her like this. "No, ma'am, she's not in any trouble. I just want to talk to her."

"What about?" the woman asked, without the slightest hesitation or concern for propriety.

Nicole smiled politely. "Well, please forgive my rudeness, ma'am, but that's between Brady and me."

"You're the one," the woman said, pointing her arthritic finger at Nicole.

"Excuse me?" Nicole said, confused.

"You." This time the woman's hand shook with the force of her word. "You're the one that has her all discombobulated. She hasn't been right since she came home last time. She prowls around her place all hours of the night, doesn't go out anymore, and just sits on the patio and stares into space. She wastes the food I bring her and pretends she's eating it."

"And I've done all that...how..." Nicole asked carefully.

"By not doing what you were supposed to do. Not doing what she wanted you to. Hell, for all I know she declared her love and you didn't say it back. How in the hell do I know?" She moved closer until her finger was poking Nicole's chest. "But what I do know is that you hurt that girl, and she don't deserve to be hurt."

"I'm sorry you think that way...Mrs..." *God, what was her name*? "Mrs. C."

"How do you know my name?" the woman asked, taking a quick step backward.

"Brady told me." Mrs. C looked skeptical and said as much. "She told me. She talked about you and your husband. She painted your house." When Mrs. C nodded, Nicole continued. "Oh, and you're the neighborhood busybody."

"She didn't call me that." Mrs. C frowned.

"I never called her that." Brady's voice echoed the words.

Nicole swung her gaze to the left, and walking toward her was the most wonderful woman in the world and she hoped she wasn't too late.

Nicole laughed and winked at the old lady. "You're right, Mrs. C. She didn't call you that. Several other wonderful and endearing things, but not that."

"Brady, get this awful woman whose only manners are to be disrespectful to an old lady off my grass. Shoo, now go. Both of you. I've got better things to do than to referee your lovers' quarrel." And with that, Mrs. C calmly walked into the house, her cane tapping on the stone sidewalk.

"Are you trying to get me in trouble?"

My God, Brady looked good. Her hair was shorter and very becoming. She was wearing a dark-green, short-sleeve T-shirt with a female fisherman on the front and baggy cargo shorts. Her feet were bare, and she was the sexiest woman Nicole had ever seen.

"That's what Mrs. C asked. She's pretty protective of you, you know." Nicole's nerves were kicking up again.

"The feeling's mutual," Brady replied, not moving any closer from where she'd stopped a few feet away.

Now she was really nervous. "How are you?"

"Fine."

"Flick's report said you were sent home." Nicole studied Brady from head to toe, looking for anything amiss. "Are you okay?"

"Flick reported it?" Brady practically spat out the words.

"He's required to."

"And you came here to what? Check up on me? See if I'm screwing the company out of time? Well, I'm not. It wasn't my idea to leave, and for the record, I hate it." Brady was angry.

"Brady, no, that's not it at all. I was just concerned...worried... afraid you were hurt." Nicole sputtered. She didn't understand why Brady was so defensive.

"Well, as you can see," Brady turned in a complete circle, showing Nicole she was in fact not injured, "I'm fine." She held her position, feet wide, arms extended out from her sides.

Brady wasn't making this easy. But why should she? Nicole had practically thrown her out of her office. She swallowed and looked around. The front yard was immaculately mowed and trimmed, and she suspected it was Brady's doing. A swing hung on the porch, but this conversation was not meant to be overheard.

"Is there someplace we can talk?" Nicole held her breath while Brady contemplated her answer. *Please say yes. Please give me a chance.*

Brady dropped her arms and studied her. Her dark eyes were hard, and Nicole felt like she was being probed. She forced herself to stand still while Brady made a decision.

"We can go upstairs," Brady replied, indicating the direction of the stairs. "It's a little cooler than out here."

Nicole agreed and somehow managed to put one foot in front of the other and follow Brady across the brick path toward the stairs. Jasmine clung to the trellis on her right, the sweet scent of new buds tickling her nose. Large pots of daisies and hibiscus framed the bottom of the stairs.

Once inside Brady motioned for Nicole to sit. "Can I get you anything?"

"No, thank you, I'm fine." Actually Nicole thought she'd probably choke if she tried to drink something, her throat was so dry.

She sat there for several minutes, too nervous to notice the interior of Brady's apartment. Brady was in no hurry to talk, which wasn't surprising, since she'd more than likely said everything there was to say in her office.

Suddenly Nicole was tongue-tied. She had so much to say she didn't know where to begin. Should she start with the moment she realized Brady was right? How about that she used to be strong and didn't like the woman she'd turned into? Should it be when she decided to take back control of her life? Or that Brady had given her the strength to take it back? Then there was that little thing about how crazy she was about Brady. How much she wanted her in her life.

"You were right," Nicole said, needing to stand and move around. "I was a coward. I hid behind my scars to keep from getting hurt again. But I'm tired. Tired of fighting to be something I'm not. I hide the fact that I'm falling apart behind appearing totally put together. I have nightmares and panic attacks, and I sleep with every light on in the house. I hadn't been anywhere near a job site in six years. I can barely get on an airplane and can't even enjoy a fucking campfire and toast marshmallows."

Nicole stopped in front of Brady. "And do you know how many people know any of those things? Just one of them?" She held up her hand, the tip of her thumb and first finger coming together to make a zero, emphasizing her point. "No one. Not one person knows even one of those things." She paced a few laps and stopped in front of Brady again.

"And then there's you. Brady Stewart, a woman who could have any woman she wants. A woman who's unlike anyone I've ever met. Who takes my breath away, makes me crazy, and turns me into a jumbled mess of nerves. The one who gives me the strength to be who I am. The only one."

Brady's eyes were dark, almost black. Nicole knew that look and her shattered nerves calmed. "I can't fight this anymore. It's been so long I've forgotten what I was even fighting for."

Nicole paused. This was it. The moment for which there was no turning back. "I'm not afraid anymore." She unclenched her hands and reached for the top button of her shirt.

CHAPTER TWENTY-NINE

"No," Nicole said firmly. Brady dropped her hands and stepped back. She had stood and moved to her the instant Nicole's intent was clear.

"I have to do this myself." Nicole was adamant that she would be the one to share all of herself with Brady. She had to remove every piece of camouflage, every cover-up, disguise, and smoke screen. She trusted Brady like no one ever before. Brady wouldn't look away in disgust. Brady wouldn't recoil at the texture of her skin. Brady would never tell her no.

After days of shaking, Nicole's hands were steady as they moved from one button to the next, Brady's eyes fixed on her movements. She pulled first one arm, then the other, from her shirt and dropped it to the floor. Her nipples hardened under her thin T-shirt. Brady saw it too.

She slid her belt through the loops on her pants, the pewter tip on the end clicking lightly on the buckle, drawing Brady's attention. Brady's jaw slackened, and she wasn't sure if her reaction gave her confidence or made her more self-conscious. Brady's eyes were glued to her zipper as Nicole lowered it, then dropped her pants to the floor.

Slowly Brady's eyes traveled up from the top of her feet to the place covered only by her lace panties. Her expression never changed and her gaze never lingered over the scar just above her left knee or the pale, puckered skin on her right thigh.

Taking a deep breath of courage, Nicole pulled her T-shirt over her head and dropped it on the floor on top of her pants. The final piece of clothing quickly followed, and for the first time in six years she was standing naked in front of a woman. Only one item remained before her entire being was bared to Brady. Her hands steady, she reached up and removed her wig.

This was about more than being naked, more than exposing her damaged body to Brady. Her vulnerability to rejection was her Achilles's heel. If Brady trusted her enough to risk her goals and everything she'd worked for, then Nicole owed it to her to do the same.

"You are absolutely beautiful," Brady said, her voice barely above a whisper. Brady hadn't moved but her eyes were everywhere, finally settling on Nicole's. "Beautiful."

Brady stepped closer, the flame in her eyes burning brighter. Nicole believed her this time and her confidence soared. Her legs were steady as she closed the remaining distance between them. The scent of sweat and Brady filled her, and she slowly kissed her waiting lips. She wanted to go slow, savor every minute. But the instant their lips met she needed to feel Brady's hands on her, her mouth on her breasts, Brady's arms around her when she came.

With little patience Nicole pulled Brady's shirt from her waistband and slid her hands over the smooth, hard body that had tormented her memory for weeks. Brady inhaled sharply, wrapping her arms tight around her neck. Nicole quickly managed to get Brady's pants on the floor and her shirt on top of that. When their bodies touched Nicole reveled in the sensation.

She dragged her mouth away from Brady's hot lips. "Is there a bedroom in this place?"

Brady grinned, took her hand, and led the way.

Brady pulled back the covers on the small bed. Nicole slid in, pulling Brady with her. The weight of Brady's body as she shifted over her took her breath away. Brady moved against her, and Nicole slid her leg between Brady's. She was wet and Brady's thigh slid easily. Nicole was on the verge of coming.

"Touch me," Nicole said. "Please, I need you to touch me." She didn't care if she sounded like she was begging. It didn't matter. What mattered was the wonderful, marvelous way Brady was making her feel.

Brady kissed her chin and neck, and between her breasts. Her hand traveled up and down Nicole's side and stomach, drifting closer to her clit with every stroke. Nicole arched instinctively and Brady continued her exploration. Warm lips circled one nipple, and when Brady started to suck, Nicole came hard. She pulled Brady's lips closer as she cried out over and over.

Brady's hand slid between them and glided into her like air. Nicole cried out again, this time not from orgasm but from the sheer joy of pleasure. It had been so long since she'd allowed herself to feel this way, and in this very moment she vowed to never let something as trivial as her body stand in the way of intimacy again.

Brady shifted and worked her way down Nicole's body, kissing and biting her stomach, abdomen, the inside of her thighs. She didn't push Nicole's thighs apart but simply looked up at her as if asking permission. In that instant Nicole knew she had fallen absolutely crazy in love with Brady Stewart.

"Brady." Nicole met her gaze. "Take me to that place I thought I'd never find."

When Brady lowered her head Nicole knew nothing other than the sensation of Brady's lips and tongue. Her orgasm rocked her to her core, left her breathless, blinded her with flashing light. Wave after wave rolled through Nicole until she thought she might die from the experience.

As her climax began to recede Brady released her and quickly gathered her into her arms. Brady tightened her hold as Nicole shuddered with aftershocks of the most powerful orgasm of her life.

The need to touch Brady far exceeded the need to sleep, and Nicole pulled herself up and on top of Brady. She was determined to do to Brady what she'd just done to her. She wanted to feel Brady squirm under her fingertips, arch into her kisses, and come for her. And only her.

Nicole was alive, genuinely alive. The previous times they were together like this she'd felt desire, lust, and arousal. But there was absolutely no comparison to this, right now, this moment.

Nicole kissed a long, ragged pale scar on Brady's upper arm. She asked about it, and when Brady told her that her mother had backhanded her so hard she fell against the jagged metal edge of the kitchen table, her heart ached for the pain Brady must have endured in her childhood. When she asked about a larger scar, this one on her shoulder Brady just said, "Don't ask."

They laughed when Brady told her the story about the tattoo of the blue marlin Nicole had found the very first time they were together and their mutual love for deep-sea fishing.

"Why do you have such a small bed?"

"It's all I need," Brady responded, nuzzling her neck. Nicole shivered from the sensation.

"With all the women passing through your life I'd have thought you'd have a bigger one."

Brady stopped her tasting and looked at her. Her eyes were serious and matched the expression on her face. "I've never brought anyone here."

"Never?" Nicole asked, incredulous.

"Never. That would make it personal. And it was never personal. Until now. *You* are personal."

Nicole didn't know what to say. Brady had made love to her with a fervor Nicole had never experienced. She'd touched and kissed every inch of her body without hesitation. She'd made her laugh, made her crazy with desire, and made her cry with release. She'd made her feel whole.

Nicole needed to kiss her. To disappear in their kisses again, their bodies intertwined like nature had intended. But she had something more important to do. Straddling Brady's hips Nicole sat and pulled Brady up with her.

"What are you doing tomorrow?" she asked, holding Brady's hands in hers.

"Spending it with you."

"And the day after that?"

"I'm not sure," Brady answered, some trepidation in her voice. "Why? Do you have something in mind?"

"Yes," Nicole said, her voice both quavering with love and solid in conviction. "I want to spend tomorrow, the day after, and the day after that with you. I love you, Brady Stewart, and at the risk of sounding unoriginal, I want to spend every day of the rest of my life with you."

"Well," Brady said, twisting so that Nicole was beneath her. "If you put it that way, how can I say no?"

THE END

About the Author

Julie Cannon divides her time by being a corporate suit, a partner, mom, sister, friend, and writer. Julie and Laura, her partner of twenty-one years, have lived in at least half a dozen states, and have an unending supply of dedicated friends. And of course the most important people in their lives are their thirteen-year-old son and daughter.

Julie has ten books published by Bold Strokes Books. Her first novel, *Come and Get Me*, was a finalist for the Golden Crown Literary Society's Best Lesbian Romance and Debut Author Awards. In 2012, her ninth novel, *Rescue Me*, was a finalist as Best Lesbian Romance from the prestigious Lambda Literary Society. Julie has also published five short stories in Bold Strokes Anthologies.

Books Available from Bold Strokes Books

The Quickening: A Sisters of Spirits Novel byYvonne Heidt. Ghosts, visions, and demons are all in a day's work for Tiffany. But when Kat asks for help on a serial killer case, life takes on another dimension altogether. (978-1-60282-975-6)

Windigo Thrall by Cate Culpepper. Six women trapped in a mountain cabin by a blizzard, stalked by an ancient cannibal demon bent on stealing their sanity—and their lives. (978-1-60282-950-3)

Smoke and Fire by Julie Cannon. Oil and water, passion and desire, a combustible combination. Can two women fight the fire that draws them together and threatens to keep them apart? (978-1-60282-977-0)

Asher's Fault by Elizabeth Wheeler. Fourteen-year-old Asher Price sees the world in black and white, much like the photos he takes, but when his little brother drowns at the same moment Asher experiences his first same-sex kiss, he can no longer hide behind the lens of his camera and eventually discovers he isn't the only one with a secret. (978-1-60282-982-4)

Love and Devotion by Jove Belle. KC Hall trips her way through life, stumbling into an affair with a married bombshell twice her age. Thankfully, her best friend, Emma Reynolds, is there to show her the true meaning of Love and Devotion. (978-1-60282-965-7)

Rush by Carsen Taite. Murder, secrets, and romance combine to create the ultimate rush. (978-1-60282-966-4)

The Shoal of Time by J.M. Redmann. It sounded too easy. Micky Knight is reluctant to take the case because the easy ones often turn into the hard ones, and the hard ones turn into the dangerous ones. In this one, easy turns hard without warning. (978-1-60282-967-1)

In Between by Jane Hoppen. At the age of 14, Sophie Schmidt discovers that she was born an intersexual baby and sets off on a journey to find her place in a world that denies her true existence. (978-1-60282-968-8)

Secret Lies by Amy Dunne. While fleeing from her abuser, Nicola Jackson bumps into Jenny O'Connor, and their unlikely friendship quickly develops into a blossoming romance—but when it comes down to a matter of life or death, are they both willing to face their fears? (978-1-60282-970-1)

Under Her Spell by Maggie Morton. The magic of love brought Terra and Athene together, but now a magical quest stands between them—a quest for Athene's hand in marriage. Will their passion keep them together, or will stronger magic tear them apart? (978-1-60282-973-2)

Homestead by Radclyffe. R. Clayton Sutter figures getting NorthAm Fuel's newest refinery operational on a rolling tract of land in Upstate New York should take a month or two, but then, she hadn't counted on local resistance in the form of vandalism, petitions, and one furious farmer named Tess Rogers. (978-1-60282-956-5)

Battle of Forces: Sera Toujours by Ali Vali. Kendal and Piper return to New Orleans to start the rest of eternity together, but the return of an old enemy makes their peaceful reunion short-lived, especially when they join forces with the new queen of the vampires. (978-1-60282-957-2)

How Sweet It Is by Melissa Brayden. Some things are better than chocolate. Molly O'Brien enjoys her quiet life running the bakeshop in a small town. When the beautiful Jordan Tuscana returns home, Molly can't deny the attraction—or the stirrings of something more. (978-1-60282-958-9)

The Missing Juliet: A Fisher Key Adventure by Sam Cameron. A teenage detective and her friends search for a kidnapped Hollywood star in the Florida Keys. (978-1-60282-959-6)

Amor and More: Love Everafter edited by Radclyffe and Stacia Seaman. Rediscover favorite couples as Bold Strokes Books authors reveal glimpses of life and love beyond the honeymoon in short stories featuring main characters from favorite BSB novels. (978-1-60282-963-3)

First Love by CJ Harte. Finding true love is hard enough, but for Jordan Thompson, daughter of a conservative president, it's challenging, especially when that love is a female rodeo cowgirl. (978-1-60282-949-7)

Pale Wings Protecting by Lesley Davis. Posing as a couple to investigate the abduction of infants, Special Agent Blythe Kent and Detective Daryl Chandler find themselves drawn into a battle over the innocents, with demons on one side and the unlikeliest of protectors on the other. (978-1-60282-964-0)

Mounting Danger by Karis Walsh. Sergeant Rachel Bryce, an outcast on the police force, is put in charge of the department's newly formed mounted division. Can she and polo champion Callan Lanford resist their growing attraction as they struggle to safeguard the disaster-prone unit? (978-1-60282-951-0)

Meeting Chance by Jennifer Lavoie. When man's best friend turns on Aaron Cassidy, the teen keeps his distance until fate puts Chance in his hands. (978-1-60282-952-7)

At Her Feet by Rebekah Weatherspoon. Digital marketing producer Suzanne Kim knows she has found the perfect love in her new mistress Pilar, but before they can make the ultimate commitment, Suzanne's professional life threatens to disrupt their perfectly balanced bliss. (978-1-60282-948-0)

Show of Force by AJ Quinn. A chance meeting between navy pilot Evan Kane and correspondent Tate McKenna takes them on a roller-coaster ride where the stakes are high, but the reward is higher: a chance at love. (978-1-60282-942-8)

Clean Slate by Andrea Bramhall. Can Erin and Morgan work through their individual demons to rediscover their love for each other, or are the unexplainable wounds too deep to heal? (978-1-60282-943-5)

Hold Me Forever by D. Jackson Leigh. An investigation into illegal cloning in the quarter horse racing industry threatens to destroy the growing attraction between Georgia debutante Mae St. John and Louisiana horse trainer Whit Casey. (978-1-60282-944-2)

Trusting Tomorrow by PJ Trebelhorn. Funeral director Logan Swift thinks she's perfectly happy with her solitary life devoted to helping others cope with loss until Brooke Collier moves in next door to care for her elderly grandparents. (978-1-60282-891-9)

Forsaking All Others by Kathleen Knowles. What if what you think you want is the opposite of what makes you happy? (978-1-60282-892-6)

Exit Wounds by VK Powell. When Officer Loane Landry falls in love with ATF informant Abigail Mancuso, she realizes that nothing is as it seems—not the case, not her lover, not even the dead. (978-1-60282-893-3)

Dirty Power by Ashley Bartlett. Cooper's been through hell and back, and she's still broke and on the run. But at least she found the twins. They'll keep her alive. Right? (978-1-60282-896-4)

The Rarest Rose by I. Beacham. After a decade of living in her beloved house, Ele disturbs its past and finds her life being haunted by the presence of a ghost who will show her that true love never dies. (978-1-60282-884-1)

Code of Honor by Radclyffe. The face of terror is hard to recognize—especially when it's homegrown. The next book in the Honor series. (978-1-60282-885-8)

Does She Love You? by Rachel Spangler. When Annabelle and Davis find out they are both in a relationship with the same woman, it leaves them facing life-altering questions about trust, redemption, and the possibility of finding love in the wake of betrayal. (978-1-60282-886-5)

The Road to Her by KE Payne. Sparks fly when actress Holly Croft, star of UK soap Portobello Road, meets her new on-screen love interest, the enigmatic and sexy Elise Manford. (978-1-60282-887-2)

Shadows of Something Real by Sophia Kell Hagin. Trying to escape flashbacks and nightmares, ex-POW Jamie Gwynmorgan stumbles into the heart of former Red Cross worker Adele Sabellius and uncovers a deadly conspiracy against everything and everyone she loves. (978-1-60282-889-6)

Date with Destiny by Mason Dixon. When sophisticated bank executive Rashida Ivey meets unemployed blue collar worker Destiny Jackson, will her life ever be the same? (978-1-60282-878-0)

The Devil's Orchard by Ali Vali. Cain and Emma plan a wedding before the birth of their third child while Juan Luis is still lurking, and as Cain plans for his death, an unexpected visitor arrives and challenges her belief in her father, Dalton Casey. (978-1-60282-879-7)

Secrets and Shadows by L.T. Marie. A bodyguard and the woman she protects run from a madman and into each other's arms. (978-1-60282-880-3)

Change Horizons: Three Novellas by Gun Brooke. Three stories of courageous women who dare to love as they fight to claim a future in a hostile universe. (978-1-60282-881-0)

Scarlet Thirst by Crin Claxton. When hot, feisty Rani meets cool, vampire Rob, one lifetime isn't enough, and the road from human to vampire is shorter than you think… (978-1-60282-856-8)

Battle Axe by Carsen Taite. How close is too close? Bounty hunter Luca Bennett will soon find out. (978-1-60282-871-1)

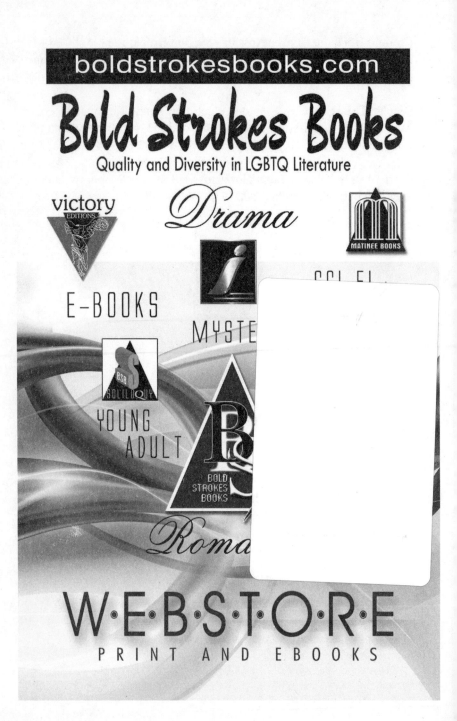